WITHOUT REGARD

THE DAY THE GOVERNMENT
NUKED LOUISIANA

John, I hope you enjoy my story.

Lauch Magruder

Lauch Magruder

Without Regard
Copyright 2007

Story by Lauch Magruder
Editing & Creative Development
by Tara McDonald-Tiner & Jubal Tiner

ISBN 13: 978-0-9795352-0-8

CoachWrite Editing & Writing
McDonald-Tiner
414-738 Gallimore Road
Brevard, NC 28712
(828) 885-6075
jubaltara@yahoo.com

ACKNOWLEDGEMENTS

During the several years I have worked on this book, I stopped work and almost gave it up many times. Dealing with intricate facts, the many hours consumed, my inexperience in writing, and my poor typing, at times, made the likelihood of a finished book seem impossible. But my wife and children and close friends would not accept that, and they pushed me to complete my work. I am deeply grateful to each of them for encouraging and pressing me. I must thank Flo Timmer, who did all the initial typing and then helped me do it myself. Thanks also to Sammie Leffler, who always with a smile ran many copies through the copy machine. The book would have never been completed had it not been for Tara McDonald-Tiner and her husband, Jubal Tiner. My heartfelt thanks to each of you.

Lauch Magruder

CONTENTS

I. Catalyst

Late Night Prep
Laurins' Opening Words
Summoned
So It Begins
Sam
Visitors
Project Apex
Westover's Opening Words
Louise
Petitioner's Team
Meeting Kay
Preliminaries
Building a Practice
The Thrill and the Challenge
Leaving for Jackson
Respondent's Team
Divorce in Shreveport
A Quick Bite
Warning

II. Neutron Bombardment

Clarence Mitchell, Jr.
Barbara
Clarence Continues
Sequestered
Grand Discovery

Estranged

Cross-Examining Mr. Mitchell

Graduation

Introducing Joseph Ross

Don't Do It Again, Sam

Ross Report for Mitchell v. IRS

Death and New Possibilities

Ross Continues

Spiritual Awakening

Cross-Examining Ross

Pleasant Company

Shock and Awe

Incomplete Restoration

Ross Cannot Be Shaken

Saying Too Much

III. Splitting the Atom

Emily's Story

Dr. Bill Poole

At Home With Kay

Dr. Poole Continues

Loss

Shea Claremore

Companions

Neely Ryder

A First Date?

IV. Plutonium Core

Petitioner Rests & Relaxes

Respondents Begin With Boggan

Cursillo Meetings

Boggan is Belligerent

Mending Good Fences

CONTENTS

Foibles With Joseph Faust
Engaged
Petitioners Evaluate

V. Fission Reaction

Ballard & Reesh
Ian's Vow
Eddie LeBlanc
A Brief Interlude
Hudgens Report for Mitchell v. IRS
Permission
Asher Thornton
Little Nibbles & Reassurance
Craig Mitchell for the Respondents

VI. Maximum Payload

The Last Night
The Other Last Night

VII. Critical Mass

Respondents Call Mr. MacGregor
Sam Takes Ian on Cross
Escaping the Aftermath
Westover Redirects

VIII. Shockwave

Closing & Chambers
A Different Kind of Celebration
Down the Aisle
A Phone Call
Next Time I See You
Concession
Fulfilled

FACT

Between 1964 and 1970, the U.S. Atomic Energy Commission performed four tests—two nuclear explosions and two gas explosions—in an underground salt dome on American soil. The first nuclear device, called Salmon, was of the Whetstone series. Sterling, the second device, was of the Latchkey series. The two other blasts were methane-oxygen explosions. The creeks ran black in that Mississippi town, and the ground and concrete rippled for miles like ocean waves. Afterwards, radioactive waste was inserted into the salt dome cavity and a deep aquifer. The Atomic Energy Commission left the area in 1972. The equipment, soil, and groundwater were all contaminated. A Remedial Investigation and Feasibility Study was conducted. Monitoring was still occurring as late as 1993. The government studied the cancer rates of local residents, though for a much later time period than the period in question, and they reported no increase in cancer rates among residents of the area at that time. They also report there is no ongoing contamination.

AUTHOR'S NOTE

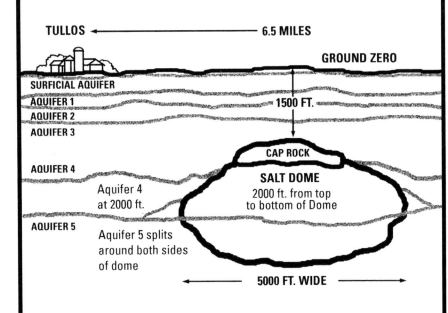

TULLOS ← ——————————— 6.5 MILES

GROUND ZERO

SURFICIAL AQUIFER

AQUIFER 1   1500 FT.

AQUIFER 2

AQUIFER 3

CAP ROCK

AQUIFER 4   SALT DOME
                 2000 ft. from top
Aquifer 4   to bottom of Dome
at 2000 ft.

AQUIFER 5

Aquifer 5 splits
around both sides
of dome

← ——— 5000 FT. WIDE ——— →

Bottom of Dome is roughly 3500 ft. down from surface

Part One: Catalyst

Chapter 1

LATE NIGHT PREP

Except for a few lights in the hall and his office, the law firm was dark. *That's to be expected at 9:00 on Sunday night,* he thought. Standing to stretch, Sam Laurins walked to the window and looked out. The city below was beginning to be deserted as people left the downtown restaurants and bars. Only a few cars were left on the street seventeen floors below. His gaze changed as he noticed his reflection, which revealed a man in good physical condition with sparkling brown eyes. With the young-at-heart smile he usually carried, Laurins appeared much younger than his 65 years. But he saw his gray hair giving him away.

As he looked across the skyline, Sam wondered how the trial would go tomorrow. He had never tried a case before this new Judge, Lansdorf, and he knew very little about him other than he had been a career attorney in the Department of Justice before coming on the Tax Court bench. To some extent, it was always a concern when the trial Judge was a career government employee, as there was no jury in a Tax Court trial. Sam's friends in the Tax Section told him that Lansdorf strictly went by the book—that he ran a pretty tight trial. That didn't bother Sam. All he wanted was equal treatment.

Even though he and the members of his trial team had been over the Trial Memorandum and other documents numerous times in their preparation, Sam had to do it once more. *It's just that this case is so remarkable.* He sat down, read and revised his opening statement, as he had already done many times. When he finally had it just as he wanted it, he re-read the Trial Memorandum for the IRS, focusing on the list of witnesses they intended to call and the testimony they expected to elicit from each.

The ring of the telephone startled him. Time had gotten away from him again. As he picked up the receiver, his wife, Barbara, said "Honey, I called to tell you goodnight. The children are in bed, and I can't stay awake. You haven't stayed this late in a while."

"I know—it is late. It's just that this the most exceptional case of my career, like nothing the Tax Court has ever seen. Would you laugh if I said this old man had night-before-the-trial jitters?"

Laughing, she affirmed him, "You'll do fine, Sam."

"I know. Thanks, honey."

"Will you be there much longer?"

"No. It is time for me to go. Sorry I've been here so long, sweetheart. I have been over this stuff so many times, I can almost recite it verbatim. I'm sure this effort is overkill. I just want to be certain I don't overlook something. This trial is so unlike anything I've ever done. But I will leave in the next 10 minutes. Don't try to stay awake for me. I will see you in the morning, sweetheart. I love you."

An hour later, Sam Laurins locked the door to his office and headed home hungry and tired. *Old habits die hard.*

Chapter 2

LAURINS' OPENING WORDS

"May it please the Court? The United States government has subjected some of Louisiana's citizens to agonizing illness and death, continually deceiving them for a period of 16 years, up to this moment, overtly covering up their deceit."

"In 1964 and 1966, the United States Atomic Energy Commission exploded two nuclear bombs in a salt dome under land owned by the decedent, Clarence H. Mitchell. This is the only instance in the history of this country where the government has conducted tests of nuclear weapons on privately-owned land."

"Representatives of the Atomic Energy Commission played on Mr. Mitchell's love for his country and civic pride to persuade him to let them use his land for Project Apex's dangerous and irresponsible testing. Those representatives of the federal government convinced Mr. Mitchell that the salt dome under his land was the only place in the United States where these tests could be conducted. They made him think that the security of the free world depended on those tests."

"They vowed to Mr. Mitchell that the government agencies involved in Project Apex had done extensive research and were certain there would be no danger to his property or to people living in the vicinity. That assertion was untrue. In fact, there were serious questions surrounding the proposed testing. No one knew to what extent the walls of the salt dome might be fractured, resulting in an uncontrolled release of radiation into the air or the water that provides drinking water in the area. This has had a devastating environmental impact on the land and timber from which my client makes his living."

"The truth is that the government people making the decisions were so intent on conducting those tests they were willing to go forward no matter what, risking the lives of unsuspecting citizens. We suspect that the CIA was involved, considering the unswerving determination to conduct the tests, regardless of the consequences to people down here in Louisiana."

"Much of the critical information pertaining to the problems and health hazards created by the testing, even descriptions of the nuclear devices exploded, are classified TOP SECRET, so we did not have access to that. Even so, from the available government reports, it is clear that the first nuclear shot resulted in serious problems, the anticipation of which was not disclosed to my client or the people in the area surrounding Ground Zero."

"Beginning a few months after the first blast, the AEC and other government agencies involved started publishing reports of results of the explosions. All of those reports have asserted that there is no contamination at or near the test site. Those optimistic reports have continued, the last one issued in January of this year."

"After the second nuclear blast, the AEC announced, with no explanation, that the third nuclear test planned for the project had been canceled. Then over the next two years, two additional blasts were made in the cavity. The AEC only revealed that they were non-nuclear, so the size and type of those explosions have never been disclosed."

"In addition to not fully revealing all the potential hazards to my client and his father, and to the health of the timber that is their livelihood, the government did not even complete the clean-up job in a safe manner."

"In August, 1971, the AEC announced that the test site would be decommissioned. The Decommissioning Report issued by the AEC reported that the disposal of all contaminated substances—liquid and solid—had been completed as directed. All contaminated liquid waste was supposed to be forced under extreme pressure into an aquifer. All vehicles, contaminated soil, protective clothing, and other equipment were to be shipped by truck and rail to the AEC nuclear disposal facility in Nevada. It appears that indeed, some liquid contamination was forced into the aquifer as directed. But instead of transporting all of the contaminated soil and equipment to Nevada, a substantial part of it was buried near the test site. With the passage of time and erosion of the soil, much of that equipment, including barrels of some type of liquid, has been uncovered."

"Additionally, their decisions to use the aquifers resulted in serious consequences that have never been acknowledged. The monumental error made by the AEC and the other governmental agencies involved in Project Apex was the decision to pump, under strong pressure, the liquid waste into Aquifer Five. To do that, liquid was pumped through the fractured salt dome shaft past Aquifers One, Two, Three, and Four, into Aquifer Five. Without researching the logical outcome, they were simply hoping and guessing that circumstances would make the liquid in Aquifer Five move in the opposite direction from its normal flow. Aquifers Two and Three, which also flow naturally to the southeast like Aquifer Five, supply drinking water to the wells of rural residents in the vicinity of the test site and for the town of Tullos about eight miles southeast of the test site."

"Incidences of cancer and death from cancer are now extremely high among the residents of Tullos and people living between there and the test site. Of the 96 families who live in that area, 83 of them have experienced at least one family member stricken with cancer since Project Apex began. Those families believe this unusually-high rate of cancer is due to nuclear contamination in the water. Our experts think they are right. Yet up to this very moment, the federal government continues to deny the existence of any problems or danger to the community, continuing to cover up the horrendous situation that exists, the ethics of which have not even been addressed."

"Before conducting the tests, the agencies involved were aware of the extreme danger that the tests might pose to people in the area, not to mention wildlife and plantlife such as the Mitchell's timber. They chose to ignore those dangers and go forward with the testing. When severe problems resulted from the first test, the government recklessly pressed on with three other blasts, making a bad situation worse. Then, to complete the disastrous project, they buried contaminated equipment, dirt, and residue, forced liquid contamination into a badly-cracked shaft damaged from the explosions, and expected the waste-filled aquifer to magically flow in the opposite direction from its natural flow straight toward the townspeople! To cover up the mistakes and hazards of the situation, which remain unresolved to this day, the AEC continues to publish false reports, denying the existence of contamination in the area."

"After all this, the Internal Revenue Service has the audacity to assert that the land of Mr. Mitchell, including the 1400 acres involved in the nuclear testing, is worth twice the value reported in his estate tax return—when in fact, it is now a wasteland he can neither use nor sell?"

Sam paused for effect, and the courtroom buzzed as people stiffened and shuffled about at this assertion.

Confidence and persistence in his voice, Sam continued in his thick bayou drawl, patient but firm, "As we prepared for this trial, with the help of our expert witnesses, we determined that the land values stated in the tax return are seriously overstated. And because the Mitchells are good citizens, honest taxpayers, and committed patriots, they never questioned whether their land had lost value because of Project Apex, since the government always told them it was clean and clear. In all these years, never once did they claim any reduction due to the contamination of the land."

"Now, for two years, we have attempted time and time again to convince the Internal Revenue Service and the Chief Counsel of the existence of nuclear contamination on the land, as well as its disastrous effect on land values and local human health. The response we have continually received is that we are nuts—the AEC claims its reports are very clear that there is NO problem and that the land values proposed by the IRS will not be compromised."

"The matter before this Court today is to determine the proper tax liability of the Estate of Clarence Mitchell. The issue is the value of 20,000 acres of timberland, of which the 1400 acres involved in the nuclear testing is a part. That 20,000-acre tract was valued in the estate tax return at $14 million. The IRS asserts that the land and timber should be valued at $30 million instead. Petitioners assert that because of the nuclear testing on the land, its value is substantially less than the $14 million originally reported."

"This will be a most atypical case for the Tax Court to hear, because in order to assess tax value, the Court must determine if there is a probability, or even possibility, that any part of the Mitchell land suffers from nuclear contamination. In the history of Tax Court, this is probably the only case of its kind. It is the only time the government has used residential property for such a dangerous purpose. In the name of patriotic duty, the trusting decision Mr. Mitchell made all those years ago to acquiesce to his government's needs now affects his family's future in terms of health, residential options, and livelihood. What the Petitioners are here to assert is that there is now a stigma attached to this land, and its ability to produce timber has been adversely affected—not to mention that no one will buy the land, forcing Mr. Mitchell between a rock and a hard place. All that being true, I ask that you please consider our request to devalue the Mitchell property tax value. Thank you, Your Honor."

Chapter 3

SUMMONED

Near the rear of the courtroom sat Ian MacGregor, a handsome, six-foot, athletic-looking man. Listening to Mr. Laurins' striking opening remarks, Ian thought, *well, if nothing else, you can't say this won't get interesting.* He intently observed everything taking place. He'd never been at a trial before. He couldn't help but wonder what role he'd be playing in all this himself.

✳

Arriving at work weeks earlier, a tall, lanky, odd-looking man was sitting on the chair outside Ian's locked office. It was early. No one else was in the building. Yet here was this stranger. Ian approached. Before Ian could ask what the man wanted, he rose, smiled half-heartedly, pulled out a piece of paper from the inside pocket of his jacket, and said, "You are hereby summoned, Mr. MacGregor."

Chapter 4

SO IT BEGINS

Thus began the unlikely tax assessment trial of Mitchell v. Commissioner in the federal courtroom in Shreveport, Louisiana, on Monday, December 9, 1984.

This was the moment the trial team for the Mitchell Estate and their expert witnesses had prepared for over the past ten months. Having completed his opening statement, Sam Laurins, attorney for the Petitioner, the Estate of Clarence H. Mitchell, returned to his seat at the counsel table, where he joined his co-counsel, Robert Fly and Claudia Stone. Both Rob and Claudia had taken notes during Sam's opening statement and had been whispering to each other. As Sam took his seat, Rob pushed his notepad in front of Sam and pointed to something on it. Sam read the scribbled note to himself, "The Respondent's crowd looks like they are at a funeral."

He smiled. *Well, here we go.*

Chapter 5

SAM

Even though he had never received career counseling to know much about it—had never even been in a law office—Sam Laurins had always desired to become a lawyer. His grandfather, who died when Sam was an infant, had earned an excellent reputation as an attorney. Sam wanted to emulate his Grandpa Joe. As Sam started his last semester of college, however, rather than register for law school, he acknowledged he wasn't ready to temper his fun-loving life enough to take on the rigors of a graduate program.

His friends in law school had to spend too much time studying, restricting their pleasure time. Sam was not yet willing to commit to that. *There is time for that later.* He had lived on a tight budget during his undergraduate years, and he wanted to change that. He wanted to go to work, make some money. So he graduated, received his commission as a second lieutenant in the U.S. Army Reserve, and went out into the real world. What he didn't know then was that it would take a tour in Korea to rekindle his passion for law.

He went to work in Monroe for a printing and office supply business owned by a friend of his father. The understanding was that when the business owner was ready to retire, he would sell the business to Sam. Monroe was a good place to be. The cost of living was low, and there were lots of pretty girls attending the college there. Why let his good looks go to waste, after all? For more than a year, Sam enjoyed the fun world of a young bachelor in a town where the social life was plentiful.

During the summer after his graduation, when he was with his

Reserve unit at their summer camp, the announcement came that the North Koreans had invaded South Korea. Everyone was restricted to the Army base. Rumors were rampant that the unit would be called to active duty immediately. But that did not happen—yet—and at the conclusion of the two week camp, they returned home. Then in December, while riding in the car with his girlfriend at the time, a news flash on the radio announced that Sam's unit had been called to active duty effective January 3.

The unit was sent to Fort Jackson, South Carolina, but Sam and three other young officers were sent to the Infantry Officers School at Fort Benning, Georgia. Sam and his friends spent a lot of time pursuing the many fun opportunities for single young officers that Columbus, Georgia, and its neighboring town, Phoenix City, offered. Upon completion of their 16-week training, they rejoined their unit at Fort Jackson. Again, they found a lot of adventures in Columbia and on weekend trips to Myrtle Beach.

Sam enjoyed Army life. While the days were busy and active, he liked the men he worked with and loved being outside and serving as a platoon leader. Life was great. It was so enjoyable that Sam secured paperwork to apply for a regular Army commission. Then came that day in December when he received orders to go to Korea.

His tour of duty in Korea was unpleasant, of course, but with his attitude of optimism, Sam could always find good in the situation. He had the opportunity to go to Japan for some R-and-R twice, and he loved that.

But it was also during his time in Korea that Sam was exposed to several regular Army officers and did not like what he saw. He encountered some West Point graduates he felt were less able than some of the reservists he knew, yet it was clear that the superior officers would give the West Pointers special considerations and advancements. He could see that even if he was a regular officer, when competing against a West Point graduate, he would not be given equal treatment by some senior officers. He did not like the politics of the system. It was how tight you were with your superior, not how you performed, that mattered.

The war experience, together with the disenchantment with prejudices he saw in the Army, revived Sam's interest in becoming a lawyer. He remembered what he had read about his grandfather, how he started his law practice and built it into something significant. As a lawyer, Sam knew he would make it or not based on his ability, without having to butter up or placate a superior. When he made the decision, he applied to Tulane Law School and was admitted to start in the fall.

Chapter 6

VISITORS

Counsel, witnesses, and others were seated in the courtroom awaiting the Judge. Coming to sit in the first row behind the government counsel table were four employees of the DOE who had apparently joined the Respondents since lunch: Kenneth Van Skiver, Chairman of the Nuclear Defense Program; Emily Carter, Van Skiver's Assistant Attorney; Kyle DeLoach, former Manager of Project Apex; and Ian MacGregor, Chief Engineer of Project Apex.

Also with the DOE crowd was Lieutenant General Aaron Bruce, Commander of the Department of Defense Advanced Research Project Agency, and Jack Erwin, Director of the Highlands Radiation Laboratory, a CIA front organization.

While listening to Laurins' opening statement, Erwin, with a sneer, turned to Emily and whispered in a voice loud enough to be heard across the room, "Can you believe that jerk, Laurins?" Emily, a bit nervous, half smiled and gently brushed him off.

Chapter 7

PROJECT APEX

In 1960, at the first meeting of the people who would make up the Project Apex Group, the AEC told Ian and the other team members their plans for underground testing of nuclear devices and the proposed location. Ian had concerns. As time moved along and plans were formulated, Ian worked harder, making more calculations, studying more. From his research, MacGregor concluded that to explode a 5-kiloton bomb in the proposed location, a salt dome in a residential area, would be a mistake—maybe a deadly mistake. Even though he was the most junior member of the Group, he voiced his strong objections to Project Apex.

At every meeting of the project group over the next two and a half years, Ian urged the them to reconsider the proposal to explode a nuclear device in the Mitchell salt dome. Referring to his studies and voluminous calculations he had made, he showed them the many unknown results. He asserted the very real possibility that the salt dome would be fractured by such a large explosion, which could result in an invasion of the water table by the nuclear residue from the explosion. He pleaded that residents of the test area could be placed in great danger. Ian urged that if the tests were absolutely necessary, they be moved to another salt dome located nearer the coast in an uninhabited area. But try as he might, Ian was shouted down by other members of the Group each time.

At the final planning meeting of the Project Apex Group, Ian made one more attempt to convince them to recommend Project Apex be canceled. Kyle DeLoach, Manager of the Project, explained to Ian and the other members that such a recommendation would mean nothing, that the President was determined to conduct the tests. As the group meeting broke up, DeLoach asked Ian to stay to talk with him.

"Ian," Kyle said, "I know you have carefully and minutely calculated the possible impact on the salt dome. I understand your fear of the damage the explosion may cause to the subsurface and the ground in the vicinity of the test site. Truthfully, as I have studied your research, I am convinced that there is cause for your concern. You may well be right. I wrote the higher-ups a memo reciting your findings and fears, and recommended we reconsider the Apex project. After discussing it, they took my recommendation as far as President Kennedy. But the CIA is pushing hard for the testing. They want it done now. The President said, 'Apex is important—do it as planned.' So we have no choice but to proceed."

✳

Ian thought about his wife, Kay, and the long list of other families living in the vicinity of the test site who had suffered from Project Apex—*are still suffering or are already dead*, he corrected himself.

Chapter 8

WESTOVER'S OPENING WORDS

"Do you have an opening statement, Mr. Westover?" Judge Hubert E. Lansdorf asked.

"Yes, Your Honor," replied Bob Westover, Counsel for the Commissioner of Internal Revenue, as he walked to the lectern. "We are here to present facts to the Court, not the fairy tales suggested by Mr. Laurins. There is not now, and has never been, any leakage of contamination from the Project Apex test site. The Atomic Energy Commission's reports of their continuous testing are consistent in their conclusions."

"Mr. Laurins correctly stated that we have adamantly refused to consider any reduction in the land values asserted by the IRS. There is no basis for any devaluation of the Mitchell lands. The federal government has spent millions of dollars over the years following the Project Apex tests to monitor soil, air, and water at and near the test site and protect its citizens as promised. We have reams of written reports of those monitoring efforts, and all of them reach the same conclusion: there is no contamination. It is preposterous for Mr. Laurins to assert that the land is contaminated and ludicrous to suggest that people living near the test site have become ill from contamination in the water. We are here to talk about facts, not fiction—reality, not rumors."

"In the Court today, we have representatives of the Nuclear Regulatory Commission, formerly the Atomic Energy Commission, as well as others who will testify to debunk the myth of contamination leakage and cover-up. The tax liability of the Mitchell Estate has been properly assessed based upon $1500 per acre, the full value of that land. Respondents ask the Court to uphold that assessment. Thank you."

Chapter 9

LOUISE

Arriving back home from Korea, Sam was discharged from the Army. A week later he started law school.

Being on a college campus again was invigorating for him, especially after a year in the desolation of Korea with very few associations with American women. Much of the first week of school was spent in registration and indoctrination. That first Friday night, though, merchants in the area held a street dance. At the dance, he saw a beautiful olive-skinned gal with black hair standing in a group of girls. Gathering up his courage, he went to her, introduced himself, and asked her to dance. They talked and danced long enough to learn a bit about each other. Louise Dennent was a junior at Tulane. Before the evening ended, Sam danced with Louise a few more times, and told her he wanted to call her soon. Agreeing, she gave him her phone number.

The following afternoon, Sam called Louise, and they talked for about 30 minutes. Toward the end of their conversation, he asked her to go to dinner with him the following night. As he hung up the phone, a feeling of excitement came over him as he anticipated an evening with this girl.

Despite some first date jitters, that Sunday night went well. Both Sam and Louise enjoyed each other's company. They talked over dinner and for several hours afterward, sharing some of their past and their dreams for the future. Sam learned that Louise was getting over a breakup with a former boyfriend. She said she was not interested in a new love at this point. She did, however, seem to find Sam very attractive and interesting—at least enough to go out again.

Over the next several months Sam and Louise continued to see each other. As time passed, they were together more and more, and then their friendship bloomed into love for each other. They married the following June.

At the end of his first year in law school, Sam became interested in specializing in Tax Law. After much investigation, it became clear that to pursue that specialized practice, he must get advanced education. By going to summer school each year, Sam graduated early and enrolled in the graduate division of New York University to study for a Masters of Law Degree in Taxation.

By that time, a little one was on the way. Sam, Louise, and baby Nell moved into an apartment building owned by the school, located on Washington Square. Neither Sam nor Louise had ever been to New York, so they were awed by it size, the hoards of people, the noise, and the expenses of living up north. Their lack of money restricted them in what they did for entertainment, but they still made friends with other student couples from around the country who were in like circumstances. The year flew by. Sam received his Masters degree and accepted a job with a firm in New Orleans that did a lot of tax work.

Chapter 10

PETITIONER'S TEAM

Sam had thought long and hard about whom to invite to participate in a case as large and unique as Mitchell v. IRS.

At 34, Robert Fly was much younger but an extremely bright and able trial lawyer. Sam had been greatly impressed with Rob's demeanor and self-confidence around the office even though they had never worked together on a case before this Project Apex business.

Rob and Sam shared a military background as well as similar motivations for pursuing a career in law. While attending Furman University, Rob was in the Air Force ROTC program. When he graduated, cum laude, he received his commission as a Second Lieutenant. His first duty assignment was an enjoyable one with the Strategic Air Command at Barksdale Air Force Base in Bossier City, Louisiana. So pleasant, in fact, that like Sam, he considered applying for a regular commission to make the Air Force a career, but after a year, he was reassigned to the 43rd Missile Deployment Group based near Cheyenne, Wyoming. It was there that he encountered Lt. Colonel James McGee, a man Rob described as an "arrogant, incompetent ass." McGee never let anyone forget that he was a graduate of the Air Force Academy. Rob felt that McGee had friends higher up who looked after and protected him—otherwise, he would have been forced out. McGee made life miserable for Rob and all the other men and women in their group. Like Sam, it was this experience that convinced Rob to reconsider the plan he'd once had to go to law school.

After receiving his discharge from the Air Force, Rob enrolled in law school at Vanderbilt. His passion was for the trial practice he did in Moot Court. Rob won the National Moot Court competition. He graduated that year number one in his class. In the fall after graduation, Rob married his sweetheart, Rebecca. Two years later, they had their first child—eventually they had three. Sam was very pleased to observe what a devoted and loving father Rob was. Sam was always amused when going into Rob's office. The walls were covered with the paintings and drawings by his kids, and each week a new work of art was added to the collection.

Sam had also asked Claudia Stone, a senior associate in the litigation section, to assist in the case. Claudia, an extremely bright and effective litigator, was an honors graduate from the University of Mississippi Law School. Even though she had been with the law firm for only four and a half years, she had impressed everyone in the litigation section with her genius and skill in the courtroom.

Claudia was single but had recently become engaged and planned to be married in June. She was very focused on her work and had a warm and pleasing personality. Sam wanted Claudia to handle some of the witnesses, as she was really in her element in front of the Court.

The last member of the trial team was Florence Long, one of the law firm's senior (and best) legal assistants. Florence had been with the firm for almost 20 years, having started work there soon after graduating from Centenary College. During those years with the firm, Florence had coordinated the document preparation, handling, and management in many of the largest cases. She was the best, and Sam knew her talents were critical for this case because of the huge number of documents and technical data to be handled prior to and during the trial.

Florence was a real character around the office. She always had conversation for whoever came by her desk. She was friendly, informal, and on cozy terms with all she met, never knowing a stranger—referring to everyone as "honey." What the trial team needed was someone who would help keep them in line, and Sam knew that when pushed, Florence would tell them very frankly, "Now just cool your jets, people." *She'll keep us organized and on our toes,* he thought.

Chapter 11

MEETING KAY

Ian stared out the window, looking at, but not seeing, the cold December drizzle. His thoughts were fixed on Kay. He remembered that day in late May of 1963 when he first saw her. She was the most beautiful girl he had ever seen. He had gone into Slim's Café in Tullos to eat lunch. When she came to his table to take his order, he could not take his eyes off her. She had pretty dark hair, azure blue eyes, smooth skin. She was wearing a red and white checked uniform like the other waitresses, white ankle-length socks and black and white saddle oxfords. Her uniform was close fitting, which showed off her small waist, full bosom, and rounded hips. Her shapely, suntanned legs completed her perfect figure.

Filled with embarrassment over his being so smitten with her looks, he stammered, "I'll take an iceburger and tea."

She laughed softly.

With his eyes still fixed on her, he corrected himself best he could. "I—uh, I—I mean a hamburger and iced tea."

"Coming up," she replied, with a smile.

A couple of times while waiting for his order, Kay saw Ian watching her move. She smiled at him out of the corner of her eye. When she brought him his lunch, she asked if he was new to the area or just passing through. Ian said yes he was new here, that he had come to Tullos working on a government project.

"Will you be here long?"

"Two or three years, maybe longer."

After he had eaten the hamburger, she brought him his check and said, "My name is Kay. Come back again when you can."

Somewhat clumsily, he responded, "My name is Ian, and I will come back soon."

Backing out the door so as to be able to watch her as long as possible, he collided with a customer entering the café, apologized, turned around quickly so Kay wouldn't see his red face, and nearly sprinted to his truck. Once inside his truck, he looked through the closed glass door of the café and reaffirmed to himself that truly he had seen an angel—no human could be that gorgeous. *And she smiled at me.*

Ian went back to Slim's Café for lunch the next day and the next and for each of the next three days after that. True, there was not but one other restaurant—well, two if you count Dairy Queen—in Tullos, but had there been a hundred, Ian would still have gone only to Slim's. Each time he went, Kay waited on him, and each time, they talked more and more.

Kay Hughes lived near Tullos on a 30-acre farm with her father and mother a few miles west of town. She was 22 years old, single and unattached. Kay had finished two years of nursing school. She was working and saving her money so that she could complete her last year of school and become a nurse. She had received a scholarship that paid most of her school bill, but she needed money for extra expenses, so she worked at Slim's.

On Friday, his fifth straight lunch at Slim's, overcoming his shyness and fear of rejection, Ian asked Kay to go out with him the next night. To his great delight, she accepted.

That Saturday night when he went to her home to pick her up, he met Kay's mother and father, visiting with them long enough for them to determine it was alright for their daughter to go out with him. They drove to Winnfield, where they ate dinner at Western Sizzler and then went to a movie. On the way home, Kay sat close enough to Ian that he could smell her perfume. Once at her home, they sat on the front porch and talked for over an hour. As Ian left her at the front door, Kay squeezed his hand and kissed him on the cheek. Ian floated home on a cloud.

✷

Ian slowly returned his attention back to his battered red notebook marked PROJECT APEX, taking out his handkerchief to wipe his wet eyes, glad he was alone. *I don't want to be here. I don't want to testify.* "Damn it," he said out loud to himself.

Chapter 12

PRELIMINARIES

Judge Lansdorf asked, "Anything further, Counsel?" Receiving negative responses from Laurins and Westover, Judge Lansdorf asked if they had a Stipulation of Facts to submit to the Court.

"Your Honor, we do have a Stipulation of Facts to submit into evidence at this time," Westover said. "This Stipulation contains 141 exhibits numbered 1-A to 141-EK."

The Court Clerk handed to the Judge the written Stipulation and an index describing the documents covered by it. Judge Lansdorf slowly and carefully reviewed the Stipulation and list of documents. When he completed his study, he announced that he admitted those exhibits into evidence, and then turned back to the two counsels.

Both the Petitioner and the Respondent had filed pre-trial Motions with the Court to exclude certain evidence the other party proposed to introduce—Motions in Limine. Sam wanted to dispose of the Motions before the trial started.

"Your Honor, will you hear arguments on the Motions in Limine at this time?"

"No, Counsel. I have reviewed those Motions and have determined not to consider them. I am not going to exclude any of the evidence either party proposes to introduce. You can argue your position to exclude on briefs. Do you have anything further?"

"No, Your Honor."

"Mr. Westover?"

"No, sir."

"Gentlemen, it is now 11:00. I think that rather than begin testimony and soon interrupt it, we should adjourn for lunch now. So we will recess until 12:00 p.m."

Chapter 13

BUILDING A PRACTICE

Law practice was exciting to Sam from the first day. He loved the lawyers in his firm, but especially Meyer Stein, who became Sam's mentor and close friend. Almost four years after starting to work with the firm, Sam received a call one night at home. It was one of the partners in the firm telling Sam that Meyer had suffered an aneurysm of the brain and was not expected to live through the night. Sam was devastated. When Meyer died the following night, Sam was the first person to visit the funeral home. He spent a lot of time there the following day and served as a pall bearer at the funeral.

A few months later, the senior partner came to Sam to tell him that the partners had decided to make Sam a partner in the firm at the end of the year. It was thrilling news.

Sam could not get very enthusiastic, however. Things were not the same since Meyer died. Over the following two weeks, he did a lot of soul searching and talked it over with Louise. They agreed that they were not real happy living in New Orleans. Even though their second child was just a small baby, he and Louise decided that if they were going to leave, now was the time, before the kids were in school and before Sam became a partner. He gave notice to the partners that he would be leaving in two months.

Louise found a house in Shreveport that she liked. Sam contacted a friend of the family who was retiring from the Internal Revenue Service after 25 years of service to see if he wanted to form a partnership to practice Tax Law. They created the law firm of Laurins & Briscoe and opened their doors. The firm was successful from the beginning. They had lots of work that kept both of them busy. They soon gained a reputation of being the best, and began to grow, adding new attorneys to the practice slowly. Clients came to them from all over the state and from neighboring states.

A very disciplined person, Sam always shared with the younger lawyers in his firm that his highly successful practice was a result of his dogged determination, the many hours he worked, and his strongly disciplined life. He practiced what he preached to his younger associates: to be the best, you need to study earnestly, strive for perfection, and work as long as necessary to do the job well. He insisted that everyone in the firm give the clients the best representation possible and do it promptly.

Each of those younger lawyers had been well schooled by Sam: "We never answer a client that it cannot be done. If we can't do exactly what the client asks, we will find another way to accomplish the desired result." His success in his practice was not without its price, however. Sam's law practice virtually consumed his life and was usually placed before family and friends.

As the practice required more and more time, Sam would leave home at 6:30 or 7:00 each morning and frequently did not get back home until 7:00 in the evening. It became normal for him to work 12 hours a day, Monday through Friday, and several hours on weekends.

His youngest baby, Sandra, grew and grew, but Sam hardly had time for her or Nell since starting the firm. Now with two little children to care for, Louise asked him to spend more time with her and the kids. He responded, "My work produces income that we need to live on. We are blessed that the work is there, and I have to do it. Maybe I can slack off some next year." She began to create a life for herself and the girls without him.

✳

In 1974, Sam had the opportunity to merge Laurins & Briscoe with the largest firm in the state. Soon, he was a partner in that firm as well. His quiet, confident, easy-going manner was very appealing to others. When engaged in a controversy with IRS representatives, however, Sam's quiet nature disappeared as he became a tiger, advocating the interests of his clients.

All in all, Sam had now lived in Shreveport for most of his 65 years. He knew nearly everyone in town and was well-liked. He was admired for his work throughout the state. During his 38 year of law practice, he'd become known for being an excellent counselor to his clients and a thorn in the side of his constant adversary, the IRS agents and attorneys. *Just how it's supposed to be.*

Chapter 14

THE THRILL AND THE CHALLENGE

Representing the Mitchell estate in this case was note only a great challenge but also a once in a lifetime engagement. No lawyer had ever before represented a taxpayer in a fight with the government arising out of the government's testing of nuclear explosions on the taxpayer's land. This was, after all, the only incident in history of the use of privately-owned land for testing such devices. For a case like this to end up in Tax Court was more than rare.

What made this case even more challenging, though, was that the government had all the information that Sam needed to prove his theory. Virtually all of that information was classified TOP SECRET and not available to Sam. Even if the Mitchell Estate had been given access to the test site for its own testing (which it was denied), the cost would be prohibitive, so it was totally impractical. They could only take the government reports that were available, interpret what they said and did not say, and reach their own conclusions. From their detailed study and investigation of the government information that was available, the Petitioner's expert witnesses were completely convinced that the tests had fractured the salt dome, resulting in seepage of nuclear contamination into aquifers carrying drinking water in the area.

What infuriated Sam was that the IRS attorneys had stonewalled him—refused to listen to his theory of the serious problems, vehemently denying the existence of any concern. They declined to concede one penny's reduction in the proposed tax deficiency.

Does Bob Westover really believe that there is no contamination problem, or is he being directed by his supervisor to take that position? Sam could not explain the stance his old buddy Westover was taking. They knew each other well, and usually Bob was a reasonable man. What was going on?

Chapter 15

LEAVING FOR JACKSON

Since arriving back in this area of the country, Ian was having difficulty sleeping. As he lay there, he remembered the many hours he had spent together with Kay. In vivid detail, he thought of the first time they slept together and made passionate love most of the night. He felt again the emptiness in the pit of his stomach as he recalled the day Kay told him that it was almost time for the fall semester of nursing school to begin at the University of Mississippi in Jackson and must enroll there in two weeks. Even though Jackson was no more than 175 miles away, at that moment it seemed as far away as the moon.

Ian took 10 days' vacation from Project Apex so he and Kay could be together every minute before she left for school. He took her to the beach in Destin, Florida, for a week and was thrilled and amazed at Kay's excitement over the white sandy beach and the crystal clear water. She had been to the Mississippi Gulf Coast on her high school senior class trip, but Kay had never been to Florida before, and she reveled in every moment.

Most of the days, they swam, sat in the sun, walked the beach, and looked for shells. One day Ian dove for sand dollars and found a bucketful that Kay meticulously cleaned and packed to take home. At night they went out to dinner, then back to the motel. And though exhausted from the day of touring around Florida, each night their affections ignited new energies, and they made love with such ardor that the previous night paled in comparison with the present.

All too soon their week was up, so with sad hearts, they drove back to Tullos.

On the morning she left for Jackson, Kay told Ian that she loved him with all her heart, that she would write him often, and asked him to come to see her on weekends when she was not on duty. Ian had said he loved her more than life itself and assured her that he would write her often and come to see her every chance he had. As she drove away that morning, he felt an emptiness in his life unlike anything he had experienced since his mother's death.

Chapter 16

RESPONDENT'S TEAM

Nodding cordially toward the Petitioner's counsel, Westover moved back to the government's counsel table and sat down following his opening remarks. Seated there were Donald Lawrence, Chief Counsel of the Internal Revenue Service, and Mark Levin, Assistant Secretary of the Treasury, and a younger lawyer, Elizabeth Pensa.

Bob Westover was one of the senior trial attorneys assigned to the Birmingham office of the Chief Counsel of the Internal Revenue Service, having been in that office for more than 20 years. After graduating from the University of Alabama Law School, Westover applied for a job with the Chief Counsel's office in Washington. He was accepted and served there for six years. When a position in the Alabama District Counsel's office came open, he sought it and got the job.

Somewhat introverted, Westover was not an easy person to know. At times his quiet countenance might be taken as total disinterest in what was going on around him. Sam wondered how Bob would handle this case because of its extreme complexity.

Over the years Westover and Laurins had been on the opposite sides of many tax controversies. While they were frequent adversaries, each had great respect for the other as lawyers and as individuals. Each knew the other to be exceptionally able in representing their clients.

Elizabeth Pensa was new to Sam—well, new to the profession, actually. A very pretty brunette, Sam guessed she was in her mid-twenties. He knew she was from Texas. When Bob had introduced her, Sam had chatted with her a bit. She'd grown up around Dallas and gone to school at Texas University. She had been working for the Chief

Counsel's office for only three years—ever since she graduated.

"Pensa must be pretty good for them to hire her right out of school," Sam had mentioned to Rob, "but she seems so young and inexperienced." Even Rob had thought she looked nervous.

Sam was more familiar with the rest of the team. Donald Lawrence had served as Chief Counsel for three years. Before accepting that position, he was a tax partner in the law firm of Wallace & Lipton in Lincoln, Nebraska. Lawrence had been very active in the Tax Section of the American Bar Association and several professional tax organizations. His choice as Chief Counsel was a popular one with tax lawyers across the country, including Sam. They knew him to be very competent, objective, and committed to protect and enhance the tax system. As the Chief Counsel, he was responsible for all litigation in the Tax Court. Even so, it was most unusual for the Chief Counsel to actively participate in a trial, as Lawrence was doing here.

What was even more unusual was for the Assistant Secretary of the Treasury to be actively participating in a trial. Sam was very curious as to why Mark Levin was there. He knew Levin but had not seen him in many years. Levin was a career Treasury Department employee. He and Sam had opposed each other some 15 years ago in a criminal tax trial when Levin was with the Department of Justice Criminal Division. Their personalities had clashed pretty violently, and when that trial was completed, neither of them was anxious to see the other again. Yet, here was Levin back in Sam's life.

After graduating from Columbia Law School in 1960, Levin went to Washington to be employed by the Department of Justice. He was assigned to the Tax Division and had worked in various divisions of Justice until President Carter appointed him Assistant Secretary of the Treasury. Levin's philosophy made him worlds apart from Sam Laurins.

When, just before the trial started, Lawrence and Levin had walked into the courtroom, Sam had been very surprised, wondering why these two top-level officials of the Treasury Department were there to participate in this trial.

Chapter 17

DIVORCE IN SHREVEPORT

Sam was filled with satisfaction from his work. It was challenging, calling for the best he could offer, and he loved it. He was so passionate about his job that over time, it began to occupy so big a place in his life there wasn't room for much else. Slowly, he and Louise drifted apart until they had no relationship at all. The time Sam spent at home was very uncomfortable, so he stayed away.

One weekend when Louise and the children were away, he moved out of the house. Ugly accusations were thrown back and forth, heaping hatred upon each other, until, late in the summer of 1967, their relationship dissolved in divorce. Sam began to realize how his children were on the sidelines observing their parents fighting, and he tried to avoid any communications with Louise when the children were present. He spent time with the children each weekend, doing all he could to reassure them that he loved them deeply, even though he did not love their mother any longer.

Louise and the children, then 11 and 7, continued to live in Shreveport for almost a year. Sam spent time every weekend with his children, finding that he enjoyed being with them now more than ever. He took them to California, where they visited Disneyland, San Diego, and San Sandraco, traveling in a convertible he had rented. They laughed and had fun. Their time together was precious. But the day after they returned home, his girls broke the bad news to him that they were moving to their mother's former home in Tennessee. It felt as though someone had hit him in the stomach with a baseball bat. For the first time he could remember, Sam cried.

For several months, Sam grieved. He had never felt so lonely. He called his daughters frequently and went to visit them one weekend each month. As the children got involved in school, and had been away from him longer, he became aware that his oldest daughter, Nell, was becoming more distant. It seemed clear to Sam that Nell was being influenced by others. That worried him deeply, but he did not know what to do about it. Efforts to talk to Louise about it were fruitless, as they always ended up shouting at each other. He accused Louise of turning his children against him, but she denied doing anything like that. No matter the cause, the result of the divorce was losing touch with his children, too.

During the lonely times that followed, Sam was determined to be totally self-sufficient. For years, he thought he didn't need anyone.

Yet periodically, when he was trying to go to sleep, he would recall an incident before the divorce. His daughters wanted him to take them to the zoo. It was a pretty Saturday afternoon. He was working at home, preparing for a lawsuit. He told them that he had to work, but the girls persisted in asking him to take them. Finally, he blew up, yelling, "No," louder than he intended. Nell and Sandra went crying to their rooms. That event haunted him. He wished that he could go back and undo his callous actions.

Chapter 18

A QUICK BITE

Sam suggested that Rob Fly, Claudia Stone, Clarence Mitchell and their star witness, Joe Ross, go to the University Club with him for lunch. They could go through the buffet and eat fast. While enjoying lunch, Sam finally wondered aloud, "Why are the Chief Counsel of the IRS and the Assistant Secretary of the Treasury here for this trial? It is true that there is a lot of money at stake, but not enough to justify the two of them to come from Washington. I have tried a number of cases involving more money than this, and the big dogs didn't come for those trials."

"Do you know them personally, Sam?" Clarence asked.

"Yeah. I have known them both for a good while. Don Lawrence and I served on a couple of committees of the Tax Section of the American Bar Association and have spent a lot of time together. He is a fine man, an excellent lawyer, a straight-shooter. Don agreed to leave his law practice to serve the government, and he's been doing an excellent job as Chief Counsel."

"I met Mark Levin a number of years ago when he was in the Criminal Division of the Department of Justice. He was handling a criminal tax fraud case where I represented the taxpayer. At that time, Mark was not long out of law school and had not yet learned that legal issues are not often black or white. He had all the answers, and he loved the authority vested him by his job. We did not get along well and to this day are not very friendly. I guess the burr he has had in his saddle all these years is that in that first encounter, as hard as I tried to show him he could not convict my client, he insisted on forcing us to a trial. The Jury was out only 30 minutes and acquitted my client. Mark was crushed. He and I have had other encounters over the years, none of which have been very pleasant. Whatever it is, he just doesn't like me, and I must admit, the feeling is mutual."

Following a few moments of quiet, Sam continued his line of inquiry, "Could it be that, for some reason, the DOE wanted them here to observe this trial?"

They just looked at each other.

The conversation then turned to talk about the opening statement. Sam expressed disappointment in his statement. "I should have emphasized more strongly the failure of the government to insure the safety of the people living in the area of the testing."

"Hey, I feel like your point was made clear to the Judge. He was listening intently," Claudia said.

Clarence agreed, "The Judge was very interested in what you were saying, and so were the government lawyers."

Rob asked, "Joe, do you have any comments about the opening statement or suggestions of points we want to emphasize as we go along?"

"No, I thought the opening was very effective—can't think of anything I would add or change."

Claudia said, "Well, I guess we will know where our emphasis should be as we proceed through the testimony."

Glancing at his watch, Sam said, "It's almost time to go. Clarence, you are the first up. Do you have any questions about what we will cover through your testimony?"

"Nope. I am ready."

"Okay, so let's go."

Chapter 19

WARNING

Over the following months, Ian and Kay remained in close contact. They talked on the telephone two or three times a week and wrote letters on the days they did not talk by phone. Then there were the weekends that he went to Jackson to be with her. Many of those weekends, they hardly left the Holiday Inn Medical Center where he always stayed.

It was on one of those weekends together in November that Ian told Kay about Project Apex and his work. Prior to that discussion, he had always been very secretive about his work around Tullos and the activities of the government team he worked with. Now, Ian revealed that he worked for the Atomic Energy Commission, and that he was a part of a group that had been assigned the task of preparing for and conducting underground tests of nuclear bombs in the Mitchell salt dome near her hometown.

He confided in her his deep concerns that the plan for the project was seriously flawed and was being rushed ahead without concern for the safety of the people around the test site. Ian told Kay of the many hours of research and study he had done on the project, the permeability and elasticity of the salt dome, his calculations of the likelihood that the dome would suffer one or more serious fractures from the explosions, and his fear that the drinking water in the area would become contaminated with nuclear properties. He told her of his red notebook filled with all of his research. Further, he told Kay how he had shared all of his research with the members of his group and the staff of the AEC, begging them not to go forward with the project, at least until they proved his research faulty. Ian related how he had given a memorandum to Kyle, the Manager of the Project Group, reciting his findings, and of his subsequent conversation with Kyle, who had said he'd taken Ian's memo all the way to the President, but that the President had said Apex was too important.

"Kay," he said to her, "You and your family must move away from the Tullos area. It is too dangerous. People who live there could be made very ill, even die, from the contamination from the nuclear tests if there is leakage."

"Where would we go? My father is the third generation to live on that land. He would be hard to move. Besides, my family has no money to move and start again. Everything we own is tied up in that home and the 30 acres of land."

"Please, Kay. You must speak with your parents. I'm really concerned."

She promised Ian that she would talk to her father and mother about it.

✳

His thoughts then shifted to the present and the reason he was back in Louisiana, the first time since Kay's death. What would he say on the witness stand? He remembered the direction given him and the other government witnesses by that creep, Jack Erwin, at the preparatory sessions last weekend.

Erwin said, "There's no danger from Project Apex. Every facet of the project was thoroughly researched, and the team *unanimously* agreed that there was no possibility of any safety hazard."

At this remark, Erwin had caught Ian's eyes with a stern look, then he continued with the story they were all supposed to stick to.

"The tests went off as planned with no problems. All investigative and monitoring reports consistently show there is no contamination, absolutely no health hazard. There is no way that Project Apex can be blamed for any contamination of the water, land, timber, or anything else."

Ian didn't like Erwin and surely didn't like him telling witnesses what they must say under oath, especially when it was a lie.

Finally, Ian became sleepy. He rolled over and threw his arm around the extra pillow, and wishing it was Kay, he dropped off to sleep.

Part Two: Neutron Bombardment

Chapter 20

CLARENCE MITCHELL, JR.

"Are you ready to begin, Mr. Laurins?"

"Yes, Your Honor, but first we want to invoke the rule."

The Judge announced that, as the rule had been invoked, all witnesses and potential witnesses must leave the courtroom. He cautioned them that for the duration of this trial, they were not to talk to anyone about the case.

Ian MacGregor left, along with a host of others.

"All right, Mr. Laurins, you may call your first witness."

＊

Rising to his feet and approaching the lectern, Sam announced that as its first witness, Petitioner called Clarence H. Mitchell, Jr.

The witness came forward and was greeted by the Clerk, who said, "Please raise your right hand," which Clarence did. "Do you solemnly swear that the testimony you are about to give in this case is the whole truth and nothing but the truth, so help you God?"

"I do," answered Clarence.

"Then you may be seated in the witness chair," said the Clerk, pointing to the chair to the right of Judge Lansdorf.

"Speak into the microphone."

"Mr. Mitchell, please state your full name and address," Sam requested.

"Clarence H. Mitchell, Jr., 213 Rosewood Circle, Winnfield, Louisiana."

"What relation was the deceased, Clarence H. Mitchell, to you?"

"He was my father."

"And are you the Executor of your father's estate?"

"Yes."

"Did your father own approximately 20,000 acres of timberland in south central Louisiana that is the subject of this suit?"

"Yes."

"Is there anything unusual or unique about that timberland?"

"Yes."

"What is that?"

"The government exploded some nuclear bombs under that land."

"Are you saying that the government exploded nuclear bombs below the surface of your father's privately-owned land?"

"Yes."

"When was this?"

"1964 and 1965."

"How did those explosions come to be conducted on your family's land?"

"Representatives of the Atomic Energy Commission came to my father and asked him."

Bob Westover asserted, "I object, Your Honor. This testimony is hearsay and is inadmissible."

"This is not hearsay, Your Honor," Sam responded. "Mr. Mitchell was directly involved in all negotiations with the AEC. With a little patience, he will explain this."

"Objection overruled."

Turning back to the witness, Sam asked, "Mr. Mitchell, did you work with your father during and after 1963?"

"Yes."

"Please explain how you worked together."

"When I was discharged from the Army in 1954 after serving in Korea, I came back home and joined my father in the family business. My office was next door to my dad's. He said he wanted me to learn the family business totally so that I could assume all responsibility for management, and he could take it easy. So from that point forward, he and I both attended every conference or meeting pertaining to the business."

"Going back to the contact your father had with representatives of the Atomic Energy Commission, were you present when that contact was made?"

"Yes."

"Please tell us about that contact, Mr. Mitchell."

"In December of 1962, a Mr. Kyle DeLoach of the AEC called and made an appointment to come to talk with my father and me. On the appointed day, Mr. DeLoach, along with Taylor Sheer and Andrew Carr, showed up. They explained that the federal government wanted to lease 1400 acres of our land to conduct some nuclear testing in an underground salt dome. My dad and I were shocked with that suggestion."

"But Mr. DeLoach explained that the security of the United States was being threatened because the Soviet Union was conducting secret underground nuclear testing in violation of the Limited Test Ban Treaty, and that our government could not adequately detect those tests. The theory was that if a nuclear device was detonated at the center of our salt dome, the air would cushion the shock and relatively little of the energy would be transmitted outside the cavity wall. Therefore, the earth shock signal to distant seismographs would be extremely small. Those tests were supposed to help the United States design instruments to detect detonation signals of our enemies."

"DeLoach explained that instruments to measure ground motion would be installed at numerous locations near Ground Zero and as much as 1200 miles from the salt dome. He said that it would even be monitored by submarine seismographs in the Gulf of Mexico."

"Even though no test like this had ever been conducted, Carr and Sheer said they believed the tests could be done in such a manner that radioactive contamination would not be leaked and that air blasts and thermal radiation would be contained within the salt mass."

"DeLoach said if these tests were done, the United States could better monitor the Soviet Union's tests, and we could do our own secret testing to keep pace with the Russians. Mr. Carr said the AEC and United States Bureau of Mines had conducted an extensive survey of salt domes that would meet their criteria. He explained that their research revealed there are only four salt domes in the country where the tests could be made, and the dome under our land was the most perfect of the four. They showed us several volumes of what they said was their research on the proposed tests and the salt dome under our land, but we were not permitted to read any of it. Mr. Sheer said it was highly classified information."

"Mr. Sheer explained that in case of some unexpected result, plans had been developed for a rapid evacuation of everyone in the threatened area. The detonation was expected to create a large underground cavity, which would be filled with gas after the blast. The plan was to drill into the cavity after the denotation and release or bleed off the gas. A facility would be built at the test site which, using pipes and filters, would remove most of the radioactive material from the gas as the gas was released slowly under controlled conditions."

"Mr. Carr stated that the scientists and engineers involved in the project believed the possibility of contamination of ground water in the area was remote. All radioactivity was expected to be contained in the salt dome. They would drill the main shaft down to the salt dome and then 50 feet into the dome, drilling airshafts and other shafts for various instruments around the main shaft. The main shaft would be 17 ? inches in diameter and 2700 feet deep. The bomb was to be lowered down the main shaft by winch and exploded just above the bottom of the shaft. The original plan was to explode three nuclear devices: the first at 5KT, the second and third, 100 tons each."

As his voice trailed off, Sam asked, "What were your responses to those gentlemen?"

"My father appeared to be interested in agreeing to their proposal. But I spoke up and told the AEC people that I thought their proposal was crazy—that we were not interested in having a nuclear bomb exploded on our land. We didn't know what kind of damage the explosion would cause, and we surely didn't want nuclear waste running under and over our land. Mr. Sheer said that we should have no fears—all of their research in those books they showed us concluded there would be no danger to the surface or subsurface of our land. Before I could respond, my father said we needed time for him and me to think about this. He asked the AEC men to come back to see us in a couple of weeks. Mr. DeLoach and the others agreed. DeLoach gave Dad one of his business cards and asked us to call him by the end of the month."

"As they were leaving, Mr. Carr said to my dad, 'Mr. Mitchell, you have an opportunity to be of invaluable service to your country by agreeing to permit us to do this testing on your land. I know that you love your country. You can be very proud of the contribution you will be making to protect our national security and to save the free world. All Americans will benefit from our plan of nuclear deterrence, and we believe these plans will be advanced by testing under your land. Please remember, however, that this project is TOP SECRET, so please do not mention our conversation to anyone.' With that, they left."

"What happened then?" Sam asked.

"Over the next week or 10 days, Dad and I talked a lot about the proposal. I still objected to the idea of exploding nuclear bombs anywhere close to us. But Dad was almost obsessed with the idea that our country needed to conduct the underground tests, that our salt dome was the only place they could conduct the tests, and that it was our patriotic duty to let them use our land. About two weeks later, Dad called Mr. DeLoach and agreed. DeLoach was extremely pleased. He said the AEC office in Nevada would send us a draft of a lease that our lawyer might review. A few days later, we received the proposed lease. After Dad and I had read the lease agreement a couple of times, we sent it to the family attorney, Ms. Susan Gryder, to review." In almost a whisper, he added, "My gut feeling was always that we should not do it."

"Mr. Mitchell," said Judge Lansdorf, "You talk about a salt dome. Would you describe the salt dome for me?"

"Yes, Your Honor, the salt dome is a solid block of salt approximately 1800 to 2000 feet thick located anywhere from 200 to about 1500 feet below the surface of the ground. It is about a mile in diameter. Between the ground surface and the top of the salt dome is a limestone caprock."

"Thank you, Mr. Mitchell. Counsel, you may proceed."

"Your Honor, Exhibit 15-M of the Stipulation is a drawing of the salt dome, as well as the strata surrounding it and the aquifers above it," Laurins stated.

Clarence Mitchell related how Susan Gryder, their attorney, received a draft of the lease agreement from the Property Management Division of the AEC in Las Vegas. The lease provided that the Mitchells would lease 1400 acres of land to the United States, acting through the AEC, for a period of five years, for the purpose of underground testing. It included 160 acres located in the center of the 1400, designated as Surface Ground Zero, subject to the exclusive use and control of the AEC. The AEC would pay a monthly rental of $600, plus a one-time payment of $7500 for the road right-of-way and for possible damage to timber on the 160 acres. By the terms of the agreement, Mitchell leased to the government both surface and subsurface of the 1400 acres, with a 40-foot right-of-way through the other Mitchell land for access from the primary county road. While the lease was only for six months, it granted options to the AEC to renew the lease for as many as 10 years.

At the insistence of Susan Gryder, the Mitchells demanded that the government indemnify Mr. Mitchell from any liability arising from the government's use of the land. The lease was altered to include an indemnity, which even though not acceptable to Susan, Mr. Mitchell insisted he would accept. Susan tried to make Mr. Mitchell see that the indemnity provision of the lease was unacceptable in that it was vague in its scope. Further, the indemnity did not comply with federal laws that prohibit federal agencies from entering into open-ended obligations without specific authorization or appropriation of funds to satisfy the obligation. But Mr. Mitchell refused to insist on more. Kyle DeLoach assured him that the government so appreciated his cooperation that it would look after him, and he accepted that. The parties executed the lease on January 4, 1963, to be effective January 1, 1963. The lease agreement was introduced into evidence as a part of the parties' Joint Stipulation of Facts.

Chapter 21

BARBARA

Sam continued to go to the Episcopal Church that he and his family had attended there in Shreveport, though he attended the service and left immediately. One Sunday, as he was leaving, the priest stopped him to talk. During the conversation, the priest asked Sam, "Are you dating anyone?" Sam said no.

"Good. I want you to know a lady in our church who is a wonderful person and a Christian. Her husband died almost a year ago. Knowing the both of you, I believe that you would really enjoy each other. Her name is Barbara Campbell."

Sam reluctantly agreed to meet the lady. The priest told Sam to come to the covered dish supper that coming Wednesday night, and he would introduce them. Since he had a lot of respect for his priest, who he counted as a friend—and since he'd had nothing else on his social calendar lately—Sam showed up for the potluck. He met Barbara and talked with her a while. He learned that she had four children, ages five to nine, that her husband had died on the golf course, and that she intended to continue living at their home in Shreveport. Despite his reticence, he had to admit he liked her and she was attractive.

After that night, they talked on the phone several times, and then he asked her to go to dinner. She did not immediately say yes, but she finally agreed.

That first date was not very pleasant for either of them. Both were nervous and ill at ease, and neither ate much of their dinner. Even so, Sam found Barbara to be very enjoyable company. She was pretty, blond, trim, and had a good figure. Eventually, Sam asked if he could come to her home to visit. She agreed. He went time and again, each visit, spending more time with the children, getting to know them. As he and Barbara became more comfortable, they began to go out more. They would talk for hours about anything and everything. Two months later, they were seeing each other almost every night. Barbara was a loving person who deeply cared about other people. She readily put her own interests behind those of her children or her friends. While she had very little money, she was teaching piano and was determined to give her children whatever they needed. This was very different from Louise, who Sam, in his bitterness, felt had money and wanted to obtain more, satisfying her own desires first.

Barbara's children loved Sam, and he them. Having them in his life filled the void caused by his own children living away. One weekend when he was going to Tennessee to see his children, he took Barbara and the four children. To his great pleasure, Nell and Sandra liked Barbara and her kids. In fact, Sandra remembered fondly that she had been in Barbara's Sunday school class back at the church in Shreveport.

Sam and Barbara married in December, 1969. Following their honeymoon in Carmel and San Francisco, they came home to Shreveport and moved into their new house with her four children to start a new life. The six of them had to make adjustments in their new family, but they all did so earnestly.

Chapter 22

CLARENCE CONTINUES

Mitchell testified that the AEC moved onto the leased acreage and commenced preparations for their testing. They took bids from drilling contractors to drill exploratory holes and remove core samples to test for composition of the subsurface and how it would transmit earth shock. Neither his father nor Clarence was told anything about the testing or its results, but on May 15, 1963, the AEC gave written notice of the exercise of its option to extend the lease.

At that point the first test, originally scheduled for June 10, was put on hold for eight months. Kyle DeLoach advised the Mitchells that the delay was necessary to permit the AEC to focus its attention on the weapons testing programs in Nevada and the Pacific.

In January, 1964, the date for the first test was again moved back. From time to time, DeLoach or others from the AEC would take Mr. Mitchell to the area of the test site area to see the activity, but they never went close enough for Mitchell to be able to determine exactly what they were doing.

Clarence went on to say that between April 1 and August 31, 1964, personnel from the United States Public Health Service, who were assigned the responsibility of maintaining good public relations with people in the vicinity of the test site, made a house-to-house population survey. The purpose of that survey was to plan for evacuation. It was determined that 290 people lived within a 2.6 radius of Surface Ground Zero, 980 people lived within a 4.5 mile radius, and another 1933 people lived within a 10 mile radius from Surface Ground Zero.

During this preparation stage, a program to obtain information on dairy cattle and milk processing plants in the area was initiated. The information gathered was used to plan for the amounts of feed that might be needed if an area was contaminated. A milk-sampling program was also developed.

The AEC held public meetings with people who lived in the area of the test site to acquaint the people with what they might expect from the test and to answer questions. As time for the first test drew closer, by way of the newspaper, radio, and television, the AEC advised people of the date they expected to detonate the first shot. The date set for that first shot was September 22, 1964, but technical problems delayed the shot, and it was rescheduled for September 28 at 10:00 a.m. The weather turned bad on the night of September 27, with heavy winds and rain, so the test was further delayed. Finally, in October of 1964, the order was given to proceed with the shot.

At 05:30 hours on the morning of the first shot, people in the zero to 2.6-mile area and those in the predicted downwind sector out to five miles were evacuated to designated assembly areas. Entrance to the controlled area was barred by roadblocks manned by government agents. The first nuclear explosion, the "Sailfish Event," was 5.3 kilotons and was detonated at 10:00 a.m. on October 22.

"Did you experience any results of the explosion?" Laurins asked Mitchell.

"I was standing in the door of my office in Winnfield when I felt the whole building shake and heard windows rattle. As I looked outside at the black-top parking lot, the pavement raised and lowered almost a foot in the same movement as waves in the ocean."

"Did your office building suffer any damage?"

"No serious damage, but several buildings and many homes in town suffered damage—cracks in foundations and walls, windows broken, china and things like that knocked to the floor and broken. Remember, this bomb was 5 kilotons, almost a quarter of the power of the atomic bomb blast over Hiroshima."

"How far were you from the test site, Mr. Mitchell?" asked Judge Lansdorf.

"About twenty-six miles, Your Honor. But there was damage like that as far away as 90 miles."

Clarence went on. "After the shot, when the 'all clear' was given, Public Health Service officers escorted the evacuees back to their homes. Upon reaching the evacuee's home, each Public Health officer made a cursory inspection of the dwelling to ensure that the dwelling was safe to enter and occupy. Noticeable damage was reported to the control point."

"Our local creeks ran black. I thought that was just a rumor, so I had to have a look for myself, and sure enough. They said it was silt."

"When the shot occurred, ground motion was felt as far away as 50 miles. Cracks as large as three to five inches along the roads and drill pads occurred within a mile of Ground Zero; steep banks along a creek collapsed; huge cracks in the ground developed; several hundred mud boils occurred way out from Ground Zero, and water flowed from the boils for up to six hours; heavy objects such as concrete pads, instrument trailers, and drill rig parts were permanently displaced. "

"They reported that air sampling data taken from as far away as Little Rock and Nashville reflected an abrupt peak in gross Beta activity eight days after the shot. On October 30, 1964, the post-shot Beta activity of ground water in the vicinity was sampled from six test wells in the area. Water samples were taken from the caprock at a depth of 934 to 1006 feet and through intervening aquifers to Aquifer One at a depth of 365 to 421 feet from the surface. The results of the tests were that Beta activity of the samples was within the expected range of values for waters in the vicinity of the salt dome."

Sam asked, "That's pretty detailed information. How do you know all this technical data?"

"Well, a lot of it was in the newspapers. I know some of this from talking with the guys who worked on the project. Some was in the information the AEC gave my father when we signed the contract. Some of it I learned at the town meeting. But let me tell you, when it's happening on your land, you remember a lot of details. The neighbors had lots of questions. I wanted to know all I could."

Sam then said, "Tell us what happened next."

"Things were quiet for about 6 months. We had no direct contact with the AEC, even though there was a lot of activity at the test site. In the summer of 1965, the AEC announced in the newspaper that they were preparing for a second nuclear test before the end of the year. On Saturday, December 3, the second nuclear explosion was made, a device reported to be about a half kiloton. Maybe because it was a smaller device, the shock was not experienced as far away as the first test. Later, the AEC announced in the newspaper that the tests were a success and that they now knew secret testing could be conducted without being detected." Clarence stopped to clear his throat.

"After the first blast, the AEC found that an underground cavity had been formed, and radioactive elements had been released into the salt dome walls. The cavity was spherical, with a radius of about 17.4 meters and a total volume of 19,367 meters. The bottom was flat, covered by about 5000 tons of liquefied salt, forming a puddle. It took over 30 days for that puddle to solidify. The rock walls were micro-fractured extensively and contained some macro-fractures. The AEC concluded that the resulting cavity was stable and probably could be used for a de-coupled experiment. However, the AEC also concluded that the material around the cavity was less competent than its pre-shot condition. The strength properties and stress distribution of that rock were not known. Samples from the bottom revealed a black, highly radioactive concentrate."

Mitchell went on to relate how no results of the test were disclosed to anyone for over a year, even though there appeared to be rather frantic activity at and near the test site.

"For several months after the first explosion, no information was available from the government. But it was obvious that something had gone wrong, because they had told us the second test would be conducted soon after the first, and it was not. Some time later, we were told that problems had arisen underground due to the extreme heat in the salt dome left from the first blast. Other problems were alluded to, but no public disclosures of these were ever made."

"On February 8, 1965, sixteen Public Health Service officers were activated to participate in the post-shot activities, including cavity penetration and bleed down."

The Judge asked Mitchell to explain "bleed down."

"Bleed down is a process of controlled release of gases from the cavity. Although the AEC had predicted that there would be no radiological problem off-site, those additional people were used to keep a continuous record of the contamination background fluctuations and to provide coverage in the off-site area in the event of an unforeseen emergency."

From there, Clarence went on to explain how, prior to penetration of the cavity, the environmental sampling program was increased beginning February 15. For the purpose of coverage during drilling and cavity studies, additional air, milk, and vegetation sampling stations and radiation background recorders were put into operation within the five-mile radius of Ground Zero. When added to those sampling stations already established, that made a total of 94 stations in operation in the area of Ground Zero and outward for a radius of 50 miles.

On the morning of March 4, 1965, the drill-back began, and the cavity was penetrated at the depth of 2660 feet. The temperature of the cavity was still 400 degrees Fahrenheit—four months after the first blast. Even though the bleed down plant had been operating during drill-back, it was put into full-scale operations on March 6 and operated continuously the next two days.

In mid-November, 1965, the government started its program of notifying residents in the area of its plan to detonate the second bomb in early December. On the morning of December 3, 1965, the second shot, smaller in size than the first, was detonated. So the second test, a half-ton blast that had originally been scheduled to be made within two months of the first, had by then been delayed for 14 months.

Clarence said, "On February 2, 1969, the Department of Defense detonated in the salt dome cavity a non-nuclear gas explosion equivalent to about 315 tons of TNT. The officer in charge described it as 'the largest controlled gas explosion ever detonated anywhere.' A second such test explosion was made on April 21, 1969."

Sam Laurins interrupted his client, "Mr. Mitchell, did the AEC explain the purpose of these non-nuclear blasts to you and the towns-people?"

"No, sir. Not really. Nor did they ever say why they didn't follow through with the third nuclear blast as planned."

"Thank you. Go on."

"The AEC announced in August, 1971, that it would decommission its underground test facility and return it to us. The surface of the site was to be cleaned and decontaminated. All vehicles, equipment, supplies, movable materials and contaminated soil were to be packed, secured, and shipped to Nevada for disposal. Liquids containing radioactive matter were to be reinserted into the salt dome cavity for permanent storage. In May, 1972, the AEC announced that the clean-up was complete and that everything had been done as in accordance with the Decommission Plan. The following month, the AEC initiated a long term monitoring program to conduct environmental monitoring at and around the site."

Mitchell explained how, in documenting the decommissioning of the test site, the government and his father executed a Withdrawal Agreement. By its terms, the parties agreed that the government was concluding its leasehold interest in the property but reserving the right of ingress and egress on the property to take soil and water samples and to operate, maintain, and monitor certain wells on the property for a 10-year period, with an option to extend for another 10 years.

"Dad agreed that the government owned all salt and minerals under the 160-acre tract that was totally controlled by the government. He also agreed that there would be no surface access to anyone other than the government and us and that there would be no removal of any minerals from below the depth of mean sea level. Further, my father agreed not to permit anyone to drill, excavate, explore, or mine under any of the leased 1400 acres, nor to permit anyone to remove any materials, whether solid, gaseous, or fluid, from below mean sea level without prior written approval of the government."

Sam asked, "What happened then, Mr. Mitchell?"

"The AEC reported that no radioactive materials were found in the air, water, milk, or vegetation samples from the area, but higher than normal amounts of tritium were found."

"Was anything unusual happening to the people of the area?"

"Yes. By this time, even with those reports that everything was fine, people were getting sick. We heard more and more stories of people who lived southeast of the test site becoming ill and dying from cancer."

Westover demanded, "I object, Your Honor. This is hearsay evidence and not properly admissible."

Judge Lansdorf inquired, "Who is 'we'? Who heard this information, Mr. Mitchell?"

"My father and me, Your Honor."

"From whom did you gain this information?"

"I can remember five different families who shared with me that someone in their family had cancer and that they knew many more families in the area who had been stricken in the same way."

"Objection," cried Westover. "That is hearsay."

"Yes, Mr. Mitchell. That is improper testimony," responded Judge Lansdorf.

"Did anything else happen at that time, Mr. Mitchell?" Laurins asked.

"Yes, a lot happened. One of our employees, whose job it was to patrol a portion of our lands, including the test site, reported that something was really wrong out there. He told me of some things he had discovered on the test site: some 55-gallon drums and boxes of what looked like protective suits (gas masks, tools, etc.) had obviously been buried but were now gradually being uncovered by rain and wind erosion. He took me to see them. While there, we looked around some more and found liquid flowing out of two wells where the concrete seals had cracked. We also discovered what we believe to be some large buried equipment, maybe even a truck."

"When was this?"

"February, 1973. The problems we observed were substantiated soon after that, when the AEC reported that clean-up following the underground testing was inadequate. They said that this incomplete clean-up job was the apparent cause of the continued high radiation levels they still found at and near the test site. Their tests revealed high levels of tritium, much higher—50 times higher—than the allowable level, together with high levels of other radioactive isotopes. What angered me most was that during all that time, the government had been publishing reports to the people who lived in the area, and to my father and me, stating that there was no serious problem, that no health hazard existed."

"What happened then, Mr. Mitchell?" Sam continued.

"The AEC sent in teams of people who spent several months at the test site. In December, 1973, the AEC announced that they had cleaned up some areas near the test site, testing water in the area and finding nothing wrong. This is the same report they had put out for nine years, since the first test blast. Meanwhile, more and more people in the vicinity of the test site were stricken with cancer. There were also reports of wildlife on the property glowing in the dark and animals having other abnormalities. People were scared."

"Objection!"

"Let him finish this train of thought, and then I will rule on the objection," the Judge decided.

"Yes, we continued to receive reports of frogs with two heads or deer glowing unnaturally at night. People near the test site were seriously ill. People we knew were dying. We also saw that our livelihood was being affected: trees in the test site area were seriously stunted, if they grew at all. No other vegetation would grow there, and occasionally some kind of liquid would seem to boil out of the concrete cap of one of the test shafts. Rumors were rampant that the whole area was contaminated, and everything seemed to point to that being the case."

"I object to this testimony of rumors and hearsay, and I demand that it be stricken from the record," screamed Westover.

"Sustained."

"Mr. Mitchell, did anything happen at or pertaining to the test site after December, 1973?" asked Sam.

"We requested the AEC go onto the property and conduct extensive testing to put to bed once and for all the question of possible contamination of the area. We also asked them to do additional clean-up of the area. But the AEC put us off time and again with all kinds of excuses. They wanted to do it, they said, but their budget would not permit it—it was on their list of things to do, but other projects had higher priority—we expect to do this anytime now, and on and on."

"It is now 1984. Has the AEC ever undertaken that extensive testing and clean-up that you requested?" posed Sam.

"Apparently us filing this lawsuit got their attention, because three months after this suit was filed, the AEC asked for permission to reenter our land and advised that they would spend $50-60 million in a total clean-up effort."

"Mr. Mitchell, you testified that three months after the Petition was filed in this case, the AEC contacted you seeking permission to reenter your land in order to conduct a total clean-up effort. The Petition was filed with this Court on August 6, 1980. Is it your testimony that the government people contacted you sometime in November, 1980?"

"Yes, sir."

"Are you aware that the Atomic Energy Commission was abolished, and the agency ultimately became the Nuclear Regulatory Commission in 1974, now under the Department of Energy since 1977?" Sam asked.

"Yes, sir."

"So the government people who contacted you in 1980 were representatives of the DOE?"

"That is correct. I just always think of those people as being the Atomic Energy Commission."

"In 1973, the AEC issued their certificate that the test site was completely clean. Did they tell you why they now wanted to come back for a total clean-up of an area they had already declared clean?"

"No. I asked that question several times but was told they were ordered from higher up to do it."

Sam then questioned Clarence about how the value of the timberland was determined for inclusion in the estate tax return. Mitchell explained that they had engaged a reputable Louisiana timber management company to appraise the timberland and had used that appraised value in the tax return. The tax return was actually prepared by an accounting firm in Shreveport. Mitchell explained that he had told neither the timberland appraiser nor the accountant of the nuclear testing on the land.

"Why on earth would you not mention this testing to the professionals who were evaluating your property?"

"I just didn't think of it. The AEC had so strongly asserted for so long that the land was completely clear, I just did not see where it was important or relevant. They also always emphasized the importance of secrecy. Plus, maybe I just wanted to keep the past in the past."

"In fact, Mr. Mitchell, you did not even tell me about the nuclear activity on your property, did you? That is why we asked for a continuance on this case." Sam said.

"That's correct, sir. My father had always insisted that out of respect for our country, we should do what the government people said, and we should trust them. I guess between the AEC's admonishments about silence and Dad's faith in America, it must have really sunk in, because I just never even considered the relationship of the blasts to the tax assessment when I hired you to be my attorney."

Those present in the courtroom murmured audibly.

Chapter 23

SEQUESTERED

The witness room consisted of a large waiting room with three smaller adjoining rooms. After sitting in the waiting room and engaging in casual conversation with the other witnesses for a while, Ian took his briefcase and moved to one of the smaller rooms, closing the glass door behind him. He opened his briefcase and took from it his beat-up red notebook labeled IAN MACGREGOR, PROJECT APEX CHIEF ENGINEER: PERSONAL AND CONFIDENTIAL. In removing the book, a photograph fell to the floor. As he reached over to pick it up, he studied for some time the beautiful girl in the picture. Her dark curly hair looked almost jet black against the bright red sweater she was wearing. Her piercing blue eyes and smooth, tanned skin matched the perfectly formed features of her face, punctuated by a beautiful, loving smile. His life would never be the same.

Chapter 24

GRAND DISCOVERY

In preparing for what seemed to be a standard tax assessment case for Mr. Clarence Mitchell, Jr., Sam had stumbled onto information referencing some kind of nuclear testing right in the middle of the Mitchell land!

"Clarence!" he'd exclaimed. "Why didn't you tell me? And what's the real story here?"

Once Clarence had finally revealed the whole situation, Sam asked him, "Before you came to me, did the Internal Revenue Service or their attorneys ever discuss or suggest that they might reduce their proposed value of the timberland?"

Clarence said, "Not only have they refused to discuss any reduction of value, but they continue to say they have mountains of documents showing there is no problem with the land. They will not even consider a reduction."

Since the trial date set by the Court was only a month away at that point, Sam requested a continuance until he could understand the significance of those newly discovered facts. Sam's trial team went to work fast, with great excitement and earnestness, to locate experts who could enlighten them as to what effect the nuclear testing would have on the land and timber values. For the next 10 months, the trial team spent huge amounts of time educating themselves on the issues.

In working with Joseph Ross, their key expert, the trial team discovered that much of the documentation that could be helpful to their case was classified SECRET or higher and was not available to them. That made it necessary for the experts and the trial team to carefully review each of the documents that were available to look for information that would be helpful to them. Ross found glaring inconsistencies, inaccuracies, and critical matters not covered at all in the available documents. He also found seriously flawed basic geological assumptions made by the government. Hidden away in some of the documents were acknowledgements that tritium, antimony-125, and cesium-137 had been found at the test site and surrounding area as late as 1975.

"This is amazing—and a little frightening! I can't believe our government did something so stupid. Joe's information is a jackpot," Rob had told Sam after talking with Joe Ross.

Excited but cautious, Sam had told his younger associate, "Now, hold on there, buddy. We haven't proven anything yet."

The information Ross was able to glean from the numerous government reports was also consistent with general knowledge of the residents of Tullos: that incidences of cancer among them was extremely high. In his report now filed with the Court, Ross concluded that there was a probability of nuclear contamination on some part of the Mitchell land, that the 1400 acres leased to the government had no value, and that the value of the rest of the land would be adversely affected.

The trial team engaged another timberland expert, Shea Claremore, to appraise the land. Shea, known for her knowledge and experience in the management, purchase, sale, and valuations of timberland, was thought to be the best. In cruising the timber and inspecting the land, she was shown the test site and educated in the methods used in the testing and clean-up. Shea concluded that the highest and best use for the land was as timberland. Taking the Ross opinion as a foundation for establishing the negatives to the land, she determined that the value of the land was $8 million, not the IRS-assessed value of $30 million. Sam couldn't wait until the Judge heard this testimony.

✳

"Counsel," said Judge Lansdorf, "The hour is late. We have had a pretty full day."

The courtroom was still buzzing from the idea that the Mitchell family had been so indoctrinated by the AEC that they didn't even realize the impact of Project Apex on their property's value.

"Yes, Your Honor. We have completed Mr. Mitchell's testimony for the time being," Laurins replied.

"Very well then. We will recess and recommence in the morning at nine o'clock," Lansdorf declared.

The Clerk called out, "All rise," at which everyone in the room quickly stood, and Judge Lansdorf retired to his chambers.

Chapter 25

ESTRANGED

Barbara always went to Tennessee with Sam now for his weekend with his children. She loved Nell and Sandra, and they loved her. But Sam's daughters remained aloof from him. At times he felt a spark of love, but mostly he felt their anger. When he tried to talk to them about it, each girl would do all she could to avoid the conversation. If they said anything it was accusatory of the way he had treated their mother. It was obvious that Louise's family was angry at him over the divorce. Nell, especially, was reflecting that anger.

When they went to Tennessee, Sam would rent two adjoining motel rooms, one for Barbara and him, the other for the children. During the weekend visits, however, his children were often involved in their own activities. They sometimes didn't have much time for their dad, and the relationship was definitely strained. Sam tried to be understanding. Some weekends he saw very little of his children, so he questioned the value in making the effort to drive that long distance for a few very short moments with them.

After one of those weekends, Sam looked out the window at the desolate snow-laden fields as he and Barbara drove back home. As if she could read his mind, Barbara took his hand and sat silently. When Sam could take it no longer, he said, "When I'm with them—the girls—when I'm with them, I feel like they don't even see me—they don't even care if I come to see them or not."

"Of course they care," said Barbara. "I see the light in their eyes. It will mean something to them later, honey, that you tried. And besides, when I've talked to her lately, Louise says that they are always excited about your coming to see them, and they have a good time."

Sam thought it odd that his wife and his ex-wife were becoming friends. "You two are quite the chums, it seems?" he said.

"And why shouldn't we be? At least we have Nell and Sandra's welfare in common."

Sam knew that was true, but he just wasn't sure where he fit in.

Barbara continually reassured Sam that his children loved him. She would say "Sweetheart, sooner or later the girls will begin thinking for themselves, and when they do, your relationship with them will be restored." He wondered if that could be true.

Both Sam and Barbara felt blessed that his children loved her and that his stepchildren loved his girls. Nell and Sandra were always invited—urged to go—on family trips and vacations. While Sandra was eager to go, and did, Nell always had an excuse why she couldn't.

Sam called his girls frequently, though many times Nell did not talk to him. Sometimes Louise would answer the phone, which was unfortunate. The sound of her voice generated anger in Sam. So when there was a chance that Louise would be on the phone, Sam had Barbara talk to her. Over a period of time Barbara and Louise had indeed become cordial.

Chapter 26

CROSS-EXAMINING MR. MITCHELL

Early the next morning, Westover began by questioning Mitchell as to whether the family had sold timber from the land since the blasts, and if there was any reduction in the price because it had come from the land where the testing had been conducted.

Mitchell admitted, "Until about 1980, some timber continued to be sold from parcels of the land located a few miles from Surface Ground Zero, and that price was not affected. But since 1980, though, no one will buy my timber. Not to mention that many of the trees are now undersized and simply don't have the value they should, even if they do sell."

Westover asked Mitchell how he could determine that a tree was undersized.

"We bore plugs from trees. By counting the rings, we can determine the age of the tree. Technical information is available to tell what size a given type of tree should be at specified ages. That's how we know our timber is undersized, as well as just being in the business long enough to know from experience."

Westover quickly moved on. "Mr. Mitchell, haven't you been provided with the AEC reports showing that the tests went according to plans, that the site is completely clean, and that there were no lasting adverse effects of the testing?"

Mitchell said yes, adding, "Yeah, but some of those statements from the AEC were obviously inaccurate because of all the reports of deformed animals and stunted vegetation on the land and the very high incidences of cancer in the area. The AEC reports had to be wrong. My Dad would have been with us a lot longer if not for those tests." Here, Clarence paused.

Westover moved, "Strike that from the record," and the Judge agreed to his request.

"A week before this trial," Clarence continued, "when we were back in the area of Ground Zero with the trial team, we encountered a buddy of mine from town. He was up on a bulldozer and said he was being paid by the government to improve some roads and to uncover something buried in a mound nearby. We asked him why he was just sitting there. My friend said, 'I can't start until the government brings the protective clothing they insist I'd better wear,' which confirmed our suspicions both that there was contamination and that the government knew about it."

Sam started realizing Westover's case was going nowhere.

Trying to appear unconcerned with what the witness had said, Westover paused to look at his notepad. Sam wondered why his old acquaintance seemed so off his game. He knew Bob was a capable attorney. What was wrong?

Then, as if sensing that others could tell he was faltering, Bob Westover took his eyes off his notepad, stood up taller, and took on a sort of vigor. Sam got worried.

"Mr. Mitchell, did you know the real value of your property prior to Mr. Laurins hiring Joseph Ross to assess it, which is the report that valued your land at $8 million instead of $30 million?"

"No."

"Did you ever have your property professionally appraised on your own, prior to meeting with Mr. Laurins?"

"No."

"Then why did you ever seek out an attorney against the IRS in the first place?"

Sam stood and objected.

"Sustained," said Judge Lansdorf.

Westover pressed on, "Did you ever get a second opinion on the value of your property?"

Clarence hesitated but then said no.

"Have you, of your own accord, hired an independent specialist in environmental pollutants or nuclear contamination?"

"No, I expected that was the government's job, and besides, it would be cost prohibitive."

"Do you have any credentials or expertise to evaluate real estate or environmental pollutants yourself?

"No, but I...."

"Just answer yes or no, please, Mr. Mitchell," Bob insisted.

"No."

Westover went on, "Mr. Mitchell, did you personally read the AEC reports yourself?"

"No."

"Then if you are not an expert in this matter yourself, and you didn't read their reports, why did you ever doubt the AEC? Or did you only start questioning them once Mr. Laurins put ideas in your head?"

On his feet before Westover could even get the words out, Sam protested hotly.

"Objection sustained, and watch it, Mr. Westover," the Judge said.

Now Sam knew why Bob Westover wanted to appear to be fumbling at first. He wanted to hit Clarence hard at the end.

Westover then advised the Court that he had no further questions.

When Sam declined to question Mitchell further, the Judge excused the witness.

Chapter 27

GRADUATION

In early June, 1964, when Kay graduated—with distinction—from nursing school in Jackson, Ian and her parents, Pam and Bobby Lee, were there for the ceremony. It was impossible to determine who was most proud of Kay—her parents or Ian. Kay was the first member of either of their families to graduate from college, so Pam and Bobby Lee were beside themselves. That night, Ian took the four of them to dinner at Dennery's. Even though neither Pam nor Bobby Lee drank, Ian and Kay persuaded them to have a glass of wine to celebrate.

Kay had committed to go to work for Dr. Blair Vassar in his clinic in Winnfield. He had been the Hughes' family doctor for 30 years and had actually delivered Kay when she was born. He had encouraged Kay to go to nursing school, reminding her every time he saw her that she would be his nurse when she graduated. Kay never questioned that, nor thought about working for anyone else. She loved Dr. Vassar and wanted to live in the area of Louisiana that had always been home.

After graduation, Kay took a couple weeks off before starting to work. During that time, she got settled back in her parent's home, helped her mother do some serious house cleaning, slept late, sun bathed, and took it easy. Ian was very busy at the test site as final actions were underway in preparations for the first test. Even so, he managed to be with Kay almost every night.

It was during that summer that Ian talked with Kay's parents about moving from the area. One night, while having dinner with the family, Ian told them of his concern for their safety because of the proximity of their home to the test site. From the numerous questions she asked and comments she made, it was obvious that Pam was concerned. But Bobby Lee responded that he had attended meetings held by the government people, and they assured all the neighbors that there was no threat to the safety of the residents of the area. Besides that, he said that he could not afford to move. His home and the 40 acres were just about all that he owned, and no one would buy the property with the tests pending. He could not leave if he wanted to.

"Mr. Hughes, I hate to say it, but I am not sure the government officials told you the whole story at those meetings." Ian related to the Hughes how he had been concerned about the testing and the potential hazards to people living in the area since the beginning of the project. He told them of the research and the many calculations he had made on his own that refuted the results anticipated by the AEC.

He also told them of his efforts to stop the testing at that site and how the decision to keep going went as far up as the President and the CIA. Ian implored Bobby Lee to leave their home at least for some extended time after the tests, even if they could not move permanently, just to give some time to see what happened.

Bobby Lee said, "Ian, I admire you, and I respect your opinions," then his tone changed in way that made sure this concluded their discussion, "but the government representatives assured us that everything would be fine."

That was the last time Ian talked to Pam and Bobby Lee Hughes about the danger he perceived that they faced.

Chapter 28

INTRODUCING JOSEPH ROSS

Rob Fly stood and announced to the Court that he called Joseph L. Ross as a witness. Mr. Ross entered the courtroom, walked to the witness stand, and after being duly sworn, took his seat. He gave his full name and address and confirmed that he was a hydro-geologist with a degree in geological engineering.

"I've gained specialized knowledge and experience in the injection of waste into subsurface geological formations, especially concerning waste with radioactive properties and its effect on groundwater. I also have experience determining the impact on property values where waste has been injected into the subsurface. I evaluate property to determine what contaminants are there, what potential they have for mobility on that property (or from that property to adjoining property), and what the magnitude and degree of contamination there is."

Fly asked Ross to explain how he got into this field of work.

"I got a degree in chemical engineering from City College of New York, then after service in the Army in Southeast Asia, I attended Oklahoma University, where I earned a master's degree in geological engineering with emphasis on hydrogeology. I wrote my thesis on the underground injection and deep-well disposal of waste."

Ross continued to introduce his credentials as requested. He had been employed by an international environmental engineering firm for 20 years, working with problems of contaminated groundwater systems, hydro-geologic and water quality. Once with Oak Ridge National Laboratory, he was designated Chief of Project to evaluate the possibility of disposal of high-level radioactive waste in salt domes. As one of his duties for that project, he studied the feasibility of disposing nuclear waste in salt domes in Mississippi and Louisiana.

Sam and Rob exchanged glances. They could tell Westover's team was not enjoying how clearly well-matched Joe Ross was as a witness for this case's situation. Sam thought, *Wait until they hear the rest.*

Ross went on to explain that one of the larger issues they faced in the proposed disposal was the possible dissolution of salt domes through the groundwater system.

"What do you mean by dissolution of the salt dome, Mr. Ross?" the Judge interrupted.

"It's the melting of the salt, Your Honor. We did numerous studies to determine the long-term effects of such dissolution. Through that project and others, we were trying to gain knowledge about the effect of injecting waste into deep wells—where the waste went and what to do if it escaped."

Ross testified that he was involved in several other projects concerning characterization of groundwater contamination as a result of seepage of uranium, tritium, and other hazardous materials.

Fly then tendered Joseph Ross as an expert in environmental consulting as it applies to real estate and hydro-geology, including the groundwater transportation of contaminants, especially nuclear waste, as well as the effects on groundwater surrounding the storage of nuclear waste in salt domes, disposal of hazardous waste by injection into deep wells, and what redemption activities, data, and analysis satisfy AEC, NRC, DOE, and EPA regulations.

"Do you have any objections to his qualifications, Mr. Westover?" Judge Lansdorf asked.

"I don't agree with all those, but I agree that he is an expert in the report that he has filed in this case. He can testify from the report he has filed as an expert witness," replied Westover.

"Is there some difference between the categories you have listed and the categories in the report, Mr. Fly?" the Judge inquired.

"No, Your Honor."

"Then I am going to accept him as an expert for purposes of the report tendered."

The report identified the scope of work Ross had done for the Petitioner, Mitchell. Among other things, it described the land involved. It cited the very lengthy list of federal and state reports and newspaper clippings and other reports utilized as a database, pointing out how Ross was handicapped because many documents relevant to the issue were still classified TOP SECRET and not available. Additional sources of information consisted of aerial photographs, topographic maps, and information obtained from Ross' personal reconnaissance of the area.

Rob handed Ross a copy and asked him to identify it as his report, which Ross did. Rob asked the clerk to mark the report for identification as an exhibit to Ross' testimony, then offered the report into evidence.

Chapter 29

DON'T DO IT AGAIN, SAM

The law firm's practice was booming—to the point that they hired three new lawyers. Although he'd done better about spending time at home when he started dating Barbara, as time passed, Sam began to once again extend the hours he spent at the office until, about the time of the second anniversary of his marriage to Barbara, he was back to twelve hour days. Even when he was at home, much of the time, he was holed up in his study reading the latest tax rulings, cases, and other publications, thus creating distance between himself and family life.

It seemed that as more of his attention was turned to his work, his subconscious thoughts pushed him closer and closer into an island of self-sufficiency. The one day that Sam refused to work now, except for rare instances, was Saturday. That was the day that he and his three close friends played golf at the Country Club. Even though that meant that he was gone for much of each Saturday, Barbara was understanding and urged him to play just to see him relax and enjoy life more. She also looked for opportunities for the two of them to get away together.

One day, Barbara thought she'd surprise him with a trip to a Bed & Breakfast for a couple days. "Guess what?"

"What?" Sam replied.

"We have two nights reserved at this marvelous little B & B on the lake this weekend!"

"Oh, honey. I can't." And Sam proceeded to explain how he had yet another "big case" coming up he was "going to have to put in some extra hours" preparing for.

This wasn't the first time Barbara had had to cancel special plans she'd made for the two of them. "Sweetheart, don't you see how you are repeating the same mistakes you did with Louise and the kids, with all your energies and time focused on work so much that there's no room for anything else? Something's got to give here. We need some time for us. I mean, don't *you* feel like something is missing?"

That was just what Sam needed to hear. He stopped what he was doing right then. They had a good long talk. Somehow Barbara always knew how to make his innermost thoughts come together and coalesce so that he could really make sense of what he felt. Because, of course, she was right. In some ways, Sam thought he had the world by the tail: a wonderful and loving wife, six great children (even though his oldest daughter still remained distant), sufficient money for most things his family wanted or needed, and an excellent, lucrative, and challenging law practice. In other ways, there was indeed something missing.

Why did he always retreat from real intimacy? His soul was restless. Maybe that was why he kept some distance—time, energy, and emotion—between himself and those he loved the most.

✳

Sam had grown up Episcopalian and was frequently active in the local church's business, but he realized he did not find solace at church anymore.

Not long after having that long talk with Barbara, as fate would have it, his priest called to tell him of a new event focusing on spiritual renewal, the first such program in the diocese. Father Harkins said he knew very little about the group except it was called Cursillo, but that he'd heard wonderful responses to it being implemented elsewhere.

"It's brought about a sense of regeneration and a revitalized relationship to God and family for many individuals and parishes where people have attended. I have a brochure I want you to see. I'd like to see you and Barbara go."

Sam knew Barbara was more involved at church than he was.

"My wife's been talking with you, hasn't she?" he asked with a grin.

He knew a move closer to God and his wife was the right thing to do, so when the brochure came in the mail at work, Sam read it and put it on his desk. The next day, and again the next, he was moved to pick up the brochure to read again. The third time, he put it in his pocket and took it home to Barbara. She read it and asked Sam if he wanted to go.

"I am not excited about spending three days away from the office, but I can't explain it—I just feel a strong urging in my spirit to go. What do you think?"

When she said that she would like to go, he asked her to call Father Harkins and get them registered.

Several times after they registered and before the date of the retreat, things came up at the office that would conflict with him being away that weekend, but the pull for them to attend that Cursillo conference was so strong, Sam managed to push everything else aside. They were *going* to attend that weekend. Barbara was right, something had to give. Sam felt as if he was, for once, really listening to his inner voice. He knew he needed to be at that retreat with Barbara.

Chapter 30

ROSS REPORT FOR MITCHELL V. IRS

The afternoon before Joe Ross was going to testify, Sam sat looking over some of Joe's report. Sam knew Joe Ross was going to make an excellent witness. He had been so excited getting Ross' final report. Among the many sections in the detailed account of Joe's findings were the facts about tritium levels in residential wells in the area. *This is what is really going to make a difference to the people of Tullos*, Sam thought to himself. But he knew he had to brief the Court on the less "juicy" details as well, so he sat down to re-familiarize himself with the subsections of Joe's report labeled "BACKGROUND."

Cause for Concern

In 1962, the United States Geological Survey prepared geologic cross-sections of the test site to be used for Project Apex. Those cross-sections show Aquifer Five ending at the edge of the salt dome but not going around it. If that was accurate, water in that aquifer would not flow past the salt dome. However, an in-depth evaluation of those cross-sections revealed that, in fact, the aquifer flows around the salt dome on each side—that is, it splits at the dome, extending beyond the dome as far southeast as the Tullos-Urania Oil and Gas Fields and as far northwest as the village of Curry. A view of the site, looking down from above the ground, would clearly show that. Therefore, potential flow pathways exist, in a horizontal direction, both north and south around the dome. This leads to the conclusion that the acid and radioactively-contaminated water that were injected into well HT-2 and Aquifer Five in January, 1972, have **most likely migrated off-site.**

Description of Salt Dome and Aquifers

The salt dome, approximately 5000 feet across in diameter (about a mile across), is at a depth of about 1500 feet below ground surface in most places, though it sometimes is a mere 200 feet below the surface in places. Bayou Boeff and the Vermilion River are located very near the dome, and they drain the 1400-acre site that was used by the AEC for Project Apex. Six aquifers are located along the flanks of the salt dome. Aquifer Five, the deepest of all, at a depth of approximately 2600 feet below ground surface, contains brine. The deepest aquifer containing freshwater, number Four, is in limestone beds at a depth of approximately 2000 feet below ground surface. The overlying sandstone and clay beds above Aquifer Four contain several sand units that typically yield large amounts of water. The principal sandstone units have been designated as Aquifers Three, Two, and One. The deepest of those is number three. The sixth aquifer comprises the sand and gravel deposits blanketing most of the region. That aquifer is significant in that it maintains a high base flow in perennial streams within the area of the site, and therefore could transport contamination off the test site. The sources of drinking water for homes in the area of the test site are Aquifers One, Two, and Three.

Findings

The primary radioisotope resulting from the nuclear detonations at the site is tritium. The half-life (or the amount of time required for half of the radioactive atoms to decay) of tritium is 12.3 years. Tritium and radioisotopes like tritium, with half-lives equal or shorter than that of tritium, will decay to inconsequential levels of radioactivity within 100 to 200 years. Radiation hazard is, ultimately, a function of the radioisotope's mobility, through both the environment and in the human body. Tritium is highly soluble and volatile.

In mid-1971, as part of the plan for clean-up and deactivation of the site after all tests had been completed, well HT-2 in the southwest corner of the site was used as an injection well. The first step of the injection process was to inject 2000 gallons of 15% hydrochloric acid into Aquifer Five. The purpose of that injection was to increase the effective porosity and holding capacity of that aquifer. Following acid treatment, approximately 340,000 gallons of radioactively-contaminated water was injected into the well. Samples collected revealed that the water contained 38 curies of beta gamma emitters and 3500 curies of tritium. This was the only time during the work of Project Apex that radioactive fluids were disposed of outside the salt dome cavity and directly into an aquifer. Aquifer Five was used for brine injection at the oil and gas field located near Tullos, approximately 6.5 miles southeast of the test site.

My professional assertion is that the location of injection well HT-2 is particularly significant, because it is at the extreme southeast corner of the site, and migration of contaminated fluids most likely has extended off-site in that direction, toward the population of Tullos.

Description of Site Clean-Up Plans

In accordance with the plan, the AEC drilled a total of 39 wells on the test site and utilized one off-site commercially-drilled well as a groundwater monitoring well during January, 1964, through July, 1972. Several of those wells were drilled into the salt dome itself. As part of the deactivation, all but six of the 39 wells were plugged and abandoned. The six remaining wells were used as part of the overall groundwater-monitoring program, which has continued on a sporadic basis since the deactivation of the site. Clean-up and restoration of the test site was to be carried out in accordance with a detailed plan established by the AEC. That plan called for:

(1) Sampling and analysis of soil water, vegetation, and indigenous animal life at the site;

(2) Excavation and removal of contaminated soil, pumping all contaminated water and fluids into the salt dome nuclear cavity;

(3) Sealing the cavity by plugging all drilled entry holes with cement;

(4) Transporting all remaining solids, including materials, equipment, debris, soil, and personal property, whether contaminated or suspected of contamination, to the AEC Nuclear Storage Facility in

Nevada;

(5) Demonstrating that the site has been decontaminated and restored so far as practical to provide reasonable assurance that unrestricted use of the site surface will cause no concern in respect to radiological considerations.

Decontamination Realities

Six areas of the test site were targeted for sampling, analysis, and clean-up: Surface Ground Zero, the bleed-down plant, the drilling storage yard, and three other locations. Tests were conducted to identify the presence of plutonium, strontium, tritium, and gross beta in those areas. According to their own reports, clean-up criteria were relaxed by the AEC during the decontamination and decommissioning program. Attempts were made to excavate contaminated soils in a slush pit located near Surface Ground Zero. However, shallow groundwater was encountered, causing extreme muddy conditions, which prevented excavation equipment from operating there. Although the contamination level of the soil exceeded clean-up criteria, approval to cease operations was given by the AEC. The pit was back-filled with clean material and the contaminated soil was buried under seven feet of clean fill.

Another of the holes drilled, completed after the first nuclear blast, was to monitor the water table. Known as the post-shot No. 1 "Mouse Hole," it was an approximately 12-inch diameter hole located at Surface Ground Zero. In the clean-up process, that hole was excavated to approximately 12 feet below ground surface, where shallow groundwater was encountered. Again, even though radioactivity readings at this location exceeded clean-up criteria, approval to cease operations was given by the AEC. The hole was back-filled with "non-contaminated" pieces of concrete, on top of which was placed a horizontal concrete slab.

Long Term Monitoring

The AEC reported that the decontamination and decommissioning plan was completed in May, 1972. At that time, a long-term hydrologic monitoring program was initiated. Two events occurred after the decommissioning that led to additional sampling and testing at the test site. The first occurred when, in 1973, high tritium levels were found in samples taken east of Surface Ground Zero and west of the Bayou Boeff overflow pond. The high tritium levels demonstrated that the test site was not clean, as previously declared by the AEC.

The second event was when well HT-2M, which had also been drilled into Aquifer Five, began flowing at the surface spontaneously. It was determined that the fluid flowing at the surface was radioactively contaminated and was apparently the same fluid injected into well HT-2 several years earlier. Shortly thereafter, well HT-2 was plugged with cement (in May, 1975).

In order to address these deficiencies, approximately 159 auger holes were drilled, under AEC supervision, to obtain samples of soil, soil moisture, and groundwater. In addition, 11 permanent groundwater monitor wells were installed and included in the overall long-term hydrologic monitoring program. A special monitor well, S.P. No. 3, was drilled to obtain samples of soil and soil moisture near the location of Surface Ground Zero.

In addition to tritium concentrations, those same soil samples that were obtained during the drilling of monitor well S.P. No. 3 were tested for conductance. The determination of conductance readings is considered a good indication for the presence of salt and the level of concentration of sodium chloride. The purpose of the testing for tritium and conductance was initiated to assess whether high levels of tritium found at the test site emanated from the cavity itself or from drilling fluids disposed of from the re-entry drilling program into the nuclear cavity.

The rationale for these tests was that if high tritium concentrations and high conductance readings were found at ground surface, and tritium concentrations and conductance readings decreased with depth, then the contamination would be associated with drilling fluids left on the surface. Conversely, if the tritium concentrations and conductance readings increased with depth, then the contamination could be associated with the cavity itself.

The AEC found high tritium concentrations both at the surface and at depth. Contrary to its hypothesis, however, the AEC concluded that the high tritium concentrations found at depth were the result of residual contamination from the re-entry drilling program. They did not explain why there were also high concentrations of tritium at the surface.

Based on the results of that study, the AEC came to the conclusion that no further action was required. All drilling fluids and associated material were buried in three open pits at the test site. From 1973 to 1976, the federal government, in cooperation with the Louisiana Department of Environmental Quality, implemented a continuous long-term hydrologic monitoring program at the test site. That sampling program has shown the constant presence of radioactivity at the test site but has not demonstrated whether the radioactivity is increasing, decreasing, or staying constant at the site.

Due to the persisting environmental concerns of citizens, arising from the monitoring program, the DOE directed a Remedial Investigation and Feasibility Study (RIFS) for the test site, beginning in 1978. That study revealed continuing high levels of tritium found at various locations around Surface Ground Zero. Especially troubling was a finding of elevated levels of tritium at a site disposal pit (Pit X-3), which had been used by the contractor for disposal of waste, one of six pits to be used to bury noncombustible waste. The AEC reported after the clean-up was completed that nothing had been buried in the pits except the permitted waste, yet here were these high tritium levels.

Conclusions

Had the data in the 1978 RIFS been carefully evaluated, it would have revealed the following environmental concerns.

Prior to Project Apex, any knowledgeable professional would have been able to see the vast potential for problems associated with using well HT-2 and its associated Aquifer (Five). Afterwards, these showed every indication of grave concerns over off-site toxicity migration.

The fact that well HT-2M began to flow at the surface with radioactive contaminated liquid in 1972 (prior to being plugged in 1975), was indicative of potential serious problems with Aquifer Five. Aquifer Five consists primarily of limestone, most likely containing fractures and joints after the blasts.

When the AEC injected hydrochloric acid into the cavity of the dome, it apparently assumed that the cavity was somewhat uniform and had sufficient volume to accept the quantity of radioactive-contaminated water. No data exists that indicates the migration pathway of the acid and radioactive water that was injected into this zone. It was assumed by the AEC that the injected fluids flowed in a confined horizontal direction, but there is a serious question of whether the injected fluids flowed along pathways enhanced by the acid or migrated beyond the confines of the assumed cavity.

Therefore, another potential flow path for this fluid is vertically, which would take it from Aquifer Five into the overlying aquifers. Prior to Project Apex, tests conducted by the USGS showed that, typical of aquifers found within the Gulf Coastal Plain, the aquifers at the site were confined and under artesian pressure. Aquifer Five, beyond its natural pressure gradient, was influenced by other external processes. Approximately 6.5 miles southeast of the test site is an active oil and gas field. That oil and gas field has used Aquifer Five for brine production disposal since the early 1950s. That same USGS study stated that the tests conducted on Aquifer Five prior to Project Apex showed the influence on vertical pressures from the oil and gas field operations. The fact that well HT-2M (completed in Aquifer Five) flowed at ground surface supports this conclusion. Under this superimposed pressure differential, there very likely will be, over time if not at present, vertical migration along fractures and joints through to the aquifers above Aquifer Five, thus affecting the water supply.

The testing conducted by the AEC prior to July 1, 1978, is inconclusive. Rather, these facts strongly indicate a very high probability that those fluids have migrated to significant portions of land outside of the 1400-acre test site and due to existing migration pathways, could include several thousand acres of impacted land and the home sites of residents in the area.

Another significant concern relates to the occurrence of high levels of tritium and iodine-131 found in soils and water during the sampling program conducted by the U.S. Environmental Protective Agency in 1977.

The sampling and testing program showed high levels of tritium in two areas adjacent to Surface Ground Zero, exceeding the clean-up standards that were used in 1972 and again in 1974. Even though some radioactive levels had exceeded the 1972 levels, the site was declared "clean" a second time by the AEC, with no further action deemed necessary. The clean-up standard regarding tritium concentration in water was 300,000 pCi/l. In fact, the levels recorded during the testing done in 1974 were 1,000,000 pCi/l.

Then, following the 1974 sampling period, all intrusive material, such as drill cuttings and fluids, were subsequently buried on site. The discovery of a concentration of tritium and quite possibly other radioisotope contamination at several locations is a concern. The testing for tritium and other radioisotope contamination was made only one time a year, in April, which was not satisfactory to establish a reliable database for monitoring the levels throughout different seasons and determining whether there was natural communication between Aquifer Five and the aquifers providing drinking water to area residents.

Although all the AEC reports and documents adhere to the idea that the salt dome would and has effectively contained all radioactivity at the test site, the database should have been considered inconclusive at the time, and was still inconclusive as of July 1, 1978. Evidence strongly suggests there would be contaminant migration through surface water, groundwater, soil, and air, including to populated areas.

The USGS suggested that there existed a potential for release from the cavity, and that any such release would definitely have an effect on Aquifers Five, Four, Three, and maybe Two and One (remembering, of course, that numbers 1-3 provide drinking water).

The integrity of the salt dome cavity and how it will respond over time are in serious doubt. The post-shot inspection of the site showed the presence of long cracks in the ground surface within a range of approximately 1640 feet of Surface Ground Zero, with several hundred mud boils of water and saturated soil emanating from these cracks. Also, the ground motion from the blast was clearly felt out to a range of approximately 29 miles. These occurrences would strongly suggest some structural duress to the geologic formations and specifically to the aquifers above the salt dome. That creates the potential for contamination to migrate off-site via surface water, groundwater, and air, as well as potential contamination within the sediments associated with the surface water drainage.

Both horizontal and vertical contamination has probably resulted from the injection of radioactivity-contaminated fluids into Aquifer Five from the injection in well HT-2, because all evidence suggests the walls of the salt dome cavity were severely ruptured by the blasts, as should have been anticipated.

The site contained several unlined waste disposal pits, which may have been receptors of solid combustible and hazardous waste, against regulations. Activities on the site in conjunction with preparation, testing, subsequent clean-up, and deactivation would certainly result in residue of fuel, oils, grease, etc. It is unclear where there is a concentration of non-radioactive contamination, radioactive chemicals, hazardous waste, and heavy metals at the test site at this time.

Chapter 31

DEATH AND NEW POSSIBILITIES

When the first test was delayed, that reduced some of the urgency Ian felt that Kay should move from her parent's home. But as the date of the first test grew nearer, he became more and more insistent. Initially Kay had agreed that she would move into an apartment in Winnfield after Christmas. She needed a few months of living at home to save some money to get her own place. Things were pretty well set for her to move in January, but in early December, Pam had a serious heart attack, and Kay saw the necessity of remaining at home to look after her mother and father. The new date for her move was extended several times.

The doctors told the family that Pam had suffered extensive damage to her heart. Surgery wouldn't help. She was confined to bed to avoid any exertion. Neighbors took turns coming in during certain hours of the day to sit with Pam. Bobby Lee and Kay were there for her at night. When Pam grew weaker, the doctors told Kay and Bobby Lee that she could not last much longer. For the next month, Bobby Lee spent most of the daylight hours beside Pam's bed. At night, Kay would take over and sleep in a bed beside her mother. Many nights, Ian sat with Kay and talked with Pam, sometimes letting Kay get some sleep while he watched over her mother.

It was during one of those private conversations with Pam that Ian confided that he wanted to marry Kay. Pam was pleased and happy that they would be married and told them that she heartily approved.

Kay's mother died in August. She was buried in the tiny cemetery in Tullos. The Rev. Kennedy Watson, pastor of the First Methodist

Church of Winnfield, where the Hughes were members and regular attendants, held the service. Everyone in the area attended the funeral, then came to the home to visit with Bobby Lee and Kay.

Kay had again begun planning to move into her own apartment after Christmas that next year. She believed that even though he missed Pam desperately, her father would be able to take care of himself, freeing her to go.

Ian went on with his work with Project Apex, and the first test finally went off. He was glad to see Kay would be moving, though he still had concerns for others who would stay behind.

As Kay started packing, however, she became worried about her father. He was losing weight, did not want to eat, and had no energy.

Suspecting that his condition was caused by depression over the death of his wife, Dr. Vassar sent some anti-depressants to Bobby Lee. Even though Kay administered the medicines as directed, Bobby Lee got worse. Kay insisted that he have Dr. Vassar give him a complete physical, which he finally did later that year.

When all of the tests had come back from the labs, Dr. Vassar was grieved to learn that Bobby Lee had cancer of the liver. He asked Bobby Lee to come in for an appointment and asked Kay and Ian to come too. Dr. Vassar let the three of them know of Bobby Lee's grave condition. When Bobby Lee asked how long he could expect to live, Dr. Vassar told him he probably had no more than a few months.

Kay was devastated—first her mother and now almost immediately, her father. She decided to devote her love and attention to her father during the months that he had left, and told Ian that he would just have to understand. Ian did understand. He and Bobby Lee were quite fond of each other. So he too, spent as much time as possible with Kay and her father.

Ian and Kay were at Bobby Lee's side when he died on October 4, 1966.

✳

Startled by the ring of the telephone, Ian's thoughts came back to the present. He answered the phone to hear Emily Carter's voice.

"Ian, are you okay? You seemed distracted when you left us to get dinner alone."

"Oh, I'm fine. How was the seafood?"

"It was great. I love their crayfish." She told him of the fish and oysters they had all enjoyed at the Sea Food Shack, then added quietly that they missed him.

Not really hearing what she was trying to say, Ian replied, "Well, thanks for checking on me." He wished her goodnight, got undressed, and got into bed.

Chapter 32

ROSS CONTINUES

Knowing that all parties had reviewed the Ross Report prior to the trial, Rob Fly began with some of what he considered the most important facts from Joe's testimony.

Fly asked, "Mr. Ross, can you please explain to the Court the fundamental findings from your report about the problems surrounding Project Apex?"

"Certainly. The first issue is that the environmental status of the test site was not adequately or properly characterized at the time of deactivation and clean-up—not originally (in 1972), nor when the additional monitoring and evaluation was conducted in 1974, nor in 1977. In fact, the environmental status of the test site still remains unsatisfactorily characterized to the present time."

Westover was objecting loudly that the government of the United States had the best scientists in the world working on Project Apex. "Perhaps Mr. Ross is not of the same caliber as those who actually did the work. Surely in the pages upon pages of expert reports compiled by the AEC, we have more than enough information to properly characterize the situation…"

Judge Lansdorf interrupted to say, "Let the witness finish, Mr. Westover. Overruled."

Ross went on, "There is radioactive and chemical contamination over an indefinite area of the surface and shallow subsurface of the test site and most likely off site. Anomalously high levels of radioactive substances have been detected in three of the five freshwater aquifers at the test site. Tests conducted in 1978 showed high levels of tritium had entered freshwater Aquifers Two and Three as a result of radioactive waste having been injected into Aquifer Five, therefore affecting the drinking water of the local population."

"Objection: conjecture."

"Sustained."

Ross continued at Rob's prompting. "If any further tests have been made to determine the existence or spread of that radioactive contamination since the 1978 test, the results remain classified TOP SECRET and are unavailable to the public."

"Any flow of groundwater between adjacent aquifers, whether through natural or human-engineered pathways, will tend to be upward in the aquifers above Aquifer Two, and downward in aquifers below Aquifer Two. Groundwater flow between aquifers would tend to carry with it any radioactive materials dissolved in it. Given the likely magnitude of underground structural damage after the first blast, the possibility is strong that contamination has traveled vertically between aquifers through cracks created by the explosions, especially considering how the contamination has ended up in local wells, drinking water, streams, and other places off site."

"Tritium, a common radioactive isotope released by nuclear explosions, is an isotope of hydrogen. As such, it becomes contained within water molecules and is assumed to be more mobile than most other radioactive isotopes released, with a consequently higher chance of affecting the human environment. Many of the Project Apex tritium analyses were not performed accurately. Careful analysis of the data from the earlier monitoring and evaluations reveals an area of anomalously high tritium levels extending approximately 800 feet east to west and 1000 feet north to south over the surface at Ground Zero."

"While the surficial aquifer—the one at the surface, that is—is not suitable for drinking water because of its shallow depth, it is nevertheless the main source of potable groundwater for domestic wells in the area. A number of these off-site water-supply wells have been monitored for tritium, and some have shown anomalously high tritium."

"The path taken by the tritium in reaching the local aquifer in the vicinity of well HM-1 is not known. Two possible pathways for tritium to reach that aquifer are a natural downward leakage through the surficial aquifer or downward leakage through defective cement barriers around the casing in a nearby well. The DOE does not know how the leakage happened, and they have not made sufficient tests to make that determination."

Ross explained, "The AEC predicted that the radioactive waste injected into the limestone in January, 1972, would move only 975 feet in 75 years (13 feet per year). However, the waste was found in well HT-2M in 1973, meaning that in just 7 year's time, the waste has traveled at least 300 feet (more than 42 feet per year). This means the toxic waste traveled more than three times as fast as they calculated it would. That does not bode well for the potential of this contamination to continue traveling outward, farther and farther from Ground Zero, in the future, affecting even more populations of people, plants, and animals than it has currently."

"The present extent of the radioactive waste in that limestone, in either horizontal or vertical direction, is not known. However, tritium has been detected in surface water in a pond near Ground Zero, so it is coming up to the surface somehow."

"There is evidence of the presence of other radioisotopes in the area, including antimony-125, cesium-137, plutonium-239, potassium-40, and radium-226."

His testimony continued to reveal just how far Project Apex had gone wrong. Ross outlined from his report just what the issues were concerning each of the various radioisotopes:

Cesium-137, a product of nuclear explosions, was detected at concentrations above the limit in groundwater samples as late as 1976, but reported only as present in "negligible quantities." Proper reporting requires that the actual activity level measurements be given, rather than such subjective and vague terms as "negligible."

Traces of antimony-125, the dominant gamma-emitting isotope, were detected in all samples at the site clean-up in 1972. Even though it has a short half-life of 2.7 years, monitoring should continue.

Plutonium-239 was detected in four surface water locations near Ground Zero in 1976 and in soil samples in 1979. The tests done by the AEC and NRC were measured by gamma spectra but should have been measured by alpha spectra, because gamma spectra would not have detected most of this element.

Potassium-40 and radium-226, both naturally occurring products of uranium, have been detected at excessive levels as late as 1976. However, the AEC test results have made no mention of those isotopes since then. If tests revealed those isotopes were detected, not detected, or if no tests were made to determine their presence—none of that is known to us at this time, but that information is all critical to a proper assessment of the situation.

Joe stated, "The government contractor at the site used a slush pit, located some 2000 feet north of Surface Ground Zero, to store drilling mud. But he was not supposed to dispose of any solid matter there. After clean-up of the test site, the pit was filled and planted over with grass. Grass is not an effective barrier to radiation last time I checked."

At this, the courtroom murmured. A couple people snorted, and some quiet snickering could be heard.

"By 1973, a gully 12 to 15 feet deep had eroded into the pit, revealing barrels, boxes, and other solid matter buried in the pit—totally against regulations. Despite no recorded disposal of contaminated materials in the pit, excessive levels of tritium have been detected in water from the pit as late as 1979. That's 13 years after the last blast! The tritium source in that pit has never been adequately defined or addressed."

"The integrity of the cavity in the salt dome and how it will respond over time are grave concerns for the future. The government's own reports reveal the presence of long cracks in the ground surface as far away as 1640 feet from Surface Ground Zero, with several hundred mud boils emanating from those cracks. Those mud boils were present as late as September, 1982."

"Ground motion from the nuclear explosions was experienced out 29 miles away from Ground Zero—some say more. Those occurrences strongly suggest some structural duress to the geological formations in the salt dome. With large amounts of known radioactive contamination having been pumped into the cavity, there is no telling where that contaminated matter has flowed through the aquifers located above the cavity. It only stands to reason that if asphalt parking lots were rolling like ocean waves miles and miles away from the site, that the dome and the aquifer walls have also suffered damage enough to allow the flow of waste to places unknown."

Fly interjected, "Mr. Westover asked you about tritium, and I would like to ask you more about it. If I want to know about the presence of such things in a certain location, and I test only for tritium, could I find plutonium, iodine, or whatever else could come from an H bomb?"

"No. Each radioisotope has a special testing procedure for that specific isotope."

"In testing, when you find tritium, is that an indicator that you should test for other things?"

"Absolutely. When you find tritium, you must look for other radioisotopes."

"In the case of well HT-2M, when tritium was found, should that have alerted Project Apex officials that they must test for other things?"

"Definitely."

"Yet they did no such testing?" Fly asked.

"Correct."

"Is there reason to believe that some radioisotopes other than tritium were injected into well HT-2M in January, 1972?"

"We don't have to guess—the government reports state clearly that materials other than tritium were injected, including, but not limited to, curries of gamma and beta emitters."

"Mr. Ross, if tritium flowed out of well HT-2M onto the ground, is it reasonable to think that only tritium flowed—other isotopes did not?"

"Absolutely not. The only way to determine what was there was to test for it."

"To your knowledge, was any testing done by the government to determine what, besides tritium, flowed out onto the ground?"

"Based on all available government reports, no such testing was done. I have reviewed all of those reports carefully. Testing was done only for tritium."

Fly continued his detailed questioning. He had Ross focus on reports of the clean-up operations and Joe's conclusions that the clean-up efforts were poorly done. As evidence of his conclusions, Ross offered that, in 1977, the government was back on the test site looking for contamination—even though the AEC had certified the site was clear when it was decommissioned in 1972 and again in 1973.

"All indications are that the clean-up was done very hastily and on a limited budget. Clearly, the methods used by the subcontractor were ineffective," Ross said flatly.

Ross' testimony revealed how, because the Louisiana Geological Survey and other state agencies were concerned with the integrity of the salt dome cavity, as they well should be, in late 1976, the AEC drilled a hole into the cavity of the dome (designated Post-Shot Hole #3, or PS-3). There was fear that the cavity was leaking, as tritium-laced salt was found at the surface.

The AEC's guess was that if high levels of tritium were coming from surface sources, levels should decrease with depth. Their second hypothesis was that if they found elevated concentrations of tritium that did not decrease as they went deeper, then it could be coming from the cavity or other sources. They drilled the Post-Shot Hole to a depth of 142 feet. High levels of tritium (950,000 pico curies per liter) were found at the surface. Those levels decreased as they went deeper, then suddenly the levels elevated again. The AEC stopped the drilling and sealed off the hole when they found increased levels of tritium as drilling reached 142 feet.

The report issued by the AEC stated, "For various reasons, the monitoring well PS-3 was never completed." Reports issued by the State subsequent to that date stated that the geo-hydrology of the Mitchell salt dome was highly uncertain, there were questions concerning the dome's integrity, and the cavity status itself was in doubt.

Fly gave Ross Joint Exhibit 63-BK, entitled, "Post-Explosion Environmental Results from Project Apex," by Oliver Radiation Laboratory, and asked him what conclusion was reached in that report.

"The document concludes that there is highly radioactive material in the bottom of the cavity of the Mitchell salt dome."

"And who had that study prepared?"

"The Atomic Energy Commission."

Rob now turned to the more specific matter at hand. "Mr. Ross, how would the condition of the dome and the test site impact your evaluation of the property for a potential purchaser or an appraiser?"

"I would have tremendous concern—the value of the property would be seriously reduced. Knowing full well the facts involved—that the dome cavity contains contaminated fluids, that fluids can migrate, that four wells went down into the cavity and have only been plugged with cement (which has surely deteriorated), that the integrity of the cavity walls are now flawed, that the wells may serve as pathways or conduits to the surface or near-surface or to the aquifers themselves—knowing all this and more, I would urge people not to buy the property. Not only would much of it have no value, all of it is a liability. Any reasonable appraiser, given the background documents I was given, would arrive at the same conclusion."

"Do you have an overall assessment of Project Apex, Mr. Ross?"

Joe responded, "Based upon these findings and conclusions, I have to say Project Apex was indeed just a horrific concept from its inception. It was poorly researched and improperly carried out, as well as simply not cleaned up correctly. My biggest concern, however, is that the government has refused to conduct epidemiological testing in Winn Parish and the town of Tullos in spite of the extraordinary high incidences of cancer reported in the vicinity of the test site."

"Objection."

"Sustained."

Feeling like pushing the envelope, Fly asked, "Mr. Ross, you said you have visited Tullos recently."

"Yes."

"What did you do while in town?"

"I traced Bayou Boeff and the streams in the area, visited the Tullos-Urania oil field, and three weeks ago, I attended a town meeting of the town of Tullos."

"Tell me about that town meeting."

"The purpose of the meeting was to hear a report from a representative of the NRC about what was going on at the test site. But during the meeting, the conversation turned to the subject of the large number of people with cancer—people who had died of it or had been diagnosed with it over the past 10 years. When they…"

"I object to this entire line of questioning, Your Honor. It is pure hearsay, and this witness is not an expert in medical concerns," Westover had the air of being indignant.

"Sustained. Mr. Fly, please steer clear of the topic of Tullos residents' health."

Fly asked, "Mr. Ross, back to the pertinent tax issues at hand, what is your estimate of the value of the Mitchell property?"

"My professional opinion is that the value of the 1400 acres leased by the government is seriously impaired and has no value at all. Furthermore, considerably more than the 1400 acres is likely affected by contamination, and the value of it should be reduced significantly. As of yet, however, with so much relevant information remaining classified, I have no way of determining how many acres are so affected or the extent of the devaluation of the remainder of the property, other than to say it has most definitely been devalued to some degree."

Fly said, "Thank you, Mr. Ross. No further questions at this time."

Chapter 33

SPIRITUAL AWAKENING

July, 1972. Sam's life was never the same.

Throughout the Cursillo weekend, he and Barbara were showered with attention by the staff and love from the entire group. It was then that Sam, for the first time ever, experienced Christ's love for him.

Sam had what can only be described as a strong spiritual experience at that weekend retreat. As he explained to his golf buddies, "I felt Jesus by my side the entire weekend, constantly reassuring me that he deeply loved me just as I am, in spite of wrongs I have done in the past. I saw myself as a different person as I looked through God's eyes." And in his more private thoughts, he realized that even with his many flaws, he must be okay if Jesus loved him so much he died on the cross for him.

Barbara had a wonderful experience that weekend, too. She felt she grew as a person, a woman, and a wife. But she was especially glad to have her husband so joyful and fulfilled.

And Sam, well, he came away from the weekend a different person. He saw people around him in a new light. Regardless of who they were, no one was to be placated or ignored. People were to be respected and loved. It was also clear to him that he must give himself to Barbara—and to the children. He no longer wanted to be just their father. He wanted to be their Dad.

Sam now realized he needed to cut down on the extra time he spent at the office. He wanted to squeeze out more time to devote to the family. Another new goal was to assume significant responsibility for duties in the church. He wanted to, as best he could, share his newfound love of Christ with others.

During the weekend, through the workshops and exercises of spiritual practice, Sam spent a lot of time recalling and reliving a lot of his past. This was a painful thing, because he realized that he had been a failure as a father. He had hardly been a part of the lives of his two daughters. Now they were both away in college, and he saw very little of them. Tears came to his eyes and a lump formed in his throat anytime he permitted himself to think about how very little he had participated with, and given himself to, his children when they were young and needed him.

Sam acknowledged to himself that though he'd had a good relationship with his stepchildren, he'd been a lousy father to his own two kids. He vowed that from that day forward, he would put his daughters first and work to deepen those relationships. He prayed that he could somehow fill that void in his life, and capture some of what he had missed by not paying attention as his precious daughters grew up. Now, since Cursillo, his greatest desire in life was that before he died, he could make up to his daughters what they might have shared had his priorities been in the right place when the kids were young.

Sam shared this deep pain he felt with Barbara. She was good for Sam, and she encouraged his efforts to rebuild the relationships with Sandra and Nell. Whether it was the distance that separated them or other causes, he and his daughters had grown apart. The time had come to do something about it.

Chapter 34

CROSS-EXAMINING ROSS

At the lectern at 8 a.m. the next day, Westover commenced his cross-examination of Ross. "Mr. Ross, did you do any original investigation or research to determine the facts as they relate to the test site?"

"I relied mostly on the existing data."

"So, you relied solely on documents provided by someone else?"

"While it is true that most of the data on which my report is based was provided from other sources, I did conduct my own independent research and investigation."

"Well, Mr. Ross, what is the source of the information that you used?"

"Most of it came from the Department of Energy's archives library in Las Vegas, some from the records of the Louisiana Department of Environmental Quality, some from U.S. Department of Interior Geological Surveys, and I also made a study of a series of aerial photographs."

"Have you been to and seen the test site?"

"Yes, sir. I have walked all over the site several times."

"When did you do this, Mr. Ross?"

"I cannot give you the exact dates between 1983 and 1984, but I spent time there as recently as two weeks ago."

"I have some concerns about your thoroughness and knowledge of the project, sir. In your report, you say that the deepest freshwater aquifer in the limestone beds at the test site is Aquifer Four, at a depth of approximately 2000 feet. Aquifer Four is not a freshwater aquifer, is it?"

"It is brackish."

"Do you understand that Aquifer Four is not used for human purposes?"

"To my knowledge, that is correct."

"You say further in your report that Aquifer Four is significant in that it maintains a high base flow in perennial streams within the area of the test site, and therefore could transport contamination off the site?"

"That is correct."

"On page 18 of your report, you describe one of the aquifers as a near-surface aquifer, or surficial aquifer. Does it also include the local water supply aquifer?"

"Not necessarily."

"Would you please explain for the Court what the surficial aquifer is? It is actually the groundwater flowing on the surface, is it not?"

"It doesn't flow on the surface, no. It's within the subsurface immediately below ground."

Judge Lansdorf interrupted, "Is the surficial aquifer visible, or is it beneath the surface?"

"You would not be able to see it above ground, Your Honor. The only way you could perceive it would be if you had springs or seepage along the embankments—incised or cut areas into the aquifer itself where it is discharging into any of the streams or drains adjacent to it."

"Does it change from sub-fluvial to above the surface?" asked Judge Lansdorf.

"No, sir, it is always in the sub-surface. It will fluctuate based on the precipitation events that occur. During periods of high precipitation, it will rise, and during periods when there's not as much rain, the amount of water in the surficial aquifer will drop. While the main supply of the surficial aquifer is precipitation, it is also interactive with streams in the vicinity of the test site. If the water level of the aquifer is below the level of the stream, it will recharge the aquifer. If the water level rises in the aquifer, and the level of the stream is lower, the aquifer will discharge in the stream. So there is constant interaction between the two."

"Thank you. You may go on, Mr. Westover," Lansdorf said.

Westover continued, "And if you were to dig a hole, say six to eight feet deep, and ran into the water table, that would be the surficial aquifer?"

"Correct. Actually, when I was at the test site recently, I looked at one of the water wells that penetrates that particular aquifer, and I found water in the well about 12 inches below ground surface."

"And, the surficial aquifer has no human use, does it Mr. Ross?"

"The geological records of the state show that there are residential wells dug into the surficial aquifer off site, but not far from the test site. These are used for water supply to rural homes not on city water. These records are public. The AEC would have had access prior to commencing the blasts. So they had full understanding of what they were…"

Obviously surprised by Ross' answer, Westover interrupted sharply, "I'm sorry, you must have these wells confused. There are not supposed to be any wells dug into the surficial aquifer. It's not supposed to be used for human purposes. Are you telling this Court that you have knowledge of wells off site that bring their water from the surficial aquifer?"

People behind Sam were whispering. Everyone seemed caught off-guard. This caught Sam by surprise, too, but for a different reason. *Didn't Bob read the reports filed with the Court beforehand? All this was in those reports.*

Ross answered, "Yes, sir. If you will refer to the U.S. Geological Survey, I think about pages 111 and thereafter, you will see the reports of those wells and the use of water from the surficial aquifer for water supply. That same information is corroborated by the Louisiana Geological Survey, too, around pages 65 or 70 of their report."

"But—but, the surficial aquifer is not normally considered to be suitable for human use, is it, in any context, here or anyplace else?"

"Well, if people are using it for that purpose, I assume that the water quality used to be such that they could safely use it, prior to

Project Apex, that is."

At this remark, Westover winced, and knowing he had to recover a bit, he took a risk and asked a mostly-rhetorical question, "Therefore, if residents are using a surficial water source that is not supposed to be used for human consumption, the government cannot be held liable for contamination resulting from Project Apex, now, can they?"

Ross started in, but Lansdorf took over. "Mr. Westover, I will remind you that is not the subject of this trial."

Bob Westover headed in another direction, instead. "Mr. Ross, in your report, you conclude the surficial aquifer could transport contamination off the site. Do you have any evidence that it is, in fact, the surficial aquifer that has carried tritium contamination off the site?"

"No, sir. The very limited test data that is available from government reports is so incomplete you cannot reach any conclusion at all. That's part of the problem…"

But Westover simply said, "Just answer the questions, Mr. Ross," and went on.

Westover went through the Ross report at great length, questioning him as to each detail, all in an effort to discredit Ross. Several times, Westover asked Ross what he was basing his conclusions on and whether Ross had conducted his own tests about this or that.

"Again, all of my conclusions are based on a thorough study of every government report available. I have not conducted my own tests, nor have I been given access to the multitudes of classified reports. But Mr. Westover, there is no way that we *could* conduct our own tests. The federal government controls the actual test site. We have no access to it—only to surrounding areas. Many of the critical documents and reports on the status of the test site and surrounding property are still classified TOP SECRET. The true status of the property is locked away in the government's vaults. The only information that we or anyone else outside the government can secure is from the government reports that are available. A comprehensive study of those reports, as I have made, reveals shoddy, incomplete, and contradictory data and conclusions. Some of the conclusions reached in the government reports, on critically important issues, are questioned and even contradicted in other government reports. I believe that a reasonable person would put very little confidence in the conclusions of those reports. I have focused on the clear inconsistencies, used basic geological reports and data, together with what independent research I was able to accomplish, to reach my conclusions."

Changing direction, Westover had Ross acknowledge that tritium can be both natural and man-made, and that it is present in the atmosphere everywhere. Westover referred to government reports stating that the levels of tritium found in the area over several years following the testing were decreasing. Ross pointed out that was true only in some areas, and the studies were not responsible, as they had been taken only once a year, always at the same time of year, when the area was very dry. He pointed out further that even those studies revealed levels bouncing up and down, trending downward slightly over an 8-year period. With a half-life of 12.5 years, the levels of tritium should be disappearing, but they are not.

Ross said, "Since tritium levels are not disappearing, I can only conclude that there is still a source of tritium at the site contributing to those levels."

Westover laboriously went through Ross' report asking what seemed to be endless questions. Then he asked Ross to explain what aquifers were found in the area of the test site and how they related to each other. The witness referred the Court to attachment 41 of his report, a diagram of the aquifers at the test site. Using the diagram, Ross explained in detail.

"The surficial aquifer is closest to the surface of the earth. Below that is the local aquifer, the depth of which depends on the topography and geology at the site, but generally from 20 feet below the surface to a depth of 200 feet. Below that are Aquifers One, Two, Three, Four, and Five. Aquifer One is closest to the earth's surface, and Five is the deepest."

"While aquifers usually flow at a level relatively constant to the surface of the earth, that pattern is altered at a salt dome. Because the dome pushes the subsurface upward, that movement forces aquifers in the area to become more compacted or to flow around the dome. Aquifer Five is approximately 2600 feet below the surface. The top of the salt dome is about 1500 feet below the surface. The dome protruding toward the surface has forced Aquifer Five, and perhaps Four, to flow around the dome. As they pass the dome, the channels meet again and flow on as before. Depending on the pressure in Aquifer Five, water can flow horizontally as well as vertically (both up or down), as it encounters the dome."

"In the process of cleaning up the test site, hydrochloric acid was injected into Aquifer Five, pumping it into well HT-2. The AEC intended for the acid to increase permeability for easier transmission of fluid in the aquifer."

"Let me understand this, Mr. Ross," the Judge said. "Is permeability the quality of the material to absorb and hold the water or for the water to move through the material?"

"Basically it is to transmit the water, Your Honor. The higher the permeability, the easier the transmission of water through the system."

"I understand. Now, what happens to the acid when it is poured into the well?"

"When you inject the hydrochloric acid, Your Honor, it has a borehole effect. Some distance out from the well, it takes the path of least resistance along fractures, joints, and little seams and openings within the formation. From some undeterminable distance from the well, it cleans those seams or enhances the flow. So, it could flow in many different directions. The acid will mix with water in the aquifer and dissipate over a period of time."

"Good. One more question. Is that acid a contaminant that you are considering hazardous in this case?' Judge Lansdorf asked.

"No, sir. As a normal procedure, the Tullos-Urania oil field used hydrochloric acid to clean the wells."

"Thank you. You may proceed, Mr. Westover."

Answering the questions Westover posed, Ross confirmed that the various government reports showed that in order to dispose of the large quantity of liquid nuclear waste, the DOE pumped, under pressure, the contaminated waste into Well HT-2. They continued to so dispose of the contamination over a period of several months. The DOE intended that the waste would travel into Aquifer Five and be forced, by what they believed to be pressure from the oil field, to flow in a northwest direction, away from the community of Tullos.

Westover asked, "Which direction would Aquifer Five normally flow if not disturbed by humans?"

"To the southeast, toward the populated areas."

The Judge asked, "So liquid injected into Aquifer Five at the test site would normally flow to the southeast?"

"Correct."

"But, Mr. Ross, wouldn't that direction from the test site be reversed and flow to the northwest, because the Tullos-Urania oil field injected its brine residue into the aquifer under high pressure?"

"Yes, if the oil field used pressure. But the oil field did not use pressure to inject its brine residue into the aquifer."

Westover was making a note to himself as Ross answered the question and seemed caught off guard again by Ross' answer. "What did you say?"

"I said that the AEC simply assumed, never checking to be sure. In fact, all injections by the oil field were gravity feed, not forced by high pressure. So there is absolutely no reason to think that the salt-water injections would reverse the natural flow of Aquifer Five. Some of the contamination pumped into Well HT-2 probably escaped in every direction, due to the severe damage to the salt dome caused by the test detonation. But most of it surely flowed to the southeast, which is the direction of natural flow of Aquifer Five and the direction of the townspeople. In fact, since the AEC pumped the waste into Aquifer Five under pressure, that waste most certainly traveled to the southeast faster and further than it might have, had it not been pumped under pressure."

"Aren't you guessing now Mr. Ross? Don't the government reports clearly state that results of monitoring test wells showed that the flow of the contaminated material was to the northwest."

"Yes, there are two reports that state that. But I believe those tests were incomplete and inconclusive."

"What makes you think that?" the Judge asked.

"Your Honor, only minimal tests were conducted in two wells to the northwest, very soon after the contamination was injected into HT-2. They were never tested again. And as I said, because of the blast impacting surrounding geology, contamination likely went in all directions to some degree. Further, those reports contradict a statement contained in another government report issued later."

Obviously quite irritated, Westover asked, "Mr. Ross, have you made any tests that would show that the AEC's plan to dispose of the contamination in a manner that would flow safely to the northwest is flawed?"

"No, sir, I have no tests of my own on this. My conclusions are that the AEC made a grave error in the disposal of contamination. I reached that conclusion from the AEC's own documents and those of the Louisiana Department of Natural Resources."

"What documents are you talking about? Are they before the Court?"

"Yes, sir, they are all part of my report."

"Show them to me, Mr. Ross."

"All right, if I might have a few moments to locate them."

After searching the documents attached to his report, Ross replied, "Here they are. In the records of the Louisiana Department of Natural Resources, Exhibit 136 (a part of my report), they show that all injections by the Tullos-Urania field were gravity fed—no pressure used. Then Exhibit 172, the Long-Term Radiological Surveillance Program report of the AEC, page 88, states that after their injection of the contaminated liquids into HT-2, the AEC learned that the oil field's injections were not under pressure. That report states that when this fact was learned, they concluded that the oil field injection may or may not have had an effect on the direction of the flow of contaminated liquids pumped into Well HT-2. That statement is in direct conflict with all previous AEC reports concluding that the contaminated waste would be forced to flow, against the natural direction of gravity, to the northeast."

"Let me see those Exhibits," Westover exploded.

Judge Lansdorf asked, "Are you saying, Mr. Ross, that the Atomic Energy Commission was aware that their own continued statements were untrue? They knew the idea that the contamination was forced somehow to flow uphill to the northwest was incorrect?"

"Yes, sir, I am saying just that. Their own reports show they knew the contamination was likely to continue to flow in the direction of the population of Tullos, yet they did nothing to stop it, and they gave no warning to anyone."

Chapter 35

PLEASANT COMPANY

Ian walked the two blocks from the federal courthouse to the hotel with Emily Carter. Knowing that they were not to discuss the trial, they engaged in small talk. Emily told Ian that she would be going to dinner with her boss, Van Skiver, and the rest of the DOE team, as usual.

"You coming with us?"

Ian said casually, "No, thanks."

Though Ms. Carter seemed pleasant, Ian couldn't bear the thought of another evening with the rest of her team.

As they walked through the lobby, past the bar, they heard Van Skiver's voice above those of the many younger people there taking advantage of happy hour. They looked at each other, both thinking that he was at it again.

Emily pleaded, jokingly, "Why don't you come with me? For moral support, so I can tolerate his belligerent binge drinking?"

Ian finally told Emily, "It's not you—I just really do not want to go with Van Skiver."

"Please?"

"Well, I tell you what. I'll go freshen up and put my things away, and I'll call you if I'm going to join you."

Emily said that would have to do, and they parted ways.

As Ian settled into his room, the thought came to him that it might have been nice to have dinner just with Emily, away from Van Skiver and DeLoach or anyone else connected to this trial. *Wonder why I didn't think to ask her that?* He admitted that thought frightened him. He had hardly looked at another woman since Kay died. Now he had to acknowledge to himself that Emily Carter was an attractive woman. To think that he might go on a date with someone made him nervous. No woman could ever replace Kay in his heart. Would it be disloyal to Kay to go out with another woman? *A refreshing shower will help me sort all this out.*

After a shower, Ian felt refreshed and decided that he would join Emily and the others. He called her to say he would go. She was excited.

Ian had worked with Kyle DeLoach for over 20 years and liked him fine. In fact, DeLoach was his mentor. And Kyle had at least listened to Ian's concerns prior to Project Apex. Kyle had been the one to take Ian's research to the higher-ups. Going to dinner with DeLoach wasn't the problem—it was Ken Van Skiver and the possibility of running into Jack Erwin.

Ian met the other three in the bar, finding that many of the happy hour crowd had left. Ken was going strong, of course. DeLoach and Van Skiver seemed pleased when Emily told them that Ian was joining them for dinner. Acknowledging that the two of them had already had enough to drink, DeLoach suggested they go on to the restaurant, and Emily and Ian could have a cocktail before dinner there if they wanted. The four of them crowded into a taxi headed for the Royal Palms restaurant. Sitting next to Emily in the crowded taxi, Ian realized how good she smelled, a soft hint of a very appealing perfume. Their sides touched. He didn't know where to put his arm, so he stretched it awkwardly across his lap.

Seated at the table, the waiter asked for drink orders. A rowdy Van Skiver ordered a double vodka martini, DeLoach had scotch on the rocks, Emily asked for a gin and tonic, and Ian had a DeWars and soda. DeLoach kept up his joking around, telling the waiter they would go on and order, as some of them had already had enough to drink. Even so, Van Skiver had a second drink before dinner ever came. Over their meal, the conversation was light and friendly, mainly about the NFL playoff potential. Suddenly and with slurred speech, Van Skiver announced that he had to go to bed. He was visibly lethargic now. DeLoach helped him to the door and put him into a taxi to go back to the hotel.

Kyle returned to the table and as he finished his dinner, shared his concerned over Van Skiver's heavy drinking. He was perplexed by this, as he had known Ken for 30 years.

"While Ken has always been one to enjoy a cocktail, this heavy drinking is something recent," Kyle said. DeLoach went on to say that he knew the serious problems arising out of Project Apex were very disturbing to Ken since he was the one to give final approval.

"But," he said, "Ken's drinking started getting serious when we came back down here to review the testing around Ground Zero, and it's been even more obvious after we attended that town meeting in Tullos last month. I'm concerned."

Ian wondered if Ken was drinking heavily to hide from something.

Each of the three looked at the other, understanding that Kyle had just hit on the most likely reason for Van Skiver's heavy drinking. Each of them had attended that town meeting. They had witnessed the desperate plight of the people who lived in and near Tullos. They saw the show of hands indicating that almost every family represented at the meeting had at least one family member stricken with cancer, many of whom had died. They had heard the people agree that their water was contaminated, but that they were trapped—their homes were all they owned, and no one would buy their homes, so they had no down payment to buy a new home elsewhere, leaving them no way to escape.

Ian found this topic abrasive and unsettling. He didn't want to think about it. He knew only too well of the perilous situation of the people of Tullos.

The three finished their dinner in silence, paid their check, and caught a taxi back to the hotel. During the taxi ride, Emily asked Ian and Kyle what they would do over the weekend, since Court would adjourn Friday afternoon until Monday afternoon. DeLoach was going home to his family in Chevy Chase. Ian said he had no plans. Emily was going to Jackson to spend the weekend with her old college roommate. Back at the hotel, everyone said goodnight and went to their rooms.

Before dropping off to sleep, Ian remembered the subtle, delightful fragrance of Emily's perfume and the unsettling feeling he had while sitting next to her in the taxi, with their legs touching. His love for Kay was so strong, though. *No, I can never love again.* Even though he had known Kay only eleven years, and been married only six, their love for each other was so complete, so perfect, that he knew he could never again experience love such as that. He had sworn to himself that he would not get involved with another woman.

Emily was most pleasant to be with—and to look at, though, indeed.

Chapter 36

SHOCK AND AWE

Joe Ross sat in silence. Behind the Respondent's table, the government visitors were obviously unsettled. Donald Lawrence had bolted straight up in his chair, his mouth agape. Mark Levin glared at Ross. Van Skiver had pulled Bob aside, adamantly demanding something of Westover, who was in a state of shock. Obviously Westover's expert witnesses had not seen—or if they had, they did not inform him of—the seriousness of the contradictions in the government's position. He asked the Judge for a recess.

Looking at the clock, Judge Lansdorf determined that this was a good place to stop for the day and ordered the trial to recess and to reconvene at 9:00 a.m. the following morning. All stood as the Judge retired to his chambers.

As the attorneys and paralegals started gathering up their papers and other materials, Sam was interested to watch Bob Westover's whispered conversation with the people sitting around him. With strong emphasis, Westover was pointing to some document—what appeared to be Ross' report. As he talked, Westover became red in the face. Then he realized that Sam and others were close by. So Westover collected the papers on his counsel table and advised the others around him that they would continue this discussion later. Sam wondered again if the government people told Bob the truth about the testing and its results. *Did he know the whole story?*

Sam and his trial team returned to the law office. They each got comfortably assembled around the conference room table. Sam requested comments and thoughts from members of the team.

Clarence Mitchell, Jr. said with a smile, "Sam, I was worried when we started out, but this is going really well. Thank you."

"Don't thank me yet, Clarence."

From the discussions, it was agreed that the testimony of Joe Ross had been very effective indeed, perhaps even more so than expected, even on cross-examination.

"Westover seemed shocked by the testimony addressing the government reports," Rob said.

They settled into planning out recommendations for the next day, then members of the team went their separate ways to prepare.

Chapter 37

INCOMPLETE RESTORATION

Sam felt awake and fully alive since the Cursillo retreat. There was a new confidence in his step, more love for everyone in his heart, and kinder words in his mouth. He was grateful for his family now in ways he never knew how to be before. After the retreat, he planned and thought about how to repair his lost relationships with his daughters. He started by really being present when his daughters visited or called home to talk and share about their lives. On the phone one day, he got a chance to tell Sandra, his youngest, about his enlightenment at Cursillo. He didn't go into details, and he wasn't brave enough to ask her forgiveness yet, but he felt it was a beginning.

Finally, several months after the Cursillo weekend, Sandra was visiting for the weekend. After supper, they were sitting at the table sharing their thoughts and laughter when Sandra said, "Dad, you don't know how happy you make me these days. I see a huge change in you since you went to Cursillo. I always knew you loved us, of course, but now I can really tell just how much you care. I've never felt as close to you or seen you share your love or faith so freely before," she finished, choking back some tears.

That was the window of opportunity he'd been hoping for. He told his daughter the rest of the story of the Cursillo retreat—about him realizing he'd failed his girls when they were young. He talked about his sense of spiritual restoration. More importantly, he asked her forgiveness for not being as much of a father as he ought to have been.

When she came over and hugged him, the experience of Sandra's forgiveness was so overwhelming and wonderful.

"Sandra, I have to confess to you the emptiness in my heart from having failed to make my family the focus of my life when you girls were young. I can't go back in time, but I sure want to start fresh, starting today, and make our relationship a priority."

Sandra asked his forgiveness, too. "Dad, I know I've punished you with years of rejection after you and Mom got divorced. I'm sorry. I love you so much."

That day, both of them crying like babies, they turned things around. With Sandra, Sam had finally made a breakthrough.

✳

While Sandra was still home visiting, Nell joined them one evening at home. Barbara knew that Sandra and her sister had talked about her reconciliation with her Dad. Sam wondered how his older daughter would respond, or if he'd even get the same chance to talk so intimately with her. The setting had been perfect for opening up with Sandra. He was hoping for a similar moment with Nell.

They were sitting around the fire enjoying a snack and talking after dinner. Everyone was catching up on the latest news of their lives.

At some point, Sandra told her Dad, "Dad, I can't thank you enough for that conversation the other night. I want you to share with Nell what you told me."

Thank you, Sandra.

So he told Nell about Cursillo, his spiritual awakening, his failures. And he asked her forgiveness.

Nell hadn't said anything, but she had tears in her eyes. In fact, everyone was dewy-eyed again. Breaking the silence, Sandra said, "I have always loved you, Dad, and knew that you loved us in your way, but I questioned why you were so distant at times. I feel as though my father was lost to me before, and now I have found him again. I thank God for that." Nell just stayed quiet, though you could tell she'd been moved by what Sam had said.

As the tears and love and kind words flowed between them all,

Sam got up to hug each one of them—his kids, Barbara's kids, Barbara, all of them. Everyone was very receptive, except for Nell. Working his way around the table, he noticed that, although Nell let him hug her, she was stiff and unaffectionate.

That night he talked with Barbara about it. He said, "Well, I have now begged Sandra and Nell to forgive me, but only Sandra responded. I guess that's all I can do for now. It's in God's hands."

"I'll pray tonight that God will work in Nell's heart," Barbara said.

Sam was glad to love and be loved by four stepchildren, his wife, and so glad to be reconciled with Sandra. But he still ached for peace with Nell.

Chapter 38

ROSS CANNOT BE SHAKEN

At 8:45 the next morning, Sam, Rob, Claudia, and Florence were standing near the counsel's table with Joseph Ross. Bob Westover, accompanied by Donald Lawrence and Mark Levin, soon came into the room and moved to their table. Sam noticed that Westover did not speak to him or even look his way. Those same four people, who Sam assumed to be government employees, came in and sat behind the government's counsel table. Precisely at 9:00, the Clerk called for all to rise as Judge Lansdorf entered the room and took his seat behind the bench. Everyone took their seats, and Judge Lansdorf asked Westover if he was ready to commence. Westover asked Ross to take the witness stand again. Ross moved to the stand, and Judge Lansdorf reminded him that he was still under oath. Ross acknowledged.

Westover began a series of questions, obviously designed to try to discredit, or at least create doubts about, Ross' expert report. For several hours, Westover attacked the portion of Ross' report where he concluded that the clean-up of the test site was dangerously flawed. Westover continually emphasized the numerous government reports advising that the only isotope of concern was tritium, and because of its short half-life, it had dissipated by now. But Ross responded forcefully that those reports ignored the potential problem by refusing to seek information on the presence of the curies of beta and alpha isotopes that were disposed of in Aquifer Five during the clean-up.

Westover launched into a new topic. "How can you verify that the contamination pumped into Aquifer Five has likely migrated upward toward the surface by an artificial pathway into freshwater aquifers located above Aquifer Five? That's just a guess, isn't it, Mr. Ross?"

Ross responded, "Such migration might likely occur through the various holes drilled into the aquifers for testing and disposing of the materials. Or it could occur through cracks—the damage from the blasting. There is a multitude of possible ways migration could have occurred."

Westover jumped on that, asking, "Mr. Ross, are you suggesting that those drill holes, which were plugged with concrete, could leak?"

The calm, assured reply was, "Yes, of course. The concrete in those holes would deteriorate just like the concrete in my driveway. Some of those wells were capped before the second nuclear explosion. Given the seismic energies released in the second blast, the concrete could not only crack and fracture but might even have been rubberized."

Attempting to temper this suggestion, Westover pointed out the conflict existing between people in the DOE—some staff wanted to drill into Aquifer Five to determine its condition, while others felt they should leave it alone since it was not hurting anyone, feeling that to drill might create another artificial pathway.

Ross responded vehemently, "I don't see it as a conflict. The pin cushion is already there. The drilling has to be done, even now. There's an ethical obligation to the area residents. You still need to know what is happening out there for the long term. I would much rather drill into Aquifer Five and find out the consequences of that drilling than have the material migrate into the drinking water supplies adjacent to the salt dome. Only if you test can you find out what problems exist, so that you can fix them."

Westover went through Ross' written report, almost page by page, interrogating Ross about anything that might possibly cast doubt or questions in the mind of Judge Lansdorf as to the reliability of the report. At one point he stated, "I am looking at paragraph 8 of the lease between the Mitchells and the government, providing, in the event the Mitchells suffer any damage or loss as a result of the government's use of the land, the government will reimburse the Mitchells. This provision is commonly known as an indemnity provision. Are you familiar with that provision in the lease, Mr. Ross?"

"Yes."

"Do you know the legal effect of such a provision?"

"Yes, sir."

"Then, with this indemnity, there is no way the Mitchells could suffer any loss for any damage to the property, is there?"

"If the indemnity was enforceable, that might be true, but this indemnity you are looking at is not enforceable, since it did not comply with statutory requirements for the issuance of an indemnity by a government agency."

"That testimony should be stricken from the record, Your Honor. Mr. Ross is not an attorney."

"So be it." Judge Lansdorf agreed.

Each direction Westover turned, Ross was able to refute Westover's claims. Ross' report had expressed his serious concerns with the reliability of the studies made by the government.

Westover attacked one portion of the report by referring Ross to a 1976 Special Study, NVO-102, which reported that only minimal levels of tritium were found around Surface Ground Zero, and that it had come from contaminated salt brought to the surface during the post-shot drill back operations. That Study also revealed that no antimony-125 was found.

Ross explained that an earlier study made in 1972 reported that in that same area, salt from the dome was found to contain cesium-137, yet the 1976 study did not even test for that isotope. He questioned why, in 1976, the government selected as their isotope of concern— the one thing that they would test for and, if found, clean up—antimony-125. Ross' conclusion was that the government agents conducting the studies were either grossly negligent, or they did not want to find the truth.

While his examination of Ross covered a lot of time, Westover returned to his central theme: proof. He continued to assail Ross for his mistrusting, critical view of the many government studies and reports, asserting that there was no problem of contamination at the dome. Finally, Westover announced to the Court that he had no further questions of Ross.

The Judge asked Fly if he had any further questions of the witness. Fly responded that he did not but added, "We reserve the right to call Mr. Ross as a rebuttal witness."

"Very well, then. Thank you Mr. Ross, you may be excused. Since you may be called as a rebuttal witness, you must leave the courtroom. Ladies and gentlemen, it is now 6 o'clock and a good time to stop. Before we recess, let me advise you that I will be returning to Washington Friday after we recess, so Court will not reconvene until 2:00 on Monday. Let me further remind you that you are not to discuss this trial, any testimony that has been taken, or any evidence introduced, with any witness who has not yet testified. We will recommence at 9 a.m. tomorrow." Everyone stood as Judge Lansdorf left the courtroom.

Chapter 39

SAYING TOO MUCH

When, along with other witnesses, Ian was dismissed for the day, he put all of his documents into his brief case. Under his arm, he tucked *To Kill A Mockingbird* and slowly walked back to his hotel. As Ian passed by the door to the hotel lounge, Van Skiver—his first drink in hand, almost empty—called out to Ian to come join him.

Damn, he caught me. Ian went inside to Van Skiver's table and told him that he was going to his room to put up his brief case and wash his face. To Ken's invitations, Ian reluctantly said, "I'll be back shortly."

Ian took his time getting to his room and freshening up. He did not look forward to sitting around the bar with Van Skiver, Chairman of the Nuclear Defense Program. He certainly would try to avoid having to go to dinner with them again. When he was ready, Ian went back downstairs to the lounge. There with Van Skiver he found Emily and Kyle DeLoach. Ian joined them and ordered a DeWars and soda. Van Skiver ordered another. The others continued their conversations, something about some new regulations dealing with reporting requirements to congress. Ian was not familiar with those regulations and really had no interest in them. So he sat there quietly.

They moved on to more meaningless conversation for a while—ball games, news, and so on. Then Van Skiver, now on his fourth drink and clearly lost in his own thoughts, blurted out of nowhere, "How did that Ross guy find the bad report?"

Kyle quickly admonished him. Emily backed up Kyle, adding, "Ken, you know we are not to talk about the case."

After a few moments of uncomfortable silence, DeLoach asked if anyone had seen Erwin. No one had, but Ian asked, "Who is that guy anyway, and what interest does he have in this trial? How can he get away with directing us witnesses about what we should say?"

Kyle DeLoach took a swallow of his drink, sat back in his chair, and told the story. "Jack Erwin is a career CIA agent. He was a member of the OSS during World War II and served behind enemy lines in Germany. When the war ended, he became one of the first CIA agents in Eastern Europe. For several years, he worked in the West Berlin Station. He was at the desk that controlled a group of field agents who were operating behind the Iron Curtain. The Russians discovered the group that Erwin headed. They captured and tortured three of the field agents before they hung them as spies. With his cover compromised, Erwin was sent back to the US and assigned to the Agency Headquarters in Virginia."

"He was appointed Case Officer of the project created to find a way to conduct underground testing of nuclear weapons in a manner that could not be detected by foreign powers. But I think losing those three men did something to him. Jack devoted his entire energies and attention to this project with a single-minded determination and zeal I have never before witnessed. Because of his deep hatred for the Russians, and I guess in an effort to somehow redeem the murder of his agents, he was doggedly resolute about finding the answer."

"When the plan for underground testing in a salt dome was proposed, and appeared to have merit, Erwin became obsessed with the possibility of such a thing. He relentlessly pushed to gain approval of the salt dome testing, including using someone he knew in the White House to influence the President, who made the final decision to go."

"He not only has a deep personal interest in the testing and work that was done at the dome, but my guess is that there are some things about the dome and its testing that he does not want to come to light. That may be why he is so absorbed in this trial. He is due to retire before next June 30, and he says that he will do exactly that, as soon as this matter is completed. A lot of stories have been told of Erwin's courage and his ruthless dealings with the enemy. He is one tough guy, not one to cross."

"Wild story, huh? Well, spooky CIA agents aside, I'm getting hungry," Kyle said. The group agreed that they would go across town to the Sea Food Shack for dinner. But Ian declined, saying that he had some work he needed to do, so he would get something fast in the hotel. As the others gathered to leave, Ian walked down the hall to the hotel café, where he figured he would have a bowl of soup and a grilled cheese sandwich.

Part Three: Splitting the Atom

Chapter 40

EMILY'S STORY

Emily stopped Ian at the entrance to the hotel café.

"Mind if I join you?" she asked cheerfully and a little out of breath.

"What are you doing here—I thought you had already gone with the others to the Sea Food Shack?"

"Nah, changed my mind. I decided I wanted something simple for dinner."

Ian had no interest in being with the others they'd left behind, but spending time just with Emily did sound nice. "Well, sure, come on," he said, holding the door.

A waitress quickly appeared and asked if they would like a cocktail or glass of wine. Emily ordered a gin and tonic, and Ian asked for a scotch and soda.

"How are you holding up, sitting in the witness room all day?" she asked.

Ian said fine. Now that they were sitting here together, just the two of them, it was a little awkward.

"What do you do all day in there? Are the other witnesses nice?"

"Oh, the people are good folks, but mostly I sit alone in one of the adjacent rooms."

"Sounds pretty boring," Emily grinned.

"I keep trying to read *To Kill A Mockingbird*, but I get lost in thought half the day, it seems."

Wanting to change the subject before she asked what he was pondering alone all day, Ian asked what she was going to do over the long weekend when Court was adjourned.

She told him of her planned trip to Jackson the next day. "I am going to spend the weekend with my college roommate and best friend, Sandy Leigh, her husband and three children."

Ian asked, "Where did you go to college?"

"I went to Ole Miss. I grew up in Memphis, which is only about an hour and a half from the University of Mississippi, though it might as well have been 1000 miles apart—I did not go home to Memphis that much. There was so much happening on the campus all week, and then weekend trips with sorority sisters and friends, so I didn't go home often. But, I don't want to bore you, so…"

"No, go on. Tell me more about yourself, please."

"There isn't really much to tell. I received an excellent education at Ole Miss while I was off having a wonderful time. It is a very friendly school, a great place to be. Two years after graduation, I married my college sweetheart, once he completed Naval Flight Training."

Ian was confused. *She's married? Am I reading her signals the wrong way? Boy, I really AM rusty.*

Ian said sheepishly, "I didn't know you were married."

"Widowed, actually." Somewhat haltingly Emily continued. "After we married, we were stationed at the Pensacola Naval Air Station for several years, then we were transferred to the Pacific Air Wing in San Diego."

Her eyes sparkled as she told of the happy, carefree life they lived for six years before her husband shipped out to the Far East, with his carrier, the Enterprise. Her voice trailed away and her head dropped as she continued.

"My husband was killed when his plane crashed during a military exercise."

She was silent for a few moments as she briefly relived that grief, then cleared her throat and looked at Ian again.

He said quite earnestly, as he, too, understood grief, "I'm so sorry for your loss. And I didn't mean to make you think about something so difficult."

"No, it's okay, really." Quickly, she went on, "Both of my parents had died, and I felt I had no roots, anywhere, so a couple of years after my husband's death, I moved to Washington to live with my aunt and find a job. Through a friend on the staff of Senator John Stennis, I was introduced to a top-level Administrator in the Atomic Energy Commission. I applied for a job and was hired. I was fortunate to be promoted several times and now serve as Assistant Attorney for the Chief of the NRC."

After a pause she added, "I am excited to be going to see Sandy this weekend. We have not had a visit in a long time, and I love her children."

Declining a second drink, they ordered dinner. During dinner, Emily said, "I have told you my life story. So, now, you must tell me about yourself."

Ian really did not want to go into that, but she insisted, so he told her.

"My mother died when I was 10 years old. My father raised me until he died in the late 1950s. I went to the University of Virginia and received my undergrad and Masters degrees there. I enjoyed my college years, but I was not very involved in the social life. Not that it was not available—UVA is a bit of a party school—but I was not in a fraternity, and the whole partying business just wasn't my scene. After receiving my masters, I was given a fellowship to work on my PhD at Stanford, so I moved to Palo Alto and lived there for 2 years. When that work was finished, and I had my degree, I accepted a job as a nuclear physicist with the AEC and was sent to Washington. A couple of years later I was assigned to Project Apex."

"I was sent to Louisiana as coordinator of the original team and later was named Project Engineer. It was in the little town of Tullos that I met my wife, Kay."

Pausing, he added, "She's gone too, you know."

Emily said, "I'm sorry, Ian."

"That summer we met, Kay was working in a restaurant before going to the University Medical School in Jackson to finish her final year of nursing training. We fell in love, and the year after she completed her training, we got married. She came back home to work for her family's doctor, a friend. Kay's mother died of heart failure during that time. About two years later, after the nuclear tests began, her father died of cancer."

Choking up, he shared, "In 1974, Kay became ill. It was also cancer. It advanced rapidly, and she died soon afterward."

The two were silent for a while, then Ian said, "I can understand your happy life with your husband, because my life with Kay was almost perfect. I have never been so happy."

Ian told Emily how, after the testing was completed, he went back to Nevada, where his office was located. He preferred being far from Tullos and the problems caused by the testing. But it had been necessary for him to return to the site of Project Apex on numerous occasions. And here he was back again.

Conversation eventually turned to happier topics, standard getting-to-know-you fare. Declining dessert, the two signed their dinner checks and prepared to leave. As they walked together to the elevator, Emily asked Ian if he was going to leave town for the weekend, and when he said no, she asked if he had friends in Shreveport. Again he said no. She expressed regrets that he would be alone in Shreveport all weekend. He assured her that he would stay busy.

"I'll go over to Winnfield and maybe on to Tullos."

They rode the elevator together, and as it reached her floor, looking into his eyes, Emily took Ian's hand and squeezed it as she said good-night.

Chapter 41

DR. BILL POOLE

Petitioner's counsel was directed to call their next witness.

"Petitioner calls Dr. William 'Bill' Poole," Claudia Stone stated.

Bill Poole entered the courtroom, walked to the clerk, took the oath, and sat in the witness chair.

Claudia asked him, "Do you have special knowledge, training, and experience in valuing environmentally-impaired real estate?"

When he responded yes, she asked him to tell the Court how he gained that knowledge.

Bill told the Court, "I'm a professional appraiser, Member Appraisal Institute. I worked as an appraiser for some six years, then went back to the University of Washington, where I received a master's degree in urban economics. I was then retained as a consultant to the Weyerhaeuser Company to develop a method to evaluate land for high-yield forestry potential. After the method was developed, I was employed to inspect company lands to classify them."

"In that effort, I visited the company's lands in Louisiana, Mississippi, and Alabama. I was also involved in acquiring large blocks of timberland for the company and in determining the price to pay for those lands. Weyerhaeuser provided me with a fellowship to go back to the University of Washington for a Ph.D. Afterwards, I formed a consulting firm and did appraisals of unique properties all over the country."

Stone asked, "What do you mean by 'unique' properties?"

"Well, for example, one of the assignments I had was to appraise a site to be used for disposal of radioactive materials. From that experience, I became interested in appraising environmentally-impaired property. After several other engagements dealing with properties that had environmental problems, I did a lot of research and was the recipient of a grant from the Real Estate Counseling Group of America to conduct a nationwide study of the impact on value of real estate because of environmental impairments. After publishing a paper on valuing property that has been environmentally impaired and the methods to be used in determining that value, I became recognized by many as an authority in such appraisals. Since then, I have written several books on the subject and lectured extensively about this to government and business groups."

Stone asked if he'd ever dealt with properties affected by radioactive waste.

He acknowledged that he had done many appraisals, mainly for lenders and federal agencies, on the effect radioactive material had on property values.

Claudia then turned to the Judge and said, "Your Honor, I tender Dr. Poole to the Court as an expert in the field of valuing environmentally-impaired real estate, including concerns over radioactivity, as well as in the field of general real estate appraisal, including timberland."

"Mr. Westover?" the Judge asked.

"No objection."

"Then Dr. Poole is received as an expert in all the areas described by Counsel."

Claudia gave Poole a copy of his report, and after having it marked for identification by the clerk, asked him to identify it as the report prepared by him for this case. He looked at it and acknowledged that he had prepared the report for this case and that it represents his opinions and conclusions as it relates to this case. Claudia offered the report into evidence.

"Any objection, Mr. Westover?" asked the Judge.

"No, Your Honor."

"Then this report will be admitted into evidence as Exhibit 149, without objection, as the direct testimony of this witness."

Dr. Poole's rebuttal report was then marked for identification, acknowledged by him to be his report, and offered into evidence.

When government counsel had no objection to its introduction, the Judge said, "Very well, Mr. Westover, you may cross examine the witness."

Westover moved to the lectern and said, "Dr. Poole, in your report, you conclude that the 20,000-acre tract of timberland involved in this case is worth very little because of nuclear contamination. Tell me what independent research did you do to determine that there is contamination on the land?"

"I based my conclusions on documentation that was made available to me."

"Was the documentation you relied on the report of Mr. Ross?"

"I have taken Mr. Ross' report into consideration, as well as other reports."

"Did you rely on Mr. Ross' report to determine the scope and extent of contamination of the land?"

"Yes, partly."

"Are you aware of the huge number of reports issued by the Atomic Energy Commission, the Nuclear Regulatory Commission and the agencies of Louisiana concluding that there is no contamination of the land?"

"Yes, and I looked at many of those, enough to see the inconsistencies and erroneous conclusions."

"What is your understanding of the scope and extent of the contamination on the property?"

"I don't think anyone really knows how extensive it is, because there has not been enough testing done. That's part of the problem. It is certainly something that would trouble a prospective buyer."

In answer to Westover's question of the method used in deriving his value of the land, Poole said he'd used the three traditional approaches: cost, income, and sales-comparison, but that he relied more heavily on the sales-comparison approach, feeling that it offered better quality information. Westover bore in rather belligerently with his interrogation, assailing Poole for relying primarily on that method rather than either of the other two.

Claudia objected, "Mr. Poole has already stated that he did use all three methods, Your Honor. Mr. Westover is badgering the witness."

"Mr. Poole, can you explain why you relied more heavily on one method of appraisal?" the Judge asked.

Poole responded, "My responsibility was to determine what a willing buyer would pay a willing seller. While I did consider all three methods, I felt the sales-comparison approach was the most reliable and best model to indicate true market behavior. My appraised value of the Mitchell land is $8,540,000. I cannot simply use the cost and income methods to determine value, as I feel those are in flux until it can be determined exactly how much contamination there is on the Mitchell property and whether or not the government will ever clean it up."

Bob said, "Now, Dr. Poole, hasn't the government said they will do anything necessary to clean up this site, spending millions of dollars to do so?"

Dr. Poole said, "Well, with all due respect, I'm not sure you can always take the government at their word on things like this. The unfortunate fact of the matter is that the United States Government has a very poor track record when it comes to correcting contamination that it caused. Just look at the Hanford Reservation in the state of Washington, where for 10 years the federal government has been saying that they would clean up nuclear waste at the weapons facility. To date, nothing has been done."

Wanting to avoid any further testimony about that, Westover changed his focus. Westover tried to get Dr. Poole to agree that the highest and best use for the 20,000 acres might be obtained by dividing it into smaller parcels and selling them. If Westover could get one of the Petitioner's witnesses to agree that the best use of the land would be to subdivide and sell it as smaller parcels, the opinion of his own expert witness, who would be testifying to that effect, would be greatly strengthened. That would enable the IRS to argue for higher values and larger estate taxes.

But Bill Poole would not agree with Westover's suggestion. Poole asserted that the highest and best use of the land was as timberland, and therefore, the larger the tract, the more valuable it is.

For the next two hours, Westover attacked Poole's report. He asked if Poole had seen the property. Poole assured him that he had never rendered an appraisal without having carefully investigated the property in person. Poole told of having recently been with Mr. Mitchell near Surface Ground Zero.

"I heard a bulldozer operator say that he could not uncover something buried until the government got him protective clothing. That right there tells you the government knows the land is contaminated."

Many of Westover's questions were asked to point out that Poole had relied very heavily on the report of Joseph Ross. No matter where Bob tried to lead him, though, Dr. Poole remained steadfast, firmly asserting that any suggestion of nuclear contamination on a property would stigmatize that property for a long, long time.

Chapter 42

AT HOME WITH KAY

The next morning at 7 o'clock, looking out the window, Ian saw that it was lightly raining, so he turned over and went back to sleep. When he finally did get up, he showered, shaved, and went for breakfast. It was 9:30. *What a luxury—I am always up and going long before this.*

After breakfast, he got his car out of the hotel garage and drove to Winnfield. As he drove, the rain stopped, and the sun came out from behind the clouds. Arriving in Winnfield, he drove through town and around the square, noticing that very little had changed since he was there last. He drove on past town and headed east on highway 84. Eight miles out of town, he came to the quaint farmhouse where he and Kay had lived after they married, a place that had been in the Hughes family for generations.

He'd told Kay he would build her a nice new home, but she loved this old house. "My grandmother used to live here," she'd told him.

It appeared vacant, so he turned into the drive that led through the pasture and up to the house. He got out of the car, walked up on the porch, and peeped inside. It was empty. Then he noticed the "For Sale" sign blown over in the yard. *Well, of course. The remaining family never could sell it.*

A strong sense of the past came over him, and he sat down on the steps. He thought of the wonderful, happy days that he and Kay had known in that house, and how much she loved it. Not only did she adore their home, but there were 20 acres along with the house, and so a year after they moved in, Ian had thrilled Kay when he bought each of them a horse.

Other than Ian, Kay's passion was her horse. She also adopted all of the stray dogs and cats that wandered into their yard. On several occasions, Ian suggested that because of her love for animals, she should have been a veterinarian rather than a nurse.

As he sat there, Ian's thoughts went back to the day of their wedding. They married in the First Methodist Church of Winnfield on a very hot June day in 1966. On any regular day, Kay was the most beautiful woman he had ever seen, and every woman looks pretty on her wedding day, but walking down the aisle, Kay was angelic—breathtakingly gorgeous.

After their reception in the church hall, they had driven to Shreveport and spent their first night in a suite at the Hilton, near the airport. Ian had ordered some hors d'oeuvres and a bottle of champagne to be chilled when they arrived at the suite. After getting their luggage into the suite and settling down, sitting close together on a little loveseat, they sipped the champagne as they recalled the beauty of the wedding ceremony and some of the special people who attended.

As darkness came, and the champagne had been finished, Ian asked Kay if she was hungry. She wasn't. She suggested that if Ian was not hungry either, they didn't have to go out to dinner. That was fine with Ian. They changed into something more comfortable. Ian put on new pajamas while Kay went into the bathroom. When she came out, she was dressed in a beautiful lacy, low cut gown. The sight of her took his breath away. He took her hand and led her to the king-size bed.

The next day, they flew to Atlanta, where they caught a plane to London and on to Edinburgh, Scotland. Many times during their courtship, Ian had shared with Kay stories his father had told him of growing up there. Ian had seen hundreds of pictures of Scotland and knew the beauty of the country. He felt a strong pull to go there, and he wanted to take Kay, so she was thrilled when he suggested they go to Scotland for their honeymoon.

Ian remembered Kay's excitement over her first flight, especially the Atlanta-to-London leg. Arriving in Edinburgh, they went straight to the Mt. Royal Hotel on Princess Street, where, from their window, they had a clear view of the castle. With its commanding position towering above the area, it was truly an awesome sight. The next three days were spent sightseeing around the central part of the city. From the castle, they walked down the Royal Mile, through the Lawn Market, to St. Giles Cathedral, John Knox house, and on to Hollyrood House Palace. They climbed to the top of the Sir Walter Scott Monument and spent most of an afternoon attending a Piper Band competition at Princess Street Park. Each moment seemed to be more exciting than the last.

Every night, before going to bed, they would stand at their window captivated by the wondrous spectacle of the castle at its site atop the cliff above the city. Together with the remaining light in the sky, the floodlights on the castle created an eerie sensation that set a tone of mystery and wonder. It had been amazing, an enchanted time.

Ian and Kay picked up a rental car he had reserved so they could take a trip to his family's homestead near Lochearnhead. The first day of driving on the wrong side of the road was an experience they later recalled with lots of laughs. By the end of that first day of driving, Ian had pretty well gotten the hang of driving on the left side—except when he exited a roundabout, he always wanted to pull back to the right side of the road. Kay's squeal would bring him back to the left. The double roundabouts were a real challenge. *God, we had fun.*

In the town of Linlithgow, they went through the ruins of a castle built in 1301, the birthplace of Mary, Queen of Scots. From there, they drove to Sterling, which they found fascinating. The narrow streets in the old town leading up to the castle were most interesting. Like Edinburgh Castle, the view of the countryside from Sterling Castle was commanding.

Going back down the hill, they found the statute of Rob Roy MacGregor, one of Ian's ancestors. Driving on toward Lochearnhead, Ian told Kay some of the story of Rob Roy as he had, many times, heard it from his father. He told how, because the MacGregor Clan had been leaders in an unsuccessful attempt to defeat the British, their lands were taken from them. The King proscribed the name MacGregor, forbade a gathering of more than four members of the clan, and offered a ransom on the head of any MacGregor delivered to him. Having lost their lands, Rob Roy became sort of a Robin Hood, taking from the rich and sharing with the poor.

They found Lochearnhead to be a quiet, small town, a peaceful place surrounded by hills covered with mountain laurel, wild flowers, and heather. The charming Lochearnhead Hotel was the largest building in the town. Even though the hotel had only 10 rooms, the dining room was very nice, and downstairs was an awesome little pub. Ian had seen notices of the Lochearnhead Highlands Games posted in the hotel and asked to verify that the games would be held two days later. Being assured this was correct, they got so excited that they would be able to go!

He and Kay spent their second day roaming the countryside. They went to Balquihidder, the place where the MacGregor Clan had once lived. Though the town was tiny, the surroundings were beautiful. Situated on the banks of Loch Voil, it seemed to be enveloped by the lush growth of flowers and heather. In the churchyard close by, they found Rob Roy's grave. As they wandered around the area, Ian experienced a feeling deep inside that here with Kay, he had come home. He felt a peace in his spirit that he had never before known. When he told Kay of his feelings, she understood, because she, too, sensed a deep serenity in this place.

Breaking that solemn, spiritual mood, Kay started giggling beside Rob Roy's grave.

"What?" Ian had asked, eyebrow cocked to one side.

"Well, all this Scottish tranquility is great, but the best part about it is…" she hesitated.

"What? What!"

"You will look great in a kilt."

Kay took off laughing and running before Ian could say "no way" was he going to wear a kilt.

The next day was probably the highlight of their trip. The Highlands Games were held in a field across the street from the hotel. Even though the games did not start until noon, by 9:00, many colorful tents had been raised, the field striped, and people were everywhere. It was chilly, drizzling rain, but that was not going to detract from the fun of the event. Several bagpipe bands were there tuning up for the opening ceremony. Many men were in their colorful kilts. Kay was fascinated by the kilts. She urged and urged, and finally, Ian got one.

They spent most of the afternoon watching the various activities of the Highlands Games. Kay loved the Scottish dancing competition, Ian was fascinated by the tossing of the caber, but both enjoyed watching the sheep dogs heard the flock. They were intrigued to know that most of the events had been used in the games for more than 300 years.

When the games ended, many of the participants and spectators gathered in the hotel pub. With the large crowd, there was no place to stand at the bar, but Ian and Kay fortunately found a table. They soon were served their drinks, and as they sipped them, they listened intently to the accents of the Scots, discerning several different ones.

One of the men at a table close by overheard Ian and Kay talking, and after straining to better hear them, intrigued by their accents, he introduced himself and asked if they were from the States. Their answer led to more conversation. The man introduced Kay and Ian to his friends at his table and asked that they join them. When they did, the Scots barraged them with questions. It quickly became obvious that, together with wanting to know more about the two Americans, all the men wanted to hear Kay's sweet Southern accent. In the course of their conversations, the Scots learned that Ian and Kay were there on their honeymoon, so they ordered the bartender to bring the newly-weds a whisky on them. Kay was full of questions for them, too, about their lives in Scotland, and especially about the different kilts. Several hours passed before their new Scottish friends agreed they had enjoyed enough spirits and must head for home. The memory of that night was another that Ian and Kay cherished and frequently recalled.

Before they knew it, it was time for them to leave Scotland to return home. The thought of leaving that peaceful, beautiful country saddened both of them. Throughout the trip, Ian had an intense sensation that he had retuned to his roots. Kay was so thankful for him introducing her to a place that she instantly adored. The scenery was spectacular, the history of the place was spellbinding, the people were loving and kind, but mostly, Ian and Kay had just enjoyed the time with each other. Hand in hand each day, arms and legs intertwining each night, they had shared the experience of a lifetime. They promised each other they would return to this land of their dreams.

We never got the chance.

✳

Realizing it was past 2 o'clock, and that he was a little bit hungry, Ian decided to head back into town to find something to eat in Winnfield rather than drive the 15 miles to Tullos to eat at Slim's Café, where he had met Kay. He knew he wouldn't eat much, and he couldn't bear the thought of going to Slim's. Afterwards, he figured he'd head on back to his hotel in Shreveport for the rest of the weekend. As he walked to his car, he looked back at the house once more. Tears ran down his cheeks, and he whispered, "Kay, I miss you so much."

Chapter 43

DR. POOLE CONTINUES

"Mr. Westover, do you have more questions of Dr. Poole?"

"Yes, Your Honor."

"Then you may proceed. Dr. Poole, please take the witness stand and remember that you are still under oath."

Westover picked up where he had left off, going through Poole's expert report and picking at any and every point he thought he could discredit. He asked about the three comparable sales that Poole had used in his estimate of the Mitchell property value. Two of those sales involved situations where low-level radioactive materials were buried on the land, while the third was where PCB's were found. Westover tried to get Poole to agree that tritium found on the Mitchell land would have no more adverse impact on value than the low-level materials found in his comparable sale number one.

"Oh, that assumption would be absolutely incorrect, sir. A buyer would be much more concerned about the radioactive material on the Mitchell property, especially tritium, than they would on the comparable property we discussed. On the Mitchell property, we have radioactive material from the explosion of a nuclear bomb! If you rank various types of contamination, nuclear waste is the most feared of all," Poole replied.

Desiring to mitigate that remark, Westover attempted to assert that in Poole's comparable sale examples, since the entire tract was not affected, the value of only a portion of the land had been discounted. He said the same should be true with the Mitchell property, but Poole had devalued the entire property.

Poole answered, "While the contamination is known to exist on only a small portion of the Mitchell land, no one knows the full extent of that contamination, so no one knows how much of the land is affected. Because of that, the entire land is impacted. The real truth of the matter is that very, very few contaminated properties sell at any price. I used these comparables because they are the closest situations I could find, and they clearly show that if a contaminated property does ever sell, it sells at a very large discount. If you want my honest opinion, I don't think the Mitchells could ever sell that land—just as the residents of Tullos cannot sell theirs. I mean think about. Would you want to buy a home and move your family to a place where nukes had been exploded?"

Quickly moving on, Westover's next emphasis was directed to Poole's testimony in his report that the cost of cleaning up the contamination was unknown and that potential buyers would have no interest in buying the property once they learned the situation. He asked if Dr. Poole was aware that the government had recently announced that it would spend $12 to 13 million dollars on a Remedial Investigation and Feasibility Study of the property, and the landowners would be required to pay nothing.

Poole acknowledged that he was aware of that planned study but reminded Westover that several years prior a similar study had been conducted, and the problems continued.

When he got no concession from Poole, Westover announced to the Court that he had no further questions.

"Do you have any questions of this witness on redirect, Ms. Stone?" the Judge asked.

"Yes I do, Your Honor."

Then you may proceed."

Claudia had Dr. Poole focus on a portion of his report citing appraisals he had done for the government property in New Mexico. The properties were situated on a road where trucks hauled sealed nuclear waste. The concern that a truck might wreck and spill the waste warranted a 25% discount of the value of the land just because it was near that road.

Emphasizing the severe lack of comparable sales to use, she then asked him, "Is it possible that some contaminated lands simply cannot be sold, ever?"

"Yes, most definitely. A property that has contamination on it generally is unmarketable. A potential buyer has two considerations: uncertainty and risk. The uncertainty is that the nature of the contamination may not have been adequately quantified so that a buyer could make a well-informed purchase decision. However, even if adequate environmental testing has been done, and the nature of the problem has been well identified, then buyers must assess the risk of acquiring the property, what the cost of cleaning it up will be, whether complete restoration is even possible, what the impact on personal health could be, and what the residual stigma on the property is, etc. If they still want to buy the property, someone still has to determine how much it should be discounted. That's why they hire me."

"Furthermore, with the Mitchell land, the uncertainty is almost insurmountable. No one knows the extent of the contamination or the cost to do a full clean-up—in fact, it is not beyond reason to suggest that cleaning up the Mitchell land is simply not even possible, especially at this late date. The government has spent millions on clean-up, and it still is not free of contamination. I personally surveyed ten parties who buy timberland, each of whom had knowledge of the Mitchell's contamination problem, as to their interest in buying the Mitchell land. Seven of them had no interest in the land whatsoever. The other three might have been interested if they could have been assured the contamination had been cleaned up, but that's the thing: there's no way for me to give them that guarantee, because there's no way to certify that complete remediation is even possible. In the end, all ten potential buyers passed. The stigma is just too great."

"Thank you, Dr. Poole."

Chapter 44

LOSS

In November, 1973, she started feeling bad. Kay had a cough she could not shake and had no energy. When the condition persisted and did not respond to treatment, Dr. Vassar sent Kay to Ochsner Clinic in New Orleans.

For three days, they ran tests and sent the results to Dr. Vassar. Four days later, Kay and Ian met with Dr. Vassar to get the results. Ian's heart went cold when he saw the look on Dr. Vassar's face. He could still hear the crushing words Dr. Vassar had said to them "Kay, I am devastated to have to tell you that you have a malignancy in both of your lungs. The x-rays show that the cancer has spread beyond your lungs." Tears ran down his face as Dr. Vassar continued, "The cancer is the fastest growing type we know of. We can give you radiation, hoping to shrink the tumors, but the likelihood of any success is remote. It would take a miracle."

Ian and Kay held each other tightly as they cried. Both of them were destroyed, but each wanted to try to comfort the other. Kay was hesitant to take the radiation treatments, but Ian encouraged her. As they earnestly prayed for the miracle of her healing, she started the radiation treatments. She felt fairly good for a while, but she slowly started going down. In mid-October, 1974, she became so weak that she had to stay in bed. In late November, representatives of Hospice came to tend her until she died.

In those last days of Kay's life, Ian never left her side. He read to her, frequently from the Bible. He recalled their shared experiences, beginning with the first day he saw her, telling her again that she was then and still was the most beautiful woman he had ever seen. She knew how gaunt and sallow she was, and she did not like the wig she had bought when she lost her hair. But Ian did not see that—he only saw the inner beauty that nothing could change. They reminisced about their years together. Kay became so weak that it was difficult for her to talk, so Ian did most of the verbalizing. Much of Kay's communication was in her eyes.

In one of their conversations just days before she died, Kay took his hand and said to him, "Ian, I want you to promise me something. You are very young still, and I want you to have a fulfilled life. I want you to promise me that you will marry again."

He was shocked at the request and resisted, saying, "My love for you is so strong, there is no way that I could ever consider marrying again. There is not another woman on Earth that could fill your place in my heart."

But she was not to be denied, and said, "Remember, my one last wish is that you remarry and have children. You will be a good father, and I want you to have that joy."

She slept most of the last week before her death, with Ian sitting beside her, holding her hand. Sensing that she was slipping away, Ian held her in his arms. He saw to it that enough painkillers were administered that she didn't hurt. He told her again and again that he loved her more than life itself, and that he would love her as long as he might live.

In a moment she was gone.

Kay was buried beside the graves of her mother and father. Rev. Kennedy Watson, the same minister who had buried her parents and had married her and Ian, performed the service. Many neighbors and friends had brought food to Ian's home, so following the service, they all went back to his house. With Ian numb from the shock of an empty house, realizing that his beloved Kay was gone, all he could do was sit on the couch and acknowledge comments made to him by the others, usually with a nod of his head.

As people began to leave, Mrs. Watson, the minister's wife, urged her husband that they spend the night there with Ian. But Ian wanted to be alone. Insisting that he would be okay, he made them go. He couldn't remember much about that night alone, or even the next couple of days.

He stayed in bed. Didn't eat much. Didn't shower.

Finally, he came out of the daze and went back to work. He found that going to work was good for him. Time passed much faster than when he sat at home alone in the house he used to share with her.

She was so young, so full of life and love and potential. Damn this stupid Project Apex. Damn cancer. She's gone. Her dad died of it. Half the town's had it. I feel so responsible.

✸

Ian sat engrossed in these thoughts of the past until he realized that dark was approaching. *I've been sitting in this restaurant for hours.* He closed the book he'd been pretending to read. Most of the people who had been around him had gone or were leaving. He got into his car and left Winnfield.

Heading back to Shreveport, he went a different route, past Saline Lake and through Natchitoches, in no hurry. Pulling into the hotel parking garage, he sat for a while more in the darkness.

After breakfast Saturday, Ian came back to his room, sat in the chair, and turned on the television. *Some diversion is what I need to get my mind off the past.* Surfing the channels, he found a golf tournament from California and got interested. When the tournament ended, Ian realized that he was hungry. He washed his face and walked two blocks to the Elite Restaurant. After dinner, he became engrossed in a movie back in his room. He got undressed and got into bed. When the movie ended, he turned out the light. He could feel the weight of the long weekend wearing on him.

Finally, Sunday came. To get out of his funk, Ian decided to go to church, so he walked around the corner from the hotel to a large Methodist Church. It had been a while since he had attended church, but he felt very comfortable there. He related to the music led by the informal choir and found it touching. After church, he went back to the hotel, ate in their restaurant, changed clothes, got his car and drove to Cross Lake on the edge of the city. Stopping at a park beside the lake, he parked the car, walked for a while, then found an empty bench and sat in the sun, engrossed at the sight of the beautiful water.

Even though there were other people around the area, Ian felt totally alone. Going through this trial was like reliving all this all over again.

Chapter 45

SHEA CLAREMORE

At the lectern, speaking into the microphone, Claudia Stone said, "Petitioner calls Shea Claremore."

Claudia asked Claremore a series of questions to point out her qualifications and experience as a forester. The testimony established that she was a person of excellent credentials and an impeccable reputation. Claudia then offered Claremore as an expert in forestry and timber evaluation. Westover had no objection to Claremore's qualifications.

Stone then took a document from the Counsel table, gave it to the clerk, and asked that it be marked for identification. She showed the document to Claremore and asked her to identify it. The witness said it was the report she had prepared as an expert witness in this case. Claudia offered the document as Petitioner's Exhibit 66 into evidence.

"Any objections, Mr. Westover?" the Judge asked.

"No, Your Honor."

"Then this report, Exhibit 66, is received into evidence as the direct testimony of Ms. Claremore."

Sam was thankful to God for a trial team he could trust to do such an impeccable job.

When it was his turn, Bob Westover systematically went through Claremore's report, raising many questions, trying to find some way to discredit the accuracy of the report. When he reached the portion stating it was suspected some of the land was contaminated, Westover asked, "Ms. Claremore, have you done any research to determine the nature and extent of the alleged contamination of the land?"

"No, sir."

Growing tired of this uphill battle, Bob Westover was losing patience. Glaring at the witness, Westover asked in harsh tones, "Then that assertion in your report is totally without foundation, isn't it? It is hearsay. And if it is the basis for your appraisal, it makes your appraisal worthless, doesn't it, Ms. Claremore?"

"No, sir. I have carefully read Mr. Ross' reports filed with this Court, and I accept his conclusions as reasonable and probable."

Bob retorted hotly, "So basically, you and every witness the Petitioner has called is relying on the Ross Report, which my team has shed serious doubts on. Doesn't anyone have their own ideas?"

"Objection, Your Honor!" Stone was livid.

"Sustained. Mr. Westover, I expect a more respectful attitude in my Court."

Westover handed Shea several of the exhibits to the Stipulation filed with the Court and asked, "Have you read any of the numerous DOE Reports like these, stating that there is no contamination on the Mitchell land?"

Claremore looked at the documents that had been handed to her and answered, "In this quick glance, I cannot be sure that I have reviewed these particular documents, but I have reviewed a number of the government reports. I put very little confidence in their accuracy."

Through his next series of questions, Westover secured Claremore's agreement that most of the Mitchell land would still grow trees.

She answered, "Yes, but let me qualify that affirmation with one reservation, that on some of the land close to Surface Ground Zero, and fanning out from Ground Zero, trees were severally stunted."

Thinking that Claremore's conclusion might be conjecture, Westover pressed this point, "How can you be sure trees are stunted and not just young trees?"

Claremore explained, "I took samples from trees at differing distances from Surface Ground Zero by boring a hole and pulling out the core. Counting the growth rings in that core, and knowing the type pine in that area of the country should grow so many fractions of an inch each year, it was simple to see that those trees were severally stunted."

"Have the Mitchells continued to sell timber from their lands since the nuclear testing, Ms. Claremore?" Westover asked.

"Yes, sir, at first, but since word of the nuclear contamination problems spread in the timber industry, no one appears interested in buying the Mitchell timber."

"But, isn't that drop-off in sales merely a temporary thing until those wild rumors dissipate?"

She replied, "I expect that, in time, yes, their sales may pick up again, but my appraisal must reflect the situation as of the date of Mr. Mitchell's death. I cannot consider what might happen in the future."

Claremore's report identified the stands of timber on the 20,000 acres owned by the decedent, reflecting on maps the types of timber and the ages of each stand. She took many samples to determine ages of the trees and growth rates. In stating her opinion of the value of the timber, she used the three approaches required by the American Society of Farm Managers and Rural Appraisers: cost, income capitalization, and sales comparison.

Claudia asked, "Ms. Claremore, please tell the Court what you think an accurate value of the Mitchell timberland is."

"According to my research, the value of the timber on the Mitchell lands is worth about $3,500,000, certainly no more. This value is based upon timber within one mile of Surface Ground Zero being worth nothing. The farther the timber was from Surface Ground Zero, the more it is worth."

In his next line of questions, Westover attempted, as he'd done with a previous witness, to get Claremore to admit that the highest and best use of the 20,000 acres was to break the acreage up into smaller tracts and sell those tracts separately. But Claremore would not agree with Westover's suggestion, asserting that the highest and best use of the property was as timberland, not to mention that no one would buy any land near that area anymore because of the stigma.

When Westover announced he had no further questions, Judge Lansdorf asked, "Ms. Stone, do you want to question this witness on redirect?"

"Yes, Your Honor, I have a few questions."

"Very well, Ms. Stone, you may proceed. Ms. Claremore, let me remind you that you are still under oath." Shea nodded her agreement.

Very methodically, Claudia questioned Claremore on matters raised by Westover during his cross-examination, to clear up any uncertainty or confusion.

She asked Claremore, "Explain any differences in growing timber to be used for poles as opposed to saw timber."

The witness said, "It takes much longer to grow poles than saw timber, but the price for poles is substantially greater than saw timber. My valuation of the Mitchell's timber reflected the fact that they used much of their land to grow timber for poles, and it is apparent that at least 400 acres of their lands will no longer produce pole timber."

Claudia succeeded in leaving the Judge with a favorable impression of Claremore's testimony through her well-crafted questions and the answers she elicited. When she had raised all the questions in her trial brief, Stone announced to the Court that she had no further questions of the witness.

Judge Lansdorf asked Westover if he had any more questions of this witness. Westover did not, so Claremore was excused from the courtroom.

Chapter 46

COMPANIONS

As he came back from the lake and through the door of his room, the phone rang.

It was Emily. "Hey, I just got back. Have you eaten? I'm famished and thought we could grab a bite."

Ian had to admit it was good to hear her voice.

"I was just thinking of dinner. Why? What'd you have in mind?"

Emily eagerly said she would meet him in 20 minutes.

Having spent the weekend alone, Ian was ready to have company, and Emily sounded like she would be happy to see him, too.

Ian did not have to wait long for Emily to arrive. As she got off the elevator, she walked to him and hugged him lightly.

Over the meal, she told him all about her trip to Jackson. She had enjoyed her time with her former roommate, Sandy, and her family, but she explained that while she was with people all weekend, she had still been lonely. She asked Ian if he had had a good weekend and what he had done.

Automatically he answered, "Oh, it was fine," but he caught himself. Pausing briefly, he acknowledged that the weekend was actually a bummer. "It's just depressing to think about Project Apex again and everything connected to it—and Kay."

At Emily's insistence, he told her how he had spent the time.

Afterwards, she said, "Your love for Kay is so obvious. It reminds me of my feelings for my late husband. Tell me about her."

Initially, Ian was reluctant to disclose much about his Kay to another woman, but as he started with nonspecific information about her and their lives together, encouraged by Emily, he became more open. He told how they had met, dated and married, about their honeymoon in Scotland, Kay's illness and death, and that he would love her always.

Then he asked Emily about her husband, too. She'd shared a loss so much like his own. As they talked on, they realized they were the last people in the restaurant, and agreed that it was time to leave. Riding the elevator together, Emily took Ian's hand and thanked him for sharing about Kay.

Then she kissed him on the cheek and told him good night.

Back in his room, Ian acknowledged to himself that Emily was a very attractive lady. Not only is she quite pretty, but she is warm, caring, and intelligent.

She kissed me.

Still, he felt so much deep concern. *As much as it troubles me to admit it, I enjoy being with Emily.* He wondered if his new feelings dishonored his vows to Kay.

Alone in bed, he asked quietly, "Kay, would you have liked Emily?"

Chapter 47

NEELY RYDER

Once Claudia was finished with Shea Claremore, it was time for Sam to call their last witness.

"Do you have anything further Mr. Laurins?"

"Yes, Your Honor. Petitioner asks for leave of the Court to call Mr. Neely Ryder, who was originally here to testify as a rebuttal witness later on, if need be. Mr. Ryder has been called to return to his home in Eugene, Oregon, due to an emergency. Rather than have him take the time and incur the expense to return here next week for his brief testimony, we request that he be allowed to testify now."

Judge Lansdorf responded, "Very well. I think that we can accommodate the witness in this way. You may call the witness. Mr. Bailiff, would you please get Mr. Ryder?"

Neely Ryder entered the courtroom, stood before the clerk, took the oath, then sat in the witness chair.

"Mr. Ryder, who is your employer?" Sam inquired.

"I work for the West Coast Research Institute," Ryder said from the witness stand. "We have long term contracts with various agencies of the federal government, including the Environmental Protection Agency and Department of Energy, as well as the National Science Foundation. I am the Project Superintendent for my company. In that capacity, I work closely with all the parties involved, seeking a satisfactory solution to whatever the problem is."

"What is your role in the clean-up process at the Hanford Reservation?" Sam asked.

"Objection: relevance?" Westover claimed, hoping to keep that testimony out.

"Overruled. I'll hear the witness out," Lansdorf said.

"For the past three years, I've worked at the Hanford Reservation, the largest of the Department of Energy sites. Part of that work is trying to get nuclear contamination on the Indian Reservation cleaned up."

Sam said, "Mr. Ryder, the Petitioner in this case has asserted that the Atomic Energy Commission created a serious nuclear contamination problem on land owned by the Mitchell family. During the course of this trial, the government has responded at times that there is no contamination problem to be cleaned up, and at other times, that if there is a problem, they will simply come back and clean it up. The government's argument is that in the lease it has with the Mitchells, the government has indemnified the land owner from any expense or loss, so there is no way the Mitchells can lose property value because of Project Apex. Have you had any experience where the government has created a nuclear contamination problem and been told to come back and clean it up, but refused to do so?"

Bob Westover was on his feet again. "I object to the witness answering that question," he said. "Your Honor, to answer that question would require the witness to testify as an expert, and this witness has not been qualified as an expert."

"The testimony of this witness is not expert testimony, Your Honor," Sam replied.

Sitting upright, Judge Lansdorf said, "Well, let's make sure the question is as I understand it. You are asking him if he has personal knowledge of a situation where the government promised—but did not follow through—regarding cleaning up a contamination problem they had created. Is that correct?"

"That is correct," Sam answered.

"Mr. Westover, I think it is a reasonable question, but you may ask him why or how he knows the answer, if you like," the Judge said.

"Your Honor, I still object. The question proposed is still not relevant to the case unless it applies to the land in question."

"And I'm saying it still seems relevant to me, Counsel," the Judge stated, giving Westover a look that dared him to object again. "Mr. Ryder, do you have personal knowledge of a situation such as Petitioner's Counsel asked about?"

"Yes, I do," Ryder replied.

"In order to describe it to me, will you have to use your expertise or judgment to reach some conclusion as to whether the government did or did not do what they were supposed to do? In other words, might people disagree that it was cleaned up properly?" the Judge asked.

"I think everyone involved in the Hanford situation would agree with what I would say."

"Well, let's test that out. Go ahead and answer."

The witness explained, "I worked with the DOE, EPA, and the State of Washington trying to get nuclear waste contamination cleaned up at the Hanford Reservation in the south central part of Washington state. I was involved in this project for three years, but the DOE had been expected to clean the site up for more than 12 years. They had not yet done so."

"What is the environmental significance of the Hanford Reservation?" Sam asked.

"The Hanford Reservation was the site where many of the major components of the Hiroshima and Nagasaki atom bombs were developed in the early 1940s. It's continued to be a major production site for the AEC and later, the NRC. The site is heavily contaminated with nuclear waste that the Department of Energy was supposed to clean up."

"You say the DOE was supposed to have cleaned it up. Were they legally obligated to do so?" Sam asked.

"Yes, sir."

"Has the DOE refused to clean up the site?"

"For more than 12 years, the DOE has supposedly been 'making plans' for the clean-up, but to date, nothing has been done."

"Thank you, Mr. Ryder. That is all I have for this witness, Your

Honor," Sam said.

"Mr. Westover, what do you have?" the Judge asked.

"Mr. Ryder, tell us about the Hanford Reservation. How large is it?" Westover asked.

"It is 560 square miles."

"What are the major contaminants on the Reservation?"

"Remains of strontium, cesium, plutonium, and other deadly debris have accumulated on the floor of holding tanks, called K basins."

"How many people are involved in the process of getting the area cleaned up?"

"Probably 200," the witness responded.

"Isn't the main reason the DOE has not yet completed the clean-up because they are still searching for the affected areas within that huge 560-square-mile property?" Westover asked. "I mean, if you are searching a 560-square-mile area for contamination that has seeped into the ground since the 1940s, isn't it to be expected that it will take a long time to complete the clean-up? A bit like looking for a needle in a haystack, isn't it, Mr. Ryder?"

"No, sir. I mean no disrespect, but the major contamination areas are clearly defined. A big portion of the problem is in the K basins that I mentioned, and everyone there knows exactly where they are. The locations of the major problem areas have been known for 10 years."

"Is it possible that the delay in the completion of a clean-up plan has been caused by lack of knowledge of the types of contamination and their sources?" Westover asked.

"No, sir. We know precisely what contaminants are there and where they are."

A little frustrated with his inability to create some inconsistency in Ryder's testimony, Westover asked, "Has the Department of Energy absolutely refused to do the clean-up outright?"

Ryder responded, "I do not know if they have refused to perform the clean-up. I have never heard a representative of the DOE say they refused to complete the clean-up, nor have I ever seen anything in writing saying that. I only know that for more than 12 years, all they have done is hold conferences and talk about developing a plan to clean up their mess. They have not acted, so I cannot say I place any trust in their promises."

"Do you have any knowledge of the government's involvement in the Mitchell case, the matter before the Court today?" Westover asked.

"No, sir. I can't say anything about what they're doing in the Mitchell situation, but in my situation back at Hanford, all the government has done is talk. I have no faith in what they say anymore."

Flustered, Westover seemed to have decided that there was no way to repair the damage that had been done, and gave up on the witness. Returning to his seat, he said, "That's all I have, Your Honor."

Lansdorf turned to Sam, "Redirect, Mr. Laurins?"

"No, sir. The Petitioner rests, Your Honor."

Chapter 48

A FIRST DATE?

When the day was done, Emily rushed to the Witness Room to tell Ian they were free to go. As the two of them walked back to the hotel, Ian was finally ready to ask her out officially.

"Emily?"

"Yes?"

"Would you like to go out with me, just have dinner alone, apart from the others?"

Emily quickly agreed. "Love to." She said she would meet Ian in the lobby in 30 minutes after she dropped off her stuff and freshened up.

As he changed his shirt, Ian felt pangs of guilt to consider a date with Emily.

But it really isn't a 'date-date,' he assured himself, *not like going to the movies or something. We are just here for this trial and will just have dinner together*, he rationalized.

Ian was waiting in the lobby when Emily stepped off the elevator. He was taken aback with how beautiful she was. The blue sweater she had changed into matched her azure eyes and was a sharp contrast with her curly blonde hair. It also clearly revealed the well-shaped body it covered. For a few moments he was speechless. She took his hand and asked if they could go to the Sea Food Shack.

"I feel like some clam chowder," she said with excitement.

He agreed. "Mmm. Sounds good. Broiled flounder, I think, for me—or shrimp scampi."

So they had the doorman get them a taxi. As they waited, Ian realized they were still holding hands. Surprisingly, he was quite comfortable with that. In the taxi, they huddled close together and talked about nothing important.

Seated at their table in the restaurant, each ordered a cocktail. Ian asked how the trial was proceeding and when she thought it would be completed.

"It's going better for the taxpayer than the government, I'd say. The Judge said the trial would be completed Friday. It won't be long before you'll join us in the courtroom. Bet you'll be glad not to be sequestered back there anymore."

"Not really." Ian admitted, "Listen, Emily, I have to tell someone. I am very uncomfortable about testifying. From the very start of Project Apex, I have felt that the government had insufficient knowledge of the possible outcome of the testing. Too many things could go wrong, and we did not have sufficient answers to the problems that could reasonably be expected to arise. The testing went forward with no regard to the safety of the people who live there. Since the testing was completed, my worst fears have been confirmed, as you know. The salt dome leaked, and nuclear contamination has spread outside the test area, people were stricken with cancer caused by that contamination. All this brings back such difficult personal memories, on top of it. I just don't know if I can do what Jack Erwin has asked us to do—tow the government line."

Looking into Emily's eyes it was clear that she understood him. "Ian, you will find your way, I know. I think you should say whatever is in your heart."

In the moments of silence that followed, he repeated the thought he had held since the lawsuit was filed. "If the taxpayer's Counsel asks questions I don't want to face, how will I respond? The government people, especially that CIA guy, Erwin, are not going to like what I have to say."

She took his hand and assured him that it was alright. "If you tell the truth, and it is harmful to the government's case, I guess that's just too bad for our side. The government wins plenty of cases. You do what you have to do. This case is so unique. Maybe the government *was* wrong. I don't know. With everything I've heard and read about this case now, I'm starting to think they did something awful out there. All I know is you were there, on the inside, so I feel like you know more than I or anyone else possibly can. I trust you. Only you will know how to respond exactly. Just be honest."

After some silence, Ian finally got his mind off the trial, reminding himself he was on a date and here to enjoy this beautiful woman's company. The conversation turned more personal, as they talked about their lives and hopes for the future.

Ian braved a personal question. "What are you looking for out of life and dating and relationships?"

Emily answered, "If the right man comes along, I want to marry again. My first marriage was so fulfilling and good that I have no hesitancy to remarry. My only fear is that another husband might die, and I would have to go through that agony again." Pausing for a few moments, she asked Ian how he felt about remarriage, with all he'd been through.

Somewhat hesitantly, Ian told her of the pledge he had made to himself never to marry again. He explained, "Kay was the first and only woman I have ever loved. I gave her my heart. No one could ever replace her."

When Emily asked him, "Oh, but Ian, I don't think it works like that. No one could replace my James, either, but that doesn't mean I can't love again. Would Kay want you to remain single forever?"

He was surprised. He had to tell her the promise he made to Kay. Ian related the conversations he had with Kay shortly before she died. "She told me that she wanted me to marry again and, hopefully, have children." As he shared this with Emily, his words were suspended in space along with his thoughts. By the time he had finished, his words came only as a whisper.

Both were quiet and pensive as they rode back to the hotel.

In the elevator, Emily turned to face Ian and moved to the point that their bodies were almost touching. With their faces only inches apart, they each moved closer to the other until their lips met. Then the elevator was at Emily's floor. She whispered, "Goodnight," and was gone.

Back in his room, Ian flopped down in the easy chair, his mind racing. *What is happening? What are all these conflicting feelings? How do I deal with this?*

He undressed, got in bed, slept very little.

As the alarm sounded the next morning, Ian opened his eyes and looked around the room, still thinking about Emily and their time together the night before. He slowly rose from the bed and got into the shower. Standing there under the tepid water, his mind was a blur. As he dressed and headed to the dining room, his first thought was that he hoped he would not run into Emily. But when he looked all over the dining room and found that she was not there, he was most anxious to see her. *I am all mixed up.* After breakfast, he hurried to the court-house and to the Witness Room, by now his second home.

Part Four: Plutonium Core

Chapter 49

PETITIONER RESTS & RELAXES

Sam suggested to his group that they go to the University Club on the 21st floor of his office building for a cocktail once they were done.

Rob said, "That sounds like a terrific idea."

After gathering up all their exhibits and other documents, Florence called the office to have a runner come take the boxes back to the office. They all left the courthouse and walked the three blocks to the office building. Sam found a convenient corner sitting area in the club and was joined by Rob, Claudia, Florence, Clarence, Joe Ross, Bill Poole and Neely Ryder.

Sitting in one of the over-stuffed chairs, Clarence said to the group, "I don't know about you all, but I am looking forward to relaxing with this drink. I don't see how y'all do this for a living. I can't help but feel stressed, hanging on every word spoken at this trial."

Rob agreed and said that he might very well enjoy two drinks.

"I'll go for that," Claudia agreed.

"Where is Shea?" Sam asked.

"She told me she was going home for the weekend, but will be back Monday morning," Rob responded.

Sam said hello to some colleagues as he went back to the bar for his second DeWars and soda. Customarily, after 5:00 on Friday, all the lawyers from Sam's firm gathered at the club to enjoy a cocktail and each other's company. As Sam headed from the bar, two of the partners stopped to ask how the trial was going. Laughing, Sam said, "Look at us and you can tell. I mean, things are going well, but the tension of days and days in trial has us pretty well exhausted. It's such an unusual case for the Tax Court, you just never can tell. I do feel like our presentation has been strong, though. I'll say this: we may be here a while—it's the first time we've all been able to relax together."

After some more chit-chat, Sam went back to their table to ask his team if anyone had any observations or evaluations of the trial thus far. As they talked, it was interesting how each of them had been impressed by something different that was said or something he or she found especially interesting during the week.

They agreed it was going well.

Clarence observed, "I can't read the Judge, so I don't know what he will decide, but I sure think you have clearly given him enough evidence to show the IRS has been unreasonable in the land values they are proposing."

As things do in larger groups, soon the group discussion turned into a series of two and three person conversations. Joe Ross, Florence, and Sam were sitting next to each other. Sam asked Ross how he was faring at the hotel where he had already been for almost two weeks.

"The Sheraton is fine," he responded. "I am just getting tired of being away from my own bed and home-cooked meals. I have had some pretty good meals, but I have tried just about all of the restaurants you recommended, so I need some more suggestions."

"Well, I am sure that Florence can give you some ideas," Sam said. "She's been in this town forever."

"Sam, you make it sound like I don't cook much!" she grinned back.

"Oh, Florence, you know we all know what a good cook you are! I love those chocolate walnut cookies you always bring to the office Christmas party! In fact, I could use some of those after dinner tonight," said Sam.

Rob chimed in, "Mmm, yeah, Florence, why don't you whip some up for us?"

Ignoring the oft-repeated request for baked goods and turning back to Clarence, shaking her head and smiling, Florence said, "Sure. I will write the names of a few good places for you. And Sam, if I bake an extra big batch, can I get a raise?"

"Mmmm. Those are *really* good cookies. We'll see how this trial goes, Florence. We may all be broke by then, but if we win, I'll think about it."

"Harrummff." Florence huffed playfully and started making notes for Joe of all the good restaurants that were off the beaten path.

While she was writing, Sam asked Joe, "Hey, what are you going to do tomorrow?"

"I don't have anything planned. My first thought was to fly home for the weekend, but I couldn't get a plane until noon tomorrow. That would put me in Denver around 4 o'clock, and I would have to leave the next day to be here Monday. So I decided against it. How come?"

"I heard that you like to play golf. Would you like to play tomorrow?" Sam asked. "I have a regular gang I play with on Saturdays, but one of our guys is out of town this week. I believe you would enjoy my buddies. We've played golf together for over 25 years and are close friends."

"Yeah," Florence said, "they are known as The Foursome."

"That sounds wonderful. Can you get me some shoes and clubs?"

"No problem. We play at 10:00. Can you meet me at the course? I will give you directions from your hotel."

"Sure I can," Joe Ross said. "I won't make any promises about my performance, though."

"Ah, you'll do fine. It's just for fun, anyway. Then we are set. Meet me at the country club about 9:00 so we can get you outfitted and have time to hit some practice balls."

"That's great. I'll be there. Thank you for the invitation."

Florence said, "Well, you two are set for your day tomorrow. Must be nice. I am afraid that I will spend the day washing clothes and cleaning house. I had best go before another round of drinks—I won't be able to drive home. See you all Monday. Have a great weekend."

Sam agreed it was time for him to leave, too, so he could get to his office and perhaps return a few phone calls he knew would be waiting for him. He said goodbye to the others, urging them to relax, enjoy the weekend, and be safe about driving home. "Y'all had better leave soon, or the barkeep will be calling you a taxi," he joked. "Leave the celebrating until the end of the trial."

Back downstairs in his office, Sam found the never-ending stack of pink slips with phone messages on his desk. As he sorted through them, he picked up the phone and dialed his home number. He was pleased to hear Barbara's voice on the other end. He asked how her day had gone.

She told him she had met with her Cursillo group, and afterwards, all her friends went for lunch. The afternoon was spent shopping for groceries and doing some house cleaning. She was interested in how the trial had gone. As they talked, partly because his spirits had been lifted by relaxing with colleagues, and partly because it was Friday, Sam decided that he was ready to quit for the day.

"These phone calls can wait, honey," he told her, "I'm going to come on home." He said goodbye, thinking, *I am going to put myself and my wife first. I am going home now before I get caught up in that never-ending cycle to "get things done."*

While driving home, Sam acknowledged to himself that despite some stumbles, Bob Westover had done well in preparing for this trial, learning much about the technical aspects to the nuclear testing, geology, and such, and had done an excellent job in cross-examining his witnesses. He asked himself again the question that had haunted him. *Does Bob really believe there is no contamination on that land, even enough to create a stigma that devalues the land? Or is he being directed by his superiors to take that position? Did he have a choice in the matter? Did they give him access to the confidential documents?*

Talking out loud in the car, Sam said, "Bob's a good guy. I just don't understand why he seems so angry during this trial, and why he took such a rigid, unbending stance before the trial."

Chapter 50

RESPONDENTS BEGIN WITH BOGGAN

On Monday morning, Sam assembled his trial team to discuss preparations for cross-examination of the government witnesses. "Okay, everyone. We had our turn, now they'll have a go at us. Are we ready?"

Florence had rearranged the documents that might be needed and said she was ready to locate any one of them when called for. They discussed the Respondent's expert reports, identifying what they wanted to challenge in each of them. Then they got to the last government witness.

Sam acknowledged, "Now this guy, I just don't know what to expect from."

Ian MacGregor, Chief Engineer of Project Apex, was listed as a witness the government expected to call to testify about the planning and engineering of the tests and the clean-up and decommissioning of the test site.

Rob reminded Sam, "MacGregor lived in the area of the testing a year or more before the first test. He married a local girl who died a few years later, allegedly of cancer, probably because of the tests. He should make for an interesting witness."

"Yeah, all that, but he's testifying for their side. I don't get it," Claudia said. "And have you seen him? Handsome as he is, my goodness, he looks like a ghost every time I see him—pale and stressed out."

Sam agreed, "Yes, I'd say he's the real unknown variable here."

After completing their review, the group broke up, each to once again study his or her portion of the Trial Brief.

＊

The clerk called all to rise as Judge Lansdorf entered the room and took his seat Monday afternoon. "Are we ready to resume this trial?"

Westover introduced Emile Boggan, who worked on groundwater problems and contaminant hydrogeology for DOE operations, mainly in Nevada. He also had worked some at the Mitchell salt dome. Usually, he was the principal investigator, responsible for taking care of the technical aspects of the program.

Rob cut the introductions short to advise the Court that Petitioner had no objection to qualifying Boggan as an expert in hydrogeology.

"Mr. Boggan is received as an expert hydrogeologist without objection."

Mr. Boggan's report, dated September, 1984, was marked as Respondent's Exhibit EM for identification. When identified by the witness as his report, Westover moved to have it admitted into evidence.

"Okay. Mr. Fly, what about the report?" the Judge asked.

"Your Honor, I object to the introduction of that report on several grounds. As set forth in our Motion in Limine, this report is irrelevant. Your Honor, although Mr. Boggan is well qualified as an expert witness in hydrogeology, the question before the Court is whether the value of the land should be reduced, and if so, how much. Since this witness has no expertise in the valuation of land, his testimony is totally irrelevant. He is not qualified to answer that. Second, he is a hydrologist, but his report runs the gamut among a number of different fields. Then, in his opinion, he relies largely on post-valuation events, which is not proper."

"I understand your position, Mr. Fly, but I am going to rule that this report is admissible as the direct testimony of Mr. Boggan. Your argument goes more to the weight and quality of the evidence and the confidence the Court should have in that opinion, which I will take into consideration. Those things should be argued on brief. You may proceed, Mr. Westover."

After having Boggan's report marked for identification and having the witness again identify it as his, Westover offered it into evidence, and the Judge accepted it.

"Mr. Fly, you may now cross-examine the witness based on the testimony Mr. Boggan has offered via his report," Judge Lansdorf said.

Rob Fly asked the witness several questions about the consulting firm that employed him, his duties with the firm, and how long he had done that type work. "Mr. Boggan, I believe that your employer did consulting work for the AEC at the Mitchell salt dome at different times over the past 15 years, is that correct?"

"Yes, sir."

"And your firm was paid large fees for that work, was it not?"

"Well, it depends on what you call large. We received reasonable fees for our work."

"And your firm has done other work for the AEC, has it not?" Rob asked.

"Yes, sir."

Westover asserted, "Your Honor, I object to this line of questioning. It has no relevance to this case."

With the Judge looking at him, Fly responded, "It is relevant, Your Honor, to the conflict of interest the Petitioner believes is an issue with this witness. These questions bear on the lack of independent objectivity of this witness' report."

"Objection overruled. Proceed, Mr. Fly."

"Thank you, Your Honor. Mr. Boggan, in your report, you have paraphrased portions of several documents prepared by agencies of Louisiana and the federal government regarding the nuclear testing in the Mitchell salt dome. How many of those documents have you read?"

"I guess I have read a dozen of them."

"Do you know how many of those documents exist?"

"No," said Boggan.

"Would you be surprised to learn that there are about 1200 of them?"

"Yes, I would, but I read enough to know the gist of things."

Rob continued, "So, in rendering your expert report, Mr. Boggan, how did you happen to pick the dozen you chose to read, ignoring the other 1188?"

"Well, not everything was relevant. Those I read were most important to the preparation of my report."

"How do you know that some, maybe many, of the remaining 1188 documents were not critical to the accuracy of your report?"

"I did not have time to read all of them. The ones I read were given to me because they were important."

"I see, you let someone else decide which reports would give you the 'gist' of things? You did not choose which of the 1200 you read— you merely read what you were told to read? And you have no idea what is in any of the remaining documents, many of which were things that perhaps the government did not want you to see?"

"I probably know some of what they say."

"When you're a professional and an expert, sir, 'probably' isn't good enough—unless you're a professionally-trained government witness-for-hire, that is."

"Objection!"

"Sustained."

"Mr. Boggan, have you testified as an expert for the Unites States government before?" "Yes, sir, a number of times."

"Have you received special training from the government in how to be an expert witness?"

"Yes."

"And have you received two special commendations from the Army Corp of Engineers for your service as an expert witness?"

"Yes. I have."

"So, you are trained to be a hired gun for the government?"

Westover knew Fly wouldn't get away with that. "Objection, Your Honor. That question is totally out of line."

With irritation obvious in the tone of his voice, Judge Lansdorf said, "Sustained. Mr. Fly, I will not have such conduct in my Court."

"I apologize, Your Honor. Tell me, Mr. Boggan, when the Internal Revenue Service hired you as an expert witness in this case, on what issue or issues did they ask you to opine?'

"They asked me to evaluate whether or not the value of the Mitchell land and timber should be reduced as a result of the nuclear testing, and if so, how much."

"And your opinion is that the value of the land might possibly be impacted, but you did not discuss the value," Rob said. "Is that because you are not qualified to render such an opinion?"

"I am not a qualified appraiser, so I put no value on the land. My report points out the reasons why this taxpayer's position that the land is seriously devalued is a fallacious concern. Furthermore, even if there is some problem with contamination on the land, the lease requires the government to clean it up. The Mitchells are indemnified. For that reason, there is no justification in devaluing the land."

"Are you an attorney, Mr. Boggan?" Rob asked.

"No."

"Have you had legal training that would qualify you to testify on the effect of an indemnity provision given by the government?"

"No, but I have talked to lawyers who…"

"Yes or no will do, Mr. Boggan."

"No."

Boggan acknowledged that the AEC had engaged his employer to conduct a survey of people residing in area of the salt dome, as a part of the community relations plan.

Rob asked, "Is it correct that the report states that virtually all of the people in the area were concerned with the dramatic rise in cancer rates?"

Boggan tried to avoid a direct answer by replying, rather off-hand-edly, "People everywhere are concerned with cancer, Mr. Fly."

Angry at Boggan's general lack of concern about such a personal issue, especially with Clarence sitting in the courtroom (who had lost his father to that cancer), Rob pressed the witness further.

Boggan answered that he had not read that report in detail and knew nothing about cancer rates in the area.

"Would you agree, Mr. Boggan, that no reasonable person could believe that exploding nuclear bombs on a piece of property would not affect the value of that property?"

"Objection," Westover forcefully asserted. "That is outside the scope of the witness' report and outside the scope of his expertise."

"I overrule the objection. Can you answer the question?" the Judge asked.

"Yes, I believe any reasonable person would assume that an atomic testing program would have an impact on the value of a piece of property. But here, the government has been careful to make certain that no damage was done to the property. They had an elaborate plan to clean up everything when the testing was completed and have spent millions doing so. Contrary to what the Mitchell's experts assert, there is no reason to suspect any contamination outside the 1400 acres leased by the government."

"Mr. Boggan, the government conducted a study from October, 1977, through February, 1979, called the Remedial Investigation and Feasibility Study (the RIFS), and you were the manager of that study, were you not?" Rob asked.

"Yes, I was."

The witness explained to the Court that the lengthy study had been made in response to some continued findings of unusually high levels of tritium, the unearthing of some buried materials, and the unnatural flow of fluids at the site of test wells. Boggan related all of the activities included as a part of the RIFS, strongly suggesting that the study was most complete and accurate.

Rob asked, "In that report, you noted six areas that could be the source of contamination, is that correct?"

"Yes, sir."

"And your report states that there is no evidence to suggest that there may be problems outside of the test site boundary? Nothing outside of the 1400 acres?"

"That is correct."

Rob continued, "The RFIS concludes that the six source areas need further study because they may be contaminated, though, right?"

"Correct."

"Mr. Boggan, you testified that the six source areas are all inside the 1400 test site boundary, correct?"

"Yes."

"Look at Exhibit 94-CP, page 73. Where is source area six?"

"Well, it is about half a mile outside the test site boundary, but that is explainable. That site is the helicopter landing pad. We did not have any evidence of any contamination there. We included it because in other instances we have found that there might be some minor contamination where the aircraft was washed down."

"So all six of the sites are not inside the test site boundary, are they?"

"All right. I just…"

Interrupting Rob asked, "My question, sir, is now that you know there is a site outside of the test area that the DOE is going to investigate, have you changed your opinion on whether property outside of the test area has been affected in value?"

"I still have no evidence whatsoever that there is any contamination outside that 1400-acre parcel. No, it does not change my opinion."

The next series of Rob's questions were designed to create doubts as to the thoroughness of the RFIS and the conclusions Boggan reached in his report. Rob asked, "Very little has been reported about the two non-nuclear explosive shots fired in the dome cavity. Tell us about them, Mr. Boggan."

The witness' face went blank. "I don't know about them, but even if I did, I doubt it would have made any difference in my report."

Feeling more confident that he was showing this witness' incompetence, Rob relentlessly questioned the witness about post-test activities of the government, the clean-up phase, and the numerous return investigations after the government had given an all-clear report. He had the witness explain how he and his co-workers preparing the RIFS went about determining the degree of compliance by the contractor during the clean-up phase.

Rob said, "The contractors did not comply with the government's own standards for clean-up, did they?"

The witness answered, "They did the best they could. There was a huge amount of equipment and a large number of people involved. We talked to as many of those people as possible to determine the degree of compliance, but I can't say how many were contacted."

All of his answers were quite defensive of the position he had taken in his expert report, avoiding admitting to anything that might be helpful to the Petitioner's case.

Referring him to another exhibit, Rob asked the witness about the radioactive gases that his exhibit disclosed were released through drilling into the cavity. Boggan first admitted that he was not familiar with that report, Exhibit 121-DQ, then went on to say that any gases that might have been released would have been filtered through the bleed-down plant.

At that point, Judge Lansdorf interrupted, "Do you have any knowledge of what residue might be left after going through the bleed-down plant? If gas did come up from the cavity and go through the process, I assume it would go into the atmosphere, right?"

"Judge, if there were any residuals, I would expect them to be the noble gases like xenon and argon, typical of an event of this nature. The bleed-down plant is to reduce the levels of those gases to air-quality standards."

"Well, could those gases contain radioactive contaminants?" the Judge asked.

"Oh, yes. Xenon and argon are radioactive. The government went to the expense of bringing a bleed-down plant all the way from Nevada. The last thing in the world the DOE would want is exposing unsuspecting citizens to radioactive gases."

Rob asked, "Are you aware, sir, that, in fact, they did just that?"

"Yes, I am aware of the recent newspaper articles to that effect."

Westover was on his feet and shouted, "I object. I know nothing about any newspaper articles."

"Your Honor, I haven't asked the witness about any newspaper articles. He is the one that brought it up."

"I don't see the problem at this point," the Judge said.

"Are you aware, Mr. Boggan, that the Department of Energy and
the Atomic Energy Commission experimented on American citizens
by releasing radioactive gas onto people in cities without their knowledge?"

"Objection. This is clearly outside the scope of this trial, clearly
outside of the question before this Court, and outside the scope of
this witness' knowledge."

"Are you aware of that fact?" the Judge asked.

"No, I am not aware that they did it. I am aware that it is under
media scrutiny right now. I am aware, through reading the plutonium
handbook, that the United States, during World War II, did conduct
experiments on American citizens using plutonium."

"Mr. Boggan, because most of the documents about Project Apex
are still classified, do you think everyone involved could be making erroneous conclusions about the safety of the area?"

"If they were concealing anything deliberately, then yes, that could
lead to erroneous conclusions. But they aren't. I have no reason to
believe that the Department of Energy has put any false or misleading
statements in any of their documents. They have made public or made
available all of the relevant information. I know that at the time I
wrote the RIFS work plan, I was allowed free reign. I was not asked
or pressured by any agency to make any particular statement. The
only group that came in and said, 'We would like to see this in this
particular document' was the Louisiana Office of Pollution Control."

"Sir, if by the date in 1978 when the Mitchell property was valued,
the United States Congress had released a report titled 'American
Nuclear Guinea Pigs: Three Decades of Radiation Experiments on
U.S. Citizens' and if that report concludes that, as late as the 1970s,
the AEC and the DOE experimented by exposing unsuspecting
American citizens to radiation (by injection, by feeding them, through
fallout, and by releasing gases over cities and pastures)—if those things

were true, would it cause you to question whether the DOE and the AEC have told the truth about the Mitchell Dome? In fact, I want you to just assume that there is such a report. Would it change your opinion?"

Watching the reaction of the people at the government's counsel table, Sam noticed that Van Skiver squirmed in his chair at Rob's reference to that report.

Westover, still standing, objected on the grounds of relevancy. But the Judge overruled the objection and directed the witness to answer.

Trying to avoid a direct answer, Boggan said that if the individuals who authorized such activities were the same people that he worked with at the DOE, he would question the validity of the database. Those people he knew would do nothing morally or legally wrong. So the fact that some faction of the government did something wrong would not affect his opinion with respect to the work at the Mitchell Dome.

Shaking his head at Boggan's refusal to give an inch, Rob then led the witness through a review of several government documents that were included in the Stipulation of Facts. He pointed out five or six statements in those documents showing concerns of danger, such as a report that, before the second nuclear blast, radioactive gas was leaking at the surface. Due to the relentless pressure applied by Rob, the witness finally admitted that he had not read those reports.

Good. Rob is showing how unprepared and uninformed this witness is, perhaps even deliberately so by government design, in stark contrast to our well-read witnesses, Sam thought.

Rob changed his attention to other parts of Boggan's report concerning the geological formations at the test site. In his questioning, Rob pressed Boggan to admit that he did not remember what type of geological formations existed above the caprock in the salt dome. The witness did admit that the caprock had fractures in it that provided channels for water to flow faster than it would through the rock itself.

"Wouldn't a fractured caprock provide a path for contamination to move from the dome into the aquifers, Mr. Boggan?"

Boggan admitted that the caprock could be hydrogeologically connected with Aquifers Three and Four, but he adamantly asserted that this did not cause him concern that radiation might leak from the dome. He reaffirmed the statement in his report that there had been no leakage of radiation from the cavity in the dome, and there was not likely to be any in the future.

"Please look at this Exhibit 130-DDZ, which I believe you have previously seen. At the bottom of page 15, it states that before the first nuclear blast, they had already observed much natural fracturing of the caprock and the salt dome itself. Is that what it says, sir?"

"Yes, but that doesn't affect the salt dome's ability to contain the radiation."

"Would it not then make sense that, if Nature and Time had caused some cracks, then a nuclear bomb would cause significant and large fractures, allowing multiple migratory paths for waste to flow through, totally unchecked?"

Boggan just would not budge. "No," he said, flatly.

Fly then asked if there would be risk of leakage if, in addition to the fractures, there were other holes drilled in the dome, pointing out that there were 28 holes drilled into the salt dome exterior walls and three into the inner cavity itself.

Boggan replied that drilling into the dome could be cause for concern for possible leakage, not from the drilling alone but from the possibility that radioactive materials in the dome could be brought up as they pulled up the drills. He explained that as the drill bit went down, it could pick up contaminants and draw them to the surface. "This was the reason that, when preparing the work plan for the RIFS, I did not want to go in and investigate the cavity," he said.

On further questioning, Boggan admitted that he didn't know if salt in the dome had been turned into radioactive material, but when pressed by Fly, he acknowledged, "It is possible that the salt abutting the caprock has been converted into radioactive material by thermal activation."

"If that is true, there surely must be nuclear contamination out there in that dome. Doesn't this concern you, Mr. Boggan?" Fly asked.

"No, not really."

Fly continued, "And is it still your position that the possibility of contamination in the salt dome would not reduce the value of the land out there?"

"I do not believe it would have any effect on the value."

Obviously irritated by the witness' adamant position, Fly, very forcefully said. "Mr. Boggan, you are admitting that salt in the Mitchell salt dome may be radioactive material now. Are you telling this Court that the possible existence of that contamination would not affect your estimate of value of the land?"

"It shouldn't affect the value."

The witness could offer no explanation of why he had no concern about the possible presence of nuclear contamination.

"I am just not concerned about it," he testified.

As Fly continued to pound the witness and his unrealistic position, Westover stood and exclaimed, "Your Honor. I object to Counsel's brow-beating this witness. Mr. Boggan has answered the questions."

"You are right, Mr. Westover, objection sustained. Move on with your interrogations, Counsel," Judge Lansdorf said.

In answer to Rob's questions pertaining to the nuclear explosions, the witness testified that he had no idea how much radioactive material was produced by the explosions. He said that he had tried to find out but had been unable to get that information.

Coming back to the subject of the problem of fractures of the dome wall, Rob asked the witness if this should be of concern. When Boggan answered no, Fly said, "I don't understand your lack of concern. It concerns me, just as a fellow human being and a resident of planet Earth, and I don't live anywhere near the dome!"

The witness replied confidently, "The Atomic Energy Commission's Report, Exhibit 121-DDQ, states that fractures of visible size probably did not extend over 15 feet beyond the dome. Therefore, they don't present a problem."

Turning to receive a document from Florence, Rob handed Exhibit

63-BK to the witness and asked him to identify it as the report prepared by Lawmore Radiation Labs in March, 1965. He asked the witness to take a minute to review that report.

When Boggan was ready to respond, Rob asked him, "Is this report the only study of the condition of the cavity after the first blast?"

The witness agreed that it was the only one.

Then, in answer to Rob's further questions, Boggan agreed that the report stated the cavity had sustained macro fractures 45 to 60 meters from the shot point, with zones of micro fractures up to 90 meters away. Pressed by Rob, the witness agreed that if the fractures were found 60 meters from the shot point, they could possibly extend well beyond that distance.

Asked to look back at the AEC report, Exhibit 121-DDQ, Boggan answered Rob's questions that while that report cited the Lawmore Report, it completely ignored it, stating that visible fractures of the dome did not extend more than 15 feet beyond the cavity wall. Boring in on that point, Rob asked, "So at least that part of the AEC's 1970 report is false, isn't it Mr. Boggan?"

"Well, according to the Lawmore Report, uh, yes, it looks like that statement may not be correct."

"Sir, what is the significance of fractures in salt around a cavity full of highly radioactive nuclear waste?"

"I don't know that they have any significance whatsoever."

Judge Lansdorf interrupted, "Mr. Fly, it is after 6 o'clock and time to stop for the day. Can we stop here?"

"Yes, sir."

"Being faced with the need to complete this trial by Friday, I think we'd better start a little early tomorrow. I'll see you at 8 a.m.," the Judge announced.

After the Judge left and some of the other team had left, Rob stomped over to the Counsel table and threw his notepad down. "Damn it, that Boggan guy is getting to me."

"Cool down, Rob," Claudia said.

Florence chimed in, "You can't win if you lose your head."

Rob was clearly unsettled. Claudia said, "Listen, Boggan is so unrealistic! He is obviously an 'employee' of the Government. Surely the Judge won't give much credence to his report."

"It sure seems obvious to me," Rob replied. "That is why I have been pounding him so hard, trying to make his bias clear to the Judge. I irritated Judge Lansdorf when I said Boggan was a hired gun, but he really is, and I could not restrain myself!"

Sam piped in, "Well, that won't get you any brownie points with the Judge, so don't worry about it. Not to mention that I think Boggan's testimony is backfiring on him. Every time he ignores the obvious evidence at hand, it adds to the impression that he hasn't researched this situation well enough to know what the heck is going on. He hasn't read anything! Did you count how many times he answered that he hadn't this or didn't know that? It makes him appear clearly coached on what the 'acceptable' answers are. Rob, you are doing great up there! You are just too close to the witness to realize how this guy's stubbornness is making him look bad. I think we're doing fine."

Feeling better now, Rob was glad for his colleague's insights and compliments to bolster his assessment of how it had gone.

Counsel and associates began gathering up their materials. While boxing up all the exhibits, Florence commented, "I've never seen so many papers for one case. I sure won't miss keeping up with so many documents after this trial is over."

Claudia turned to her and said, "Florence, you have done a super job, by the way—being there with the right documents when we need them."

Sam agreed and added his compliment to Florence. She beamed.

Chapter 51

CURSILLO MEETINGS

The following morning, as he showered and shaved, Sam anticipated being with his men's group for breakfast. He had been a part of the group since what he now called his spiritual rebirth. The same six men participated in that group, and each was committed to attend weekly unless they had an unavoidable conflict. They had attended the Cursillo weekend retreat together, after which they willingly agreed to meet regularly to share their thoughts, actions, and feelings during each week as they tried to come closer to God. They made themselves accountable and encouraged each other in their Christian walk.

As he drove to meet the group, Sam reflected on his new life after that Cursillo weekend in 1972. How could he have thought himself so self-sufficient before, imagining, as he often expressed early in his career, that he did not need anyone and could make it fine in this world alone?

He thanked God again, as he had countless times, for leading him to that weekend experience, for it was there that he realized that God loved him even though he thought himself unlovable. That realization had made it possible for Sam to open his heart to others, beginning with Barbara and his children. He felt no remorse over the breakup of his first marriage, but he was constantly saddened by what he saw as a void in his life caused by his inability to show love to his children in their childhood as deeply as he did after Cursillo. It still tormented him to see in hindsight the precious time he could have had with his kids when they were young.

But if God forgives me, and if I expect my family to do so, I have to

*learn to forgive myself. Perhaps that's what I'll talk about this morning with
the guys.*

As he arrived, all members of the group were present, and they
began their session with a prayer. Then each person shared the spiritual aids they had used during the prior week to further their
relationship with God, the moment during the week that they felt
closest to God, and what they planned to do during the coming week
to help lead someone to Christ. After each person spoke, the group
prayed for others and themselves. Shortly before 8 a.m., they broke up
to head to work.

Sam drove to his office parking garage and walked the three blocks
to the courthouse, with thoughts of how the lessons of Cursillo could
be carried with him throughout the day. He prayed that he be given
the strength to fight for justice and prevail.

Chapter 52

BOGGAN IS BELLIGERENT

The next morning, as the Clerk called the courtroom to order, Judge Lansdorf entered from his chambers and took his seat. "Good morning ladies and gentlemen," he said. "Are we ready to proceed?"

When both Counsel responded that they were ready, the Clerk called Emile Boggan to the witness stand. The Judge reminded the witness that he was still under oath and asked Rob Fly to proceed.

"Mr. Boggan, yesterday we looked at the Lawmore Radiation Lab Report, and I want you to look at it again," Rob said. After directing the witness' attention to several portions of that report and asking questions, Rob had the witness turn to a portion of the report dealing with the cavity and asked, "Do you see, on page 29, the report says that the cavity contained approximately 1.3 million gallons of contaminated liquid?"

"Yes. I see that."

"And reading further on that page, and the next, the report says that while they believe the cavity was stable, the material surrounding the cavity was questionable, giving rise to some concern."

"I see that."

"Then, Mr. Boggan, a cavity that may be unstable and which is holding 1.3 million gallons of contaminated liquid would present a real hazard to people on and nearby that land wouldn't it?"

"I don't see it that way. I see no hazard. There is no proof of any problem on that land, so I am not concerned with that," Boggan replied.

Shaking his head again in disbelief, Rob moved on to more questions regarding the potential, even today, of leakage of radioactive material from the cavity through fractures, faults, drill holes, or other means.

Boggan repeated his thesis that there was no reason for concern.

Rob showed him Exhibit 94-CP, in which the Louisiana Department of Environmental Quality expressed major concern over possible leakage.

Again the witness treated the content of that report with disdain, "They said 'possible' leakage, and to me, that's not enough of a guarantee to merit devaluing such rich timberland."

Rob said, "Sir, I take it that you do not share the concerns of others about nuclear contamination in general, much less the problems near the salt dome?"

"Well, we are all concerned about nukes, but you have to be reasonable here. The government cleaned things up. End of story."

"You are aware, are you not, that seven months after the nuclear waste was injected into well HT-2 it was found in well HT-2M, located 300 feet away?"

"Yes."

"And the government had asserted that any injected liquid would travel at no more than 13 feet a year, meaning it should have taken more like 23 years to go between those two wells?"

"It must be true. That is what the report states," Boggan replied.

Rob handed the witness Exhibit 73-BU, an internal memo of the AEC, reporting that in 1972, well HT-2M was discovered to be flowing at the surface and had obviously been flowing for at least a month before it was capped.

"What was that liquid flowing from that well, Mr. Boggan? And where did it flow to?"

"I don't know what the liquid was. It was not identified. It probably was a very small amount, and more than likely, it just accumulated in a pool," was the answer.

Judge Lansdorf interrupted, "Could some of that liquid have sunk below the surface?"

"Yes, it could."

Pressed by Rob, the witness agreed that there had been a second flow from the same well about two years after the first. When asked if any of the overflows could have migrated off-site, he answered, "I am not aware of any migration."

"Mr. Boggan," Rob said, "if liquid was injected into the salt dome cavity today, could it possibly come back to the surface around a bore hole at either well HT-2 or HT-2M?"

Reluctantly, the witness agreed that was possible, but added, "I still say that a reasonable person interested in the Mitchell land would not be concerned about the extent of any contamination."

At this response, Rob rolled his eyes, thinking, *I can't believe this*, and said, "Turn to page 83 of your report. There you discuss how the nuclear waste that was injected into Aquifer Five would flow uphill. You claim it would go to the northwest rather than follow the aquifer's natural flow to the southeast, which is the direction gravity would take it. That sounds like a magic trick. How was that going to happen?"

Acting cocky, Emile Boggan said, "The Tullos-Urania Oil Field is located to the southeast of the test site. As is customarily done in oil fields, that field pumped saltwater, under pressure, into an abandoned well to dispose of the brine. That brine would flow past the salt dome and push liquid injected at the dome to the northwest, the opposite from its normal flow."

Rob asked, "And if that brine was simply poured into the oil well, gravity fed, whatever was in the aquifer would not flow uphill, would it, Mr. Boggan? It would follow its natural path downhill toward the residential population."

Cautiously the witness responded, "Well, it would not flow uphill as forcefully if there was no pressure."

Rob pressed hard, and Boggan turned red in the face.

Finally the witness, with a clear tone of anger in his voice, answered, "I do not know how much pressure the oil field used in its saltwater disposal, but I am convinced that it was enough to reverse the natural flow and force the waste onto the 1400 acres controlled by the government."

"As the person in charge of the RIFS, wouldn't it be very important that you know exactly how much, if any, pressure was used by the
oil field, and where the waste pumped into the dome cavity went?
Wouldn't that be a bare minimum amount of knowledge you would
have to obtain, as a professional, before proceeding?" Rob asked.

It appeared that the witness had taken this question as an attack on
his performance, which of course it was, and he bristled. "I did everything possible to secure all of the facts before the RIFS was prepared."

"Did you or anyone from your team ask the oil field whether or not
they used pressure in their brine disposal?"

"No."

"Did you go, or instruct someone to go, to the Louisiana
Department of Natural Resources to review their records regarding
the injection of saltwater into the aquifer by the Tullos-Urania Oil
Field?" Rob asked.

"No."

Rob showed the witness a document and had him read the title:
Louisiana Department of Natural Resources' Report of Injection by
Tullos-Urania Field. The Friday before the trail started, Sam's trial
team had secured this from the DNR, but since they could not authen-
ticate it, they could not introduce it into evidence.

Westover was on his feet, questioning what the document was and
what Fly intended to do with it. The Judge turned toward Rob, who
responded that he was going to use it as a hypothetical question.

Rob said, "Assume that the document you hold is a record of injections made at the oil field between the years 1970 and 1973, and…."

"I object. This question is nothing but assumptions," Westover
asserted.

Rob replied, "Your Honor, it speaks to the witness' unwillingness
to change his opinion in the face of evidence. I am asking this hypothetical question of the witness to see if, had he been aware of this
document, it would change his opinion."

"Yes, I think that is proper. Objection overruled," the Judge said.

The witness read from the report that the injection of brine at the oil field was made at zero pressure, a vacuum. Rob asked him, having this knowledge, would it change his opinion as to where the waste injected into the dome cavity was going?

Refusing to waiver from his opinion, Boggan answered, "I do not know if it would change my opinion. It would merely indicate that I need more information."

Try as he might, Rob could not get the witness to agree that his assumption of the uphill pressure against gravity was erroneous.

Finally, Judge Lansdorf, showing irritation at the witness' refusal to answer, asked, "Mr. Boggan, if the saltwater had not been injected into the aquifer, which direction would waste in that aquifer flow?"

The witness answered, "To the southeast."

"And that flow would take it outside of the 1400 acres controlled by the government, right?"

"Well, yes, Your Honor."

"Which is in the direction of the town of Tullos, correct?" the Judge continued.

"Yes, sir." The witness answered in almost a whisper, knowing that although he had successfully evaded the Petitioner's attorney, he could not evade the Judge.

With that, Rob advised the Court that he had nothing further for this witness.

Judge Lansdorf then turned the witness over to Government counsel for redirect examination.

Bob Westover approached the lectern, asking the witness a series of questions about the AEC community relations plan, having the witness agree that the purpose of that plan was to inform the community and dispel secrecy or any idea of a cover-up.

Boggan testified that in no document he had seen was there any suggestion of any contamination that endangered anyone. He stated that in the 1983 work plan, the DOE had designated only the six aforementioned areas as possible sources of contamination, covering a total of 305 acres.

Counsel went into lengthy questioning about the structure of the dome, designed to down-play concern of damage to the structure of the salt dome. Westover worked hard to help the witness try to assert that there was no possibility of any upward migration of nuclear waste from Aquifer Five to the freshwater aquifers.

Boggan testified that he saw no problem with the fractures found in the cavity after the detonations. He said, "Salt is like plastic in that, in time, it will heal itself and revert to its natural state. Over a period of time, the fractures in the cavity will heal."

Finally, Westover questioned the witness at length to refute Ross' assertions that the tests made by the government for dangerous radioisotopes were incomplete and ineffective. As expected, Boggan was resolute in his testimony that the DOE had carefully prepared a work plan designed to test for any and every radioisotope that could be hazardous to people or property in the area. Those tests had located only those isotopes covered in the reports.

When Westover had completed his questions, the Judge asked Rob Fly if he had any further questions of the witness on re-cross. Rob advised that he did.

Fly then had the witness go to the section of his report stating that there had never been anything but background radiation found off-site and had him agree that it was a true statement. Rob gave the witness Exhibit 58-BF, asking him to look at page three, which contained results of vegetation samplings taken before and immediately after the first bomb explosion. The document stated that at five different locations, the background radiation increased an average of 16 times.

Asked to verify this finding, the witness answered, "That was what the document said, but I would need more information to verify it. Still, looking at a piece of paper such as this would not cause me to change my opinion of the property value. I would want to dig into that deeper to determine the basis for that report."

"Of course you would, wouldn't you?"

"Yes."

"And you haven't done it, have you?"

"No. I wasn't aware of that particular information."

"When you came to tell Judge Lansdorf that there was no problem out at the test site, you hadn't researched much at all, in fact, had you?"

Obviously quite agitated, Boggan answered, "I did not come here to tell anyone that there is no problem out there at the site. What I have stated is that, yes, they conducted nuclear testing at the site, that they had contamination as a result of the testing, and that they are going to spend $7-$9 million of taxpayer money to go there and once again investigate a site they have investigated and investigated, all just to make sure it's totally clean. I trust my government to do that, Mr. Fly. Don't you?"

Ignoring this remark designed to play on patriotic loyalties instead of focusing on the truth, Fly pressed onward. "After all the investigations, there is stall a raft of uncertainties, isn't there Mr. Boggan?"

"Yes. And that is because you cannot prove everything to everybody."

"I guess that's true. And those people buy real estate, don't they, Mr. Boggan?"

"Some of them do, yes."

"That is all I have, Your Honor."

"Mr. Westover, anything further?"

"Nothing else, Your Honor."

"All right, thank you, Mr. Boggan. You may step down."

Chapter 53

MENDING GOOD FENCES

As time passed, Sam amazed himself with his new life pattern. Before Cursillo, he had no time, nor inclination, to have more than a superficial relationship with those outside his small band of family and friends. Afterwards, he desired to reach out to others, even strangers. Though he'd always been a churchgoer, prior to his conversion experience, Sam felt that his relationship with God was strictly personal, not to be talked of with anyone. Afterwards, to his wonder, he was speaking to groups all over town, sharing his discovery that Jesus loved him and all about the change it had made in his life. He was also remembering what was really important in life these days, placing a much higher priority on family and close friendships than ever before. He found it easier to leave work at the end of the day, not trying so hard to fit in "one last thing" before going home, which used to wind up meaning longer and longer nights at the office. His law practice was important, but it had a place, and he had *a real life* outside work now.

Forgiveness gives us freedom, he thought. *I have asked and been granted forgiveness from all those I have hurt, save one. Now, if only I had Nell's forgiveness, too.*

✳

In July 1973, a year after attending Cursillo, Sam revealed to Barbara a reoccurring thought about his ex-wife, an idea that could not be dismissed from his mind. "I think that I must ask for Louise's forgiveness for any hurt I have brought to her. Not for the divorce—I have no reason to regret that—but for all these years, there has been so much anger and bad blood and harsh words between us. I will feel better asking her to forgive my un-Christian like behavior."

Proud of the way her own Christian leadership had helped her husband grow, too, Barbara hugged him, telling him that she was thrilled. "I know in my heart it's the right thing for you to do."

Sam said, "I have thought about this a while, but I tell you what holds me back. I imagine how stupid I will feel if she rebuffs or berates me or laughs. But now, I've decided that once I ask for forgiveness, if she doesn't accept it, that's her problem."

"I feel sure she will take it seriously and forgive you. She's different now. Louise shared with me that six months ago she spent a week at a Catholic Retreat Center. Much like you lately, she is a changed person."

A couple of nights later, with Barbara at his side, Sam called Louise. As she answered the phone, he felt the heat of anger, like an old habit from past phone calls, welling up in him. Quickly he reminded himself why he was calling.

As they talked about Nell and Sandra, chatting casually, each of them became more relaxed, and their voices got calm when they saw the other did not intend to attack. Sam asked how she was. In her reply, he heard a surprising serenity he remembered from their youth, something he had not heard from her in years.

"How are you and Barbara and the kids?" Louise asked.

He answered honestly that he had never been better, sharing how his life had changed since he and Barbara attended Cursillo.

"That is what prompted this phone call, Louise. I called to ask your forgiveness for all the pain I have caused you over the years. I have been a real jackass about a lot of things. You may think this is a joke, but it's not. I am sincere. I'm a different person now, and I regret a lot about my past. I hope you will forgive me," he said.

He heard nothing.

As the pause got to be more and more awkward, Louise finally responded. "Yes, Sam."

She paused and began again slowly. "Yes, I will forgive you. And I need to ask you to forgive me. I have been a hateful bitch at times myself. I have done things to hurt you, and I am sorry."

Sam said quickly, relieved and overjoyed, "Oh, of course. Barbara and the Cursillo meetings—and probably just the passing of time—have all helped me see that I should have been there for you and the kids more, should have been more interested and involved in family life, more supportive and helpful at home. I especially did the children a great disservice. I apologize. At the time, I thought I was doing the best I could, the only way I knew how to be, but I was wrong. God and my family were asking more of me, and I failed."

Louise took him very seriously. "Like you, it was a spiritual experience that spurred me on toward recognizing how I could have been different back then," she said. She talked of how she'd been callous and back-biting, resentful of his job and full of rage toward him over the years. "I didn't know back then what to do with all the anger and loneliness I felt, so it came out in inappropriate ways. Now I know I could have handled myself and my emotions better, could have been kinder, especially after the divorce, and especially for the sake of our kids. I'm so glad you opened the door for this conversation. Thank you."

Feeling the weight of years of bad tidings lifted like sandbags off his shoulders, Sam was now able to talk to her comfortably. The awkwardness both had felt for years had now passed, and they expressed great relief. They talked a little more, and then finally he said he'd better say goodbye, as Barbara wanted to talk. Grateful for the friendship his wife and ex had built over the years, now realizing how it was the stepping stone to his own healing, he handed the phone to Barbara, smiling.

✳

Barbara met Sam at the door as he arrived home. "Dinner will be about 45 minutes. Let's sit and have a drink while we wait for it."

"Sounds good to me," he said, "this Project Apex business is wearing this old man out!"

"Project Apex?" she asked.

"Oh, just this case I've been working on. It's like nothing any tax lawyer has ever done before. But you know what? Let's not talk about work. How was your day?"

She said, "I had a long talk with Louise."

"And how is she?"

"She has been having a lot of headaches lately. Her doctor says they are migraines. But emotionally and spiritually she is fine. You know what she mentioned, though? After all this time, she said again that receiving your forgiveness freed her of her guilt, and she was thankful for the new relationship she has with you now, and with me."

"I'm glad. Tell her likewise next time you see her," Sam said.

Chapter 54

FOIBLES WITH JOSEPH FAUST

Reconvening the trial, the Judge asked Bob Westover to call his next witness. Westover had Elizabeth Pensa approach the counsel stand and call Joseph Faust to testify. It would be Pensa's first time working directly with a witness.

Faust told the Court of his formal education (a Bachelor of Science degree in mechanical engineering), his work experience, and his current employment as an Environmental Program Manager with the Department of Energy in Las Vegas, where he had served for four years.

"In my job, I am responsible for conducting environmental assessments at the department's facilities under the auspices of the Nevada operations office. That includes both the Nevada test site and several locations throughout the United States. During my 22-year employment with the DOE, I've worked as a planning engineer for civil works construction at the Nevada test site, for engineering activities on geothermal investigations throughout the U.S., and for some engineering responsibilities associated with decommissioning inactive nuclear test sites."

"Mr. Faust, you were not involved in the original testing program at the Mitchell salt dome, but you are now responsible for the environmental assessment program there, correct?" Pensa asked.

Faust affirmed that this was correct.

"Mr. Faust, what is the DOE's policy regarding inactive facilities, and what have they done to implement responsibilities for clean-up at the Mitchell Dome?" Pensa asked.

"The policy of the DOE is to bring all of its inactive facilities, such as the Mitchell site and others in Colorado and Nevada, into compliance with current laws. Doing so requires a very structured and graduated approach to determining the nature of contamination, if any. It's a slow process. We are currently in this phase at the Mitchell site. While I was not involved in the original decommissioning phase at the Mitchell site, I am aware of it, because I was doing similar work at other sites at the time. I know what they did to remove the surface contamination. In that process at other sites, any radioactive materials or debris were transported to the Nevada storage facility. What we do is restore the site to a state where it could be used for its originally-intended purpose," Faust replied.

Sam stood, "Your Honor, I object and move to strike this witness' testimony. It is my understanding that this gentleman will not be offered as an expert witness. He has just told us that he has no personal knowledge of the Mitchell Dome. An expert witness may perhaps tell you what has been found and what he has heard, but a fact witness may not."

"Ms. Pensa, Mr. Laurins has made a good observation. Is this witness being offered as a fact witness, or is he being offered as an expert witness, or both?"

Elizabeth Pensa had worked for the government for only a short time. She was just three years out of law school. Clearly flustered, she replied, "Well, Your Honor, he is—uh, I can offer—I listed him as an expert in our report to the Court and can offer him as an expert, if necessary. But as he has testified, his job with the DOE is to run the environmental management at the Mitchell Salt Dome, so he does have a connection there."

"You have not answered my question. You said you could offer him as an expert. What are you offering him as at the moment?" the Judge asked.

"Well, at this point, I was offering him as a fact witness because of his own personal knowledge of what is going on."

"Are you planning also to offer him as an expert, separately?" Judge Lansdorf asked.

"I will, so long as it pleases the Court."

"I am certainly not encouraging you to offer him one way or the other—that is up to you. But Mr. Laurins is going to be confused as to how he should relate to this witness until we know what you are offering him as."

As the Judge was talking, Pensa turned toward Westover, her eyes pleading *help*. Westover nodded to her, and she said, "At the present time, I do not offer him as an expert. I am offering him as a fact witness."

Judge Lansdorf responded, "All right. Mr. Laurins, do you have something further?"

Having stood quietly during all of that, Sam said, "Your Honor, the question Ms. Pensa was asking the witness was about the clean-up at the Mitchell Dome during the decommissioning process. He clearly stated that he was not there, so he has no personal knowledge and cannot testify as to those facts."

"All right, Mr. Laurins, do you want to take the witness on voir dire?" the Judge asked.

Behind the Respondent's table, Van Skiver leaned over and whispered to Emily, "What is that—voir dire?"

She whispered back to him, "That is a procedure where the lawyer can, before a witness testifies, ask him questions to determine his competence to testify as a witness."

"Yes, sir," Sam replied, "just to determine his competence as a fact witness and a potential expert witness."

"Very well, go ahead."

"Thank you, Your Honor." Sam turned to the witness and asked, "Mr. Faust, what were you doing with respect to the Mitchell Salt Dome in 1972?"

"I was not involved with it."

"I renew my objection, Your Honor."

"All right, Ms. Pensa," Judge Lansdorf said. "How do you respond?"

Somewhat indignantly, she said, "That is not the question I asked, Your Honor. What I asked the witness was what the DOE has done to implement its responsibilities for clean-up at the Mitchell Dome."

"Well, you really ought to lay a better foundation before you even ask him a question concerning what he knows about the Mitchell Dome or how he acquired his knowledge," the Judge responded.

Sam turned to the Petitioner's table with a look at Rob and Claudia, as if to say with his eyes, *I don't know what Westover's team is doing fumbling this badly, but it sure is to our benefit.*

Pensa proceeded to ask the witness a series of questions intended to now lay a proper foundation.

Faust testified that he worked for the division responsible for decommissioning the Mitchell Dome test site, that he peripherally had knowledge of the original activities there, that he had access to all the history and activities at the Mitchell Dome, and that his office had all records and reports dealing with that test site, though he had no in-depth knowledge of those reports because he had not read them.

"Now, Your Honor, I submit that Mr. Faust, by his occupation and his experience, has personal knowledge of what happened and is happening at the Mitchell Dome test site, and I therefore offer him as a fact witness."

"Ms Pensa, I think it would be better if you asked him a question to see," the Judge said. "Now that we know his background, why don't we measure that against your questions, see what you want out of him, and if he has any useful knowledge about what you are going to ask him."

Counsel asked the witness what the DOE had done to carry out its responsibilities for environmental management and protection at the Mitchell Dome test site.

Laurins objected that the question was overly broad until there was a time frame established.

When the Court sustained the objection, it looked like Pensa was ready to run out of the courtroom and disappear. She shot an angry glance to Bob Westover for letting her get into a predicament like this—why had he not given her better direction and more help to avoid this awful situation? During the next few seconds, she regained her composure and asked, "Mr. Faust, what has been done since 1972 to decommission the Mitchell Dome test site?"

Laurins objected to the question on the grounds that the witness had no personal knowledge of that.

With a steely glare directed at Laurins, she responded, finally with some strength in her voice, "Mr. Faust does have personal knowledge—he is head of the department and has all the records and information."

"Are all those records a part of the record in this case?" Judge Lansdorf asked.

"Many of them are stipulated in this case—a lot of them, most of them," Pensa replied.

The Judge said, "Ms. Pensa, Mr. Laurins makes a valid objection. I don't see how he can cross-examine your witness about what Mr. Faust read if it is not in this record or if Mr. Faust is relying on things that are not before the Court. If you bring him forward to testify about documents of his agency that he is familiar with, he can tell us about them, but you are asking him what happened, and that is not proper. If you stay within those parameters, you may proceed."

Sam thought she was almost totally dispirited, but Pensa took a few moments to recompose herself, shuffled through her notes, then began a line of questioning pertaining to the lease the DOE had with the Mitchell family and the fact that the government was obligated in the lease to clean up and restore the land.

Faust testified that no private landowner had ever been asked to clean up a test site. "The government has always cleaned up their messes," he said.

Again Sam objected. "Counsel is attempting to wedge into the record the witness' opinion of liabilities and the government's trust-worthiness, and that is clearly inadmissible, Your Honor."

"I am going to allow a few more questions to see where this is going."

From the ensuing questions, it became clear that Counsel was indeed attempting to have the witness testify that the DOE would bear all responsibility, so the Judge sustained Sam's objection.

Ms. Pensa then attempted to introduce into evidence through the witness a new lease between the Mitchells and the DOE, executed in 1983.

Of course, Laurins objected on the grounds that the date for determining the value of the land was the date of Mr. Mitchell's death (December 28, 1978), and at that date, terms of a lease executed in October, 1983, could not be reasonably foreseen.

With all the courage she could muster, Elizabeth Pensa argued strongly that the lease should be received into evidence, but the Judge sustained Sam's objection.

Elizabeth asked the Court for a few minutes recess to confer with her co-Counsel and the Judge complied.

After a brief conference with Westover, she announced to the Court that she had no further questions of the witness. He was permitted to leave.

Sam and Rob just looked at each other. *Wonder what that was about?*

Chapter 55

ENGAGED

In late 1983, Barbara told Sam that Nell was beginning to talk about marrying the young man she had started dating in college. Nell had lived in Atlanta for about two years now, and with each of the telephone conversations Barbara had with Nell, she talked more and more of the possibility of marriage. During one of their talks, Nell said that she was thinking of eloping so that she did not have to go through all the planning and fuss of a formal wedding.

Barbara said, "Oh, honey, please don't deny your Dad the pleasure of seeing you marry and walking you down the aisle."

"Well, to tell you the truth, the way things are between us, I'm really not sure I would want my father to give me away. If we elope, I won't have to face that decision."

Barbara urged Nell to give that a lot of thought, saying, "It is your decision, but your Dad would be deeply hurt if he could not be there for that part of your life or walk you down the aisle. He loves you very much, Nell. I pray every day that you can release your anger over your parents' divorce. It was between them, honey—it had nothing to do with you, and it certainly did not indicate that he did not love you. Even though he was not good at showing you his affections at the time, in his way, your Dad has always idolized you and Sandra."

One evening in May, 1984, Nell called to tell Barbara that she was engaged. They wanted to set the date of the wedding for the first or second Friday of January, 1985. She said that the church was available either of those dates, and both were good for her and her mother, so Nell asked Barbara to see if she or Sam had conflicts with either weekend.

Barbara said, "I can't think of any possible conflict, but let me get my calendar. Do you want to talk to your Dad while I find it?" When Nell said that she did, a surprised Barbara called Sam to pick up the telephone.

Sam asked how she was, and they chatted a bit.

Then Nell said, "Dad, I am going to get married in June to Lyn— you know, the guy I have been dating for three years. I asked Barbara to check your calendar to see if either of you have a conflict with the two possible dates. I know that you will have to look at your calendar at the office too. Let me know as soon as you can." She hurried through everything she said, not letting Sam break in, even to congratulate her.

Finally, he burst out, "Sweetheart, I am so happy for you! Barbara and I like Lyn very much. He is a very nice young man. Oh, I'm so excited! Congratulations."

"Thank you, Dad. What about the dates?"

"Well, let me think. I have a big law suit this December, but it will be over before the end of the year. If I have a conflict with your date on my calendar, I will just change my schedule. We will do it when- ever you want. Tell Lyn how happy I am for you two! He is a lucky man. Do you want to marry at our church here?" Sam asked.

"No, thanks. I have been away from Shreveport for so long. Lyn and I are members of St. Philip's Cathedral here in Atlanta and will marry there. We are to start our pre-marital counseling in September with a priest that we really like and relate to. We have started saving all the money possible for the expenses we will face, and it won't be a large wedding."

Sam replied, "You two save your money for your honeymoon or a house or whatever. I won't be deprived the pleasure of providing my daughter the wedding she desires. Don't limit what you want to do because of costs."

"I thank you, but you don't have to do that," she said.

"I know I don't have to, my love, but I want to, and if you'll allow it, I will. So you plan it like you have dreamed your wedding would be. Tell us what we can do to help you," her father answered.

"Lyn and I will appreciate anything you want to do. Thank you," Nell replied.

Nell sounded happy, but Sam still felt Nell's words were tight and drawn, holding something back between them.

Barbara was back with her calendar, so Sam told his daughter again how happy he was for her and that he loved her. He handed the phone to Barbara, who said either of the two weekends was fine. They agreed the wedding would be set for the first weekend, the 5th of January. Barbara volunteered to come to Atlanta to help any way she could in the planning, picking out clothes and so on. Then she told Nell, once again, how happy she was for them, asking Nell to hug Lyn for her.

However, neither in that call, nor in any subsequent conversation, did Nell mention Sam's giving her away. She did tell Barbara that she would be escorted as a mother of the bride and would sit with Louise and Sam. Barbara's intuition told her that Nell was not going to have her father walk her down the aisle, but she did not discuss that with anyone, especially Sam.

Chapter 56

PETITIONERS EVALUATE

As they usually did at the end of each day, Sam and his trial team packed up their files to go back to the firm's office.

Rob called over his shoulder, "I'll see you back in the war room."

In preparation for the trial, Sam had reserved one of the firm's conference rooms for the duration of the trial. The numerous files, maps, and other documents they were using were all stored in what they had come to call the "war room."

The secretary, Joyce, came in and asked if she could get coffee or a soft drink for anyone. Several requests were made and in a few minutes, she was back with a tray of coffee and Cokes. She pulled a chair close to Sam to tell him about a few phone calls of a rather urgent nature that he needed to return. Thanking her for covering for him so well, he asked her to phone three of those clients to tell them he would return their calls before he left the office, even if he had to call them at home. He mumbled aloud, "Thank you, Lord, for Joyce. I don't know what I would do without her."

Florence stuck her head in the room to ask Sam if he needed her in the meeting. He replied that he wanted to double check the order of the exhibits that they expected to use the next day, but that he would go over that first so that she could get away for the evening. When the lawyers and the expert witnesses were all present, he led them through the government's Trial Memorandum, reviewing the names of the witnesses listed there. Collectively, they compiled a list of the exhibits they anticipated using the next day. After reviewing her exhibit list, Florence said, "I've got each of them ready to go."

"Does anyone have anything else you need to talk to Florence about?" Sam asked.

When no one did, he told her that she could go. "Now Florence, don't live it up too much tonight. We only have three more days to go. After Friday, we will all be ready to celebrate. Can you wait until then?"

Florence laughed and walked to the door. "Yeah, live it up—right. I am going home to clean the bathroom and watch my favorite TV show."

After she left, Sam turned to assessing the trial. "Well, let's get to it," Sam said. "What do you think about today's session?"

Dr. Poole said, "I thought Rob's cross-examination of Boggan went very well. It was clear that Boggan was basically an employee of the government and was not going to admit to anything that might remotely hurt their case."

"But that's no surprise," Rob added. "We knew that going in."

They all agreed that Boggan's testimony was full of holes.

"I don't see how the Judge could give much credibility to what he had to say, and that will surely reflect poorly on his expert report," Claudia said.

"I felt so sorry for Elizabeth Pensa," Sam said. "Poor girl, she was lost, and Westover did nothing to help her."

"Oh, yeah, sure, Sam—it really looked like you felt sorry for her. You delighted in raising all those objections and making her sweat," Claudia laughingly replied.

"Hey, I still had to do my job. Let's just say I helped educate her in examining a witness." Grinning, Sam turned back to business. "Did anyone note anything that came out today that we need to turn around, or anything that didn't come out that should have—things we need to get into the record tomorrow?"

Rob said, "According to the Trial Memorandum they filed with the Court, the government will call Ballard, Reesh, LeBlanc, and Thornton next."

"Then let's review each of their reports and see what we think they'll have to say," said Sam.

For the next hour, they discussed the reports of each witness and reached a consensus about the questions they would ask of each.

Looking over the report of Eddie LeBlanc, Rob said, "I don't see anything in his report that is especially harmful. Sam, isn't he the guy who did not call you like he'd said he would when he heard from the IRS lawyers? Are you going to ask him why?"

"I think I will, just to see what reaction I get from him. I really don't see that there is much to get from that guy. But the next one, Reesh, is different. He will probably be tough. Claudia, are you ready for him?"

She said, "From his testimony in other cases, it is clear that he has a big ego and will never acknowledge any fact that might in any way vary from his conclusions. But my plan is to try to pin him in a corner so that even if he won't agree with the facts, I can at least show the Court his lack of objectivity."

"Sounds good to me," Sam said. "What about your witness, Rob— Mr. Thornton?"

"We could not find out much about him, but I expect to work on him over his failure to follow Rev. Proc. 79-24 and the fact that he is not a licensed appraiser," Rob replied.

Shea Claremore interjected, "I know of Thornton. He may be pretty good at appraising small farms, but I am really surprised that the government would use him as their principal land appraiser in something this big."

When Sam was satisfied all were comfortable with plans for the next day, the meeting broke up. Rob and several of the group headed for the University Club, while Claudia left for home, and Sam went to his office to return the important phone calls.

Two of the calls went smoothly and did not take long; the third was different. It was a client for whom Sam did a lot of work, so he knew well this call would take a while. *Ugh,* Sam thought, *I'm tired and just want to go home.* Over the years, this client had become more and more dependent on Sam, to the point that he frequently pushed Sam to make decisions for him regarding his business. But he was a loyal client, so picked up the phone. Sam spent the next 45 minutes attempting to help his client reach a decision.

When he was finally free, he called Barbara to tell her that he was heading home.

Part Five: Fission Reaction

Chapter 57

BALLARD & REESH

Elizabeth Pensa took her place at the lectern and called Tom Ballard as her next witness.

Ballard testified that he was an Estate Tax Examiner for the Internal Revenue Service, a job he had held for 22 years. Counsel asked a number of questions designed to show the Judge that the witness was experienced and quite competent. He testified that he had examined Mr. Mitchell's estate tax return and had a government engineer determine the value of the Mitchell timberland. That appraised value had been used by him for the assessment of additional estate tax, the subject of the controversy that had brought this matter into Court.

Ms. Pensa asked, "Mr. Ballard, have you worked in the area of Winnfield, Louisiana, in the past?"

"Yes, ma'am, quite a lot over the years, examining tax returns for those who live in the area, checking land records, and so on."

"From your work in that area, did you know of the nuclear testing on the Mitchell land?"

"No ma'am."

"During the audit of the Mitchell estate tax return, did you meet with the Mitchell's CPA or attorneys?"

"Yes, I did, several times."

"Did any of them ever mention to you the nuclear testing?"

"Never."

"When did you learn that the government had conducted underground nuclear testing on land owned by Clarence Mitchell?"

"Only in September of last year, when the Petitioner in this case asked the Court for a continuance of the trial because of the discovery of that nuclear testing."

"Since learning of that testing, have you reviewed and reconsidered the values you asserted for the Mitchell lands?"

"Yes. Because of the position taken by the Petitioner, it was necessary that I carefully examine all the facts to see if there was a basis to discount the value of the land. So I read all of the government's expert witness' reports and discussed with them any questions I had."

This time, Pensa was more confident and prepared. "After your reconsideration of all the facts, did you change your valuation of the land?"

"No. I am convinced by the government's expert witnesses that the nuclear testing in 1964 and 1965 does not result in a devaluation of the land—it had no effect on value. I would add that it was apparent that the Mitchell's CPA and lawyers did not think that it affected value either, since they never mentioned it. Not until the case was taken to Sam Laurins, a tax lawyer, did this question ever come up."

After a few more questions, with a smile evidencing satisfaction with her handling of this witness, Pensa turned to the Petitioner's counsel table and said, "Your witness, Counsel."

Sam rose and faced the witness.

"Were you aware that the Mitchell family's CPA and attorneys did not even know about the nuclear tests, which is why they never claimed a devaluation on the property in the past?"

"No, sir."

"Did you realize that Mr. Mitchell did not even tell me, his tax attorney, about Project Apex—believing and trusting that, like the government reports promised, there was no contamination on his property—and that I found out by accident?"

"No, I—uh—didn't realize that."

Laurins knew there was nothing of value to the case that he could ask Ballard, but because he had clashed with Ballard many times over the years, Sam hated to pass an opportunity to try to make him squirm a little. He asked Ballard some rather general questions to determine if he could create an impression that the IRS agent might not have been as thorough as he should been in preparing for testifying.

Sam said, "Mr. Ballard, in conducting your examination of an estate tax return, are you obligated to trace leads, secure information that might cause you to look more favorably on values asserted by the taxpayer, or do any other research to give the taxpayer some benefit of the doubt?"

Pensa stood and objected to the question, "This examiner and his report are not on trial here." The Judge sustained her objection, and she looked pleased.

Sam announced that he had no more questions.

When Ms. Pensa had no further questions, either, the witness was excused.

✳

Elizabeth Pensa announced that she called Brook Reesh.

Reesh testified that he was employed as an Associate Professor of Forest Resources at the University of Georgia, specializing in biometrics and mensuration (geometry applied to the computation of measuring from different angles). As he launched into his education and work training, Claudia rose and addressed the Court, "Your Honor, Petitioner will agree that the witness is an expert in forestry and biometrics, so it will not be necessary for Counsel to go through the process of qualifying him."

"Thank you, Ms. Stone," the Judge replied. "Ms. Pensa, is this witness being offered as an expert in those fields?"

"Yes he is, sir."

"Then for the record, the witness is accepted as an expert without objection."

Elizabeth then went through the procedure to have Reesh examine and identify the report he had prepared for this trial, offering the report in evidence as the direct testimony of the witness.

The Judge asked, "Ms. Stone, do you have any objection to the admission of the report?"

"Petitioners would like to ask the witness a few questions before responding to the question of admitting his report," Claudia replied.

With approval of the Court, Stone asked Reesh if he was a real estate appraiser.

"I am not."

Claudia asked the witness, "Do you have any experience in appraising real estate?"

"No."

She addressed the Judge, "Your Honor, I object to the admission of the report of this witness on the grounds that the report is basically a critique on appraisal procedures and techniques, a discipline in which Mr. Reesh just admitted he had no experience."

Ms. Pensa argued strongly that while the report did contain some of the material to which Ms. Stone objected, it was a minor part of Reesh's report. She said. "The report provides information to lead to proper assumptions used in determining the income discount method of evaluating timberland. Mr. Reesh is a specialist in forestry mensuration, the measurement of timber value, Your Honor. We believe that because of this information, his report will be very important to the Court in rendering a decision in this case."

After hearing further arguments from both Counsel, Judge Lansdorf said, "I am going to admit the report in evidence, but I assure you that I will pay no attention to any portion of it that discussed real estate valuation techniques."

Claudia announced that Petitioner had no questions for Mr. Reesh. Thanking the Judge, Elizabeth advised him that she also had no further questions of the witness.

"All right. Fine. You have had an easy day here, sir. You may step down," the Judge said.

Pensa said, "Since the government will not be recalling this witness, Your Honor, we'd like to ask that Mr. Reesh remain in the courtroom to assist during the remainder of the trial."

The Judge agreed he could stay.

Chapter 58

IAN'S VOW

Ian was aware that the Court had recessed for the day. So when Emily appeared in the hall, he was there waiting for her. As they meandered their way to the hotel together, even though it was cold and getting dark, they both felt stimulated by the crisp air.

Emily said, "I am really getting tired of sitting in the trial for so long. I'll be glad not to have to sit still all these hours each day." What she didn't say was that she was not looking forward to separating from Ian.

Ian agreed, "At least you are in the courtroom and can see and hear what is going on. It really is boring sitting in that witness room. I have now read everything I brought and whatever else I could find. I have been there too long already. I'm getting antsy."

As they arrived at the hotel, Ian asked Emily if she would have dinner with him. She quickly accepted but then remembered she had told Kyle that she would join him and Van Skiver for a drink. "Meet me in the hotel bar with Kyle and Ken, then after a drink together, you and I can go our way and have dinner alone," she said.

Even though he did not want to be with Van Skiver, he did want to be with Emily, so he agreed. They joined several people waiting for the elevator and crowded in with them.

Ian felt a rush of excitement as he and Emily were pressed together. They went to change clothes and freshen up in their rooms.

Arriving at the hotel bar, Ian found DeLoach and Van Skiver. Before he could sit, Emily entered. She was gorgeous, in a bright red knit skirt and sweater. All three of them stood as Ian motioned for Emily to sit in the chair next to him. Van Skiver had finished his drink and ordered another as the waitress took orders for Emily and Ian. As their conversation developed, Ian was acutely aware of how quiet and detached Ken Van Skiver was. He had little to say, never raised his voice, and stopped after that second drink. What a difference from his actions on other nights Ian had witnessed him in this same bar. *Hmmm. Why the switch?*

As they finished their drinks, Kyle said that he and Ken were going to the Sea Food Shack for dinner and asked Emily and Ian to join them. Relieved he didn't have to make an excuse for not going with them, Ian said, "Emily and I ate there last night."

"Well, aren't you two buddy-buddy?" Kyle smirked at her.

Emily declined comment.

Ian declined the invitation but thanked them. Ian and Emily left the two others.

"Let's walk the two blocks to Nick's," Ian said. It was a popular restaurant, and Emily agreed. They had not gone very far before Ian took her hand in his and held it as they walked.

"What has happened to your boss, Ken?" Ian asked. "He was so quiet and restrained tonight—so different than last week."

"Kyle told me today that he spent a lot of time with Ken yesterday," Emily said. "He learned that Ken has personally assumed the blame for all that happened on and around the test site. When Ken heard the people who live in the Tullos area tell of all of the incidences of cancer and their being trapped with no way to get out of that town and its poisoned water, he was devastated. Apparently, Ken's brother died of lung cancer, so it's a sensitive subject."

Ian interrupted, "You mean that guy has feelings? I'd have guessed he was just mean and grizzly all the time."

"Yeah, well, the Tullos residents' story got to him, I guess. Kyle was able to help Van Skiver see that orders for Project Apex came from so high up, it would have happened whether Ken gave the green light or not. Ken was not the one who made the final decision to test in the Mitchell Dome, so he could not bear the full responsibility for the plight of those poor people. Basically, Ken was feeling guilty for his role in all this—and somewhat at cross-purposes with the government's objective here at this trial."

"Huh, I know the feeling," Ian said.

"Kyle told me Ken really needs some professional counseling, but that he thinks he'll be okay for now."

"Well, I hope that he can get straightened out. If he doesn't, he will surely lose his job, moping around, cussing and yelling at everyone, not to mention drinking like that," Ian said.

While waiting for their dinner, they enjoyed a glass of chianti and casual conversation. During dinner, both were pensive. Emily broke the silence, "A penny for your thoughts."

He said, "I was thinking about the memories we shared last night and how we seem to be so closely connected, with such similar life stories. Here we have been brought together in this situation and have so much loss in common. Thinking about all that we talked about, I just had a hard time getting to sleep."

"Really? Tell me about it."

Hesitantly, Ian began. "For these 10 years since Kay died, I have not met a woman who interested me like you do, Emily. When Kay died 10 years ago, I thought that I could never love another woman, and I vowed to myself, at her grave, that I would never consider remarriage." Feeling bashful and assumptive for saying that, Ian qualified it with, "Not that I'm talking about marrying anyone tomorrow or anything—just that I…"

"I know what you meant," she grinned, relieving his awkwardness.

"Last night, as I stood close to you, and we kissed, something happened to me, Emily. Back in my room, I was bewildered. My heart was telling me that, like my Kay, you are beautiful inside and out. You are very special, and you stir my emotions. But my head was reminding me of my vow that I would never feel anything for another woman again. The conflict between those feelings made me toss and turn all night."

Emily reached over and took Ian's hand. Looking into his eyes, she said, "That vow you made to yourself was out of desperation and lone-liness, at the lowest point of your life, having lost the person dearest to you. But that vow was not made to Kay, Ian. In fact, you told me yourself that she made you promise the very opposite—that you *would* marry again. You probably saw your vow to yourself as a way to declare your undying love for Kay, but don't you see that you can love someone else without diminishing your love for Kay? I will never forget my James, but I am open to new feelings, too, and I know James would want me to move on and find happiness again. There is room in your heart for a living love and for memories of Kay," she trailed off and quietly added, "I hope."

He was silent.

She continued, "Well, I admit that I too spent a restless night last night. My knees went weak kissing you." She giggled a little. "I experienced a feeling that I have not known since my last days with my husband."

The corner of Ian's mouth went up in a sheepish grin.

Emily continued, "Since we both shared those feelings, I urge you to free yourself from any pangs of guilt because of that vow. Remember that Kay implored you to love again. She knew that your life would be empty if you forever clung to memories of her, that if you ran away from the love of another, living within the restrictions you imposed upon yourself, you would not be happy."

Pausing again, she added at last, "I have the memory of my husband, James, and his love, too, but also have new feelings for you. Give our feelings a chance, Ian. Let's see where they take us."

With his eyes fixed on hers, Ian again felt his stomach flip-flop. He knew that she was right. He, too, wanted to see where they would go.

Finally, he spoke, "It will take some time for me to become completely comfortable feeling this way about someone new, but I want to try with you." Following his heart and without thinking about it, Ian moved forward and lightly kissed her.

As they strolled back to the hotel after their meal, he felt a lightheartedness he had not experienced since he first met Kay. His feet were not touching the pavement. Ian squeezed Emily's hand a little tighter.

Back at the hotel lobby, he suggested, "Let's not say goodnight just yet. Have another glass of wine with me—and maybe some dessert." Even though there were not many people in the bar, they chose a table in the corner. For the next two hours, they talked about everything that came to mind. Then, realizing it was after midnight, they agreed they should get some sleep.

Ian was happy that no one was on the elevator. He held Emily very close and passionately kissed her. When the elevator stopped at her floor, he walked off with her and followed her to her room. At the door to Emily's room, with no one in sight, he held her very close, and they kissed. Hearing the elevator stopping on her floor, Ian reluctantly broke apart and said goodnight.

Ian was certain that he floated from the elevator to his room. His heart pounded as he got into bed. This night, he would not stay awake mulling over difficult feelings. He would let himself enjoy this moment and Emily's insights.

It's like she knew exactly what to say to open my heart.

He quickly went to sleep with a big smile on his face.

Chapter 59

EDDIE LEBLANC

As the Court reconvened, Judge Lansdorf asked Westover for Respondents to call their next witness. Elizabeth Pensa stood and announced that the Respondent called Eddie LeBlanc. Mr. LeBlanc walked to the witness stand, took the oath, and sat down.

In response to questioning, LeBlanc established that he was the Director of Radiological Health for the Louisiana State Department of Health and that he had signed the document entitled "Mitchell Salt Dome Radiological Monitoring," Exhibit 90-CL. His job responsibility was to direct the statewide health program. He advised that by virtue of an agreement that the Atomic Energy Commission made with Louisiana and a number of states, the Division of Radiological Health was a regulatory agency responsible for discovering and monitoring sources of radiation in the state.

Pensa asked, "In carrying out your duties, has it been necessary for you to go to the Mitchell Salt Dome and Surface Ground Zero?"

"Yes, ma'am. I have been there 50 to 60 times, and the first of my visits must have been in early 1965. Beginning in 1974 or 1975, my Division started monitoring the test site along with the EPA."

"How did you go about monitoring the site?" she asked.

"Well, we had to take environmental samples, both at the test site and off site. We analyzed them while the EPA was doing the same thing. We took our samples from hydrological monitoring holes—we refer to those holes as HMHs. The holes were drilled with a power augur six to ten feet deep, down to the water table. Each hole was numbered so that we could keep up with the location of each sample. Initially, and for some time, the samples were taken monthly, then quarterly, then starting in 1973, they went back to monthly intervals. Samples of water were taken from the various HMHs, from ponds on the test site, creeks that run on or nearby the site, and other locations. We exchanged our reports with the EPA, and then we disseminated the info to state officials, the AEC, local residents, and others."

"Once your sampling had reached a quarterly schedule, why did you go back to monthly sampling?" Pensa asked.

"Because of the unreasonably high levels of tritium that persisted. That concerned us. It should have dissipated, but it did not. We were worried about that and urged the DOE to drill a well near Surface Ground Zero, to see what they could find. They were to go to the local aquifer, a depth of somewhere around 140 feet. But they did not find the aquifer at or near the 140-foot level, so they terminated the drilling and plugged the well. That well was designated as Post-Shot Three (PS-3). The DOE drilled several other Post-Shot wells, but none were effective."

Noticeably feeling like she'd finally hit her stride with this case, Pensa asked, "Mr. LeBlanc, did your Division conduct tests to determine the presence of radionuclides other than tritium?"

"Yes, ma'am, we did. We found no other beta emitters above background levels, other than tritium, but to this day, we are concerned with the high levels of tritium. It is especially excessive in and around the REECO pits."

"Please explain to the Court what the REECO pits are."

"Those are pits that were dug fairly close to the well drilled into the cavity of the dome. They were used to catch any overflow or ground liquids from the test site. We took, and still take, water from the local aquifer and test it at least once a year. It is very troublesome that we continue to find the tritium at higher than background levels."

"Mr. LeBlanc, there have been assertions made to this Court that barrels and other materials have been seen buried at or near the test site, including some possibly in the REECO pits. Have you ever seen anything like that?" Ms. Pensa asked.

"No, I have never seen anything like that out there, and I've been out there a lot."

Government counsel continued her questioning. When she had completed her direct examination, the witness was turned over to Petitioner's Counsel for cross-examination. Sam approached the lectern, looked briefly at his notes, then asked, "Mr. LeBlanc, you said, I believe, that you had tested for radionuclides other than tritium?"

"Yes, sir."

"Were any of those test samples taken from the soil around well HT-2M?"

"Uh, yes, I feel sure they were. You know, it has been years since the soils were collected and analyzed around HT-2M."

"And if those tests were made, where would we find written results of the tests?" Sam asked.

"It would be in some of the EPA reports, I am sure."

"I see. In fact, sir, according to the reports, the soil at well HT-2M has never been tested for anything other than tritium," Sam responded.

"I can't—I don't—I am really not sure on that one," the witness said.

Sam asked, "Mr. LeBlanc, do you remember me calling you a couple of weeks ago?"

"Yes, sir."

"You told me that you had been requested to come to this trial."

"Yes."

"At that point, the IRS lawyers had not told you what they were going to ask you. Do you remember that?"

"Yes, sir."

"And you told me that you would call me back if they talked to you between then and now. Right?"

"Yes, sir."

"And you have not called me, have you?"

"No."

"Objection, Your Honor," Ms. Pensa asserted. "What is the purpose of this line of questioning?"

"Mr. Laurins?" the Judge asked.

"It goes to the objectivity of this witness, Your Honor."

"All right, continue."

"Have you talked to an IRS lawyer since the time you and I talked on the phone two weeks ago?"

"Yes, I have."

Turning to another point he wanted to raise, Laurins asked, "Sir, you told me that as early as 1978, Louisiana State officials were very concerned with the contamination at Mitchell Dome. Is that correct?"

"That is right."

"And you were asking the Department of Energy to drill more wells and do more studies?"

"Yes."

"And you told me that the whole point of doing more monitoring was to detect the possible escape and migration of contaminants from the cavity. Correct?"

"Yes."

"Mr. LeBlanc, you and other state officials would not want to do more monitoring today if there was not a risk of escape and migration, would you?"

"That is true," LeBlanc admitted.

Sam said, "Thank you, Mr. LeBlanc. That's all."

"Okay, Ms. Pensa, anything further from this witness?"

Elizabeth replied, "Only a couple of questions, Your Honor. Mr. Leblanc, did I ask you not to call Mr. Laurins?"

"You did not."

"Were you under any obligation to call Mr. Laurins?"

"I don't think so, because I checked with my attorney."

"That is all I have, Your Honor," Pensa declared.

The Judge looked at Sam, who said, "That is all I have of this witness, Your Honor."

Judge Lansdorf asked Counsel if either intended to recall the witness. Determining that neither would, he thanked Eddie LeBlanc and advised him that he was free to go.

"You may call your next witness, Counsel."

Chapter 60

A BRIEF INTERLUDE

The Wild Thyme Deli was crowded, but a table in the back soon cleared, and Ian and Emily took it. After reviewing the lunch menu, they exchanged some pleasant chit-chat, all of which seemed preoccupied with unspoken thoughts. Then they sat in silence for a few moments looking at each other or around the room.

Ian spoke first. "This morning, sitting in my cubicle, I have thought of nothing but what you said to me last night—that my vow to never open myself to another woman was not made to Kay, and that I could care for someone new without diminishing my love for her."

Pausing, he added, "I understand what you said, and I am so relieved by it. Thank you. Because the thing is, I want you to know I really enjoy your company. I feel something special toward you. Now, I think, I can be free to let that feeling take me where it will."

Reaching over to take his hand, Emily responded, "That makes me so happy, because my heart is telling me that there is something very special happening between you and me."

While eating their lunch, neither had much to say, but from the excitement they felt inside, it was apparent to each of them that something truly magical was indeed happening between them. With a little time left before 2 o'clock, when they finished eating, they slowly walked back toward the courthouse, holding hands, enjoying the warmth of the sun as they strolled. Once inside the building, looking around to be sure no one was near, Ian pulled Emily close to him around a semi-private little nook in the wall and kissed her lightly.

Then he was back to the witness room, and she left for the courtroom, smiling.

Chapter 61

HUDGENS REPORT FOR MITCHELL V. IRS

Sam felt things were going pretty well with the case. The Respondent's witnesses had not done much harm as of yet. Perhaps the most damaging so far, however, was Paul Hudgens and two timber buyers.

Westover had called as a witness a man who was a timber buyer for Georgia Pacific. The guy testified that he had grown up around Winnfield and was aware of the nuclear testing on the Mitchell property. He revealed that he had bought timber from land within five miles of the test site, and that the price was not discounted. Then another witness testified to the same thing. This one was a procurement forester and timber appraiser for Flood Timber Company and had purchased timber within five miles of the test site, paying full value for it.

The point the government was making was that lots of different timber buyers could declare there was no basis for discounting the value of timber on the Mitchell land, since timber on land close by was selling at full price.

Then came Paul Hudgens, whose report was brief, but poignant. Sam leafed through Hudgens' report for the Court, knowing there wasn't much the Petitioner's team would be able to do to combat Hudgen's testimony.

Suddenly, a random, passing thought transfixed Sam. Holding Hudgens' report in his hands, all he could think of was whether or not this paper came from the International Paper Company, and whether or not the finished paper products from timber around the Tullos area could be cancerously toxic. He sat the report down. *I'll have to make sure Joyce never orders copy paper from IPC again.*

✳

Paul Hudgens, Land and Timber Manager
International Paper Company
Central Louisiana

It is my professional opinion that there is no reason to devalue the land or timber owned by Mr. Mitchell. I work for one of the largest paper companies in the world, and we use a lot of timber. We also have a lot of experience in such matters. In my estimation, the Mitchell timber is as good as anyone else's. I think its taxable value should reflect a normal price.

I have worked for IPC for eighteen years in various locations, working my way up to Land and Timber Manager. Because I have not been in the Tullos area very long, and I live outside of town, I had not heard of the nuclear testing there. IPC owns over 5000 acres of timberland, some of which is about five miles from the test site at the Mitchell Salt Dome outside Tullos. Our company has sold timber that came from within five miles of that test site. We did not sell <u>any</u> of it at a discount. We continue to sell timber from that location at fair market value, a good price.

IPC has also sold gravel right-of-way and hunting rights on some of that property. None of that sold at a discount, either.

If IPC is going to be taxed at full value, the Mitchell Timber Company should be, too.

If indeed the entire area was affected by the nuclear testing, as many local residents claim, then all of the timber companies should be equally affected. After all, all our trees are watered by the same source and plant their roots in the same dirt. Likewise, there is no reason why one timber company should be permitted to pay a lower rate of taxation if all the area timber companies were affected by the contamination—if there is, in fact, any remaining contamination (of which I know nothing about).

I would strongly oppose allowing the Mitchell Timber Company to be taxed at a reduced rate. As a professional in this field, I know my timber, and the Mitchell timber is the same as IPC's timberlands in the area. Therefore, it ought to be taxed the same as ours. Thank you for your consideration of this report.

Chapter 62

PERMISSION

After the day's trial was done, Emily went to get Ian from the witness room. As they walked back to the hotel, it was almost dark, and the brisk wind was cold.

"Okay, where should we eat tonight?" she asked.

"There is a great, romantic Italian restaurant, Romanos, out in the suburbs, Emily. I would like to take you there. Do you like Italian food?"

"Love it."

He took her by the hand and led her to his car in the parking garage. As he drove, Ian mentioned that the government attorney, Bob Westover, had told him that they expected to put him on the witness stand the next afternoon, and he would be the final witness to testify. Neither Emily nor Ian said it, but both were thinking that with him being the final witness, they would be going their separate ways all too soon. Although they would both be glad for the trial to end, neither of them wanted to part ways.

Ian broke the silence, "When you leave here, will you go back to Washington?"

"Yes. I have reservations on a flight Friday afternoon at 5:00. Where will you go?"

"I am to go to Winnfield to direct the new testing program and to help orchestrate the new clean-up efforts at the Mitchell site. My office is still at our headquarters in Las Vegas, but I expect to be in Louisiana for most of the coming year."

They talked and talked. Dinner came and went, and they talked some more over dessert. As they were finishing coffee, Ian took her hand and told her that he hated to see their time together coming to an end. "Can't say I won't be glad this trial will be over soon, but I'm going to miss being with you every day when it's done."

Leaning toward him, Emily lightly kissed Ian. "I know. I don't want to face the fact that in two days, we'll go our separate ways. I hope, though, that it will only be for a little while."

"Hey, a guy doesn't meet a girl like you every day. I'll keep in touch."

Arriving back at the hotel, Ian walked Emily to the door of her room. As she unlocked the door and turned to him, Ian took her in his arms and kissed her. Emily pulled him inside the room and closed the door. They stood there, bodies pressed tightly against each other in a long passionate embrace. Ian became unnerved when he became aroused. It had been so long since he'd been this way with anyone. Though he sensed that she wanted him to stay, he said, "I'd better go."

They kissed once more and with a knowing smile, Emily told him goodnight.

With a spring in his step, Ian went back to his room. He could not readily fall asleep, his mind full of thoughts of Emily. It had only been two weeks, but he had to acknowledge to himself that he was falling in love with her.

As he laid there, his mind whirling, he had a strong sensation of Kay's presence.

Drifting off to sleep finally, he thought he heard Kay's voice.

Go ahead, Ian, don't be afraid. Love her.

Flooded with feelings of peace, he slipped deeper into his dreams.

Chapter 63

ASHER THORNTON

Bob Westover called for Asher Thornton. Entering the Court Room, the witness took his seat after being sworn in. From Counsel's questions, it was established that Thornton was owner of M & A Forestry Consultants, that he was a registered forester, a licensed real estate broker, and had been engaged in the business for 15 years. In addition to the management of timberlands, his company had been active in buying investment properties for clients. He explained the education and training he had gone through to become a registered forester. With some obvious pride, he informed the Court that he had served as an expert witness many times. Westover then offered Thornton as an expert witness in evaluation of timber, timberlands, and related products.

Rob Fly was standing and the Judge addressed him, "Yes, Mr. Fly?"

"Your Honor, I have a couple of questions of this witness to determine his competency before we deal with the acceptance of him as an expert."

Judge Lansdorf told Rob to proceed with his questions.

"Mr. Thornton, are you licensed as an appraiser?"

"No."

"Are you certified as an appraiser?"

"No."

"Your report filed with this Court is signed by you and a Marcus McDuff. Who is Marcus McDuff?"

The witness answered, "Marcus is a certified real estate appraiser who, at my request, did a review appraisal. After I completed my appraisal, I asked Marcus to review it, consider the logic of it, and give his opinion of my work—nothing out of the ordinary. When Marcus approved my work and concurred with my conclusions, he co-signed my appraisal."

Rob asked, "Is Mr. Marcus McDuff here as a witness or available to this Court?"

"No, not that I know of."

"Your Honor," Fly said, "I object to this man being accepted as an expert in the appraisal of real estate on the basis that he does not have proper training in appraising, he is not licensed as an appraiser, and he had someone else, who is not listed as a witness in this case and is not before this Court, sign the appraisal to lend creditability to it."

Westover argued vehemently, "In Alabama, Thornton's domicile, a license is not required to be an appraiser. The witness has rendered many appraisals, and in this instance, took the extra step to have a licensed appraiser review his work. He's gone the extra mile to lend even more credibility to his work, even though he didn't have to because of his own experience and expertise."

The Judge ruled that Thornton would be accepted as an expert in the appraisal of timber and timberland.

The report prepared by the witness was marked for identification, shown to him, and after he identified it as his, Westover moved to admit it in evidence as the witness' direct testimony. The Court accepted it. Westover then had the witness identify his rebuttal report, which he had marked for identification, and moved its admission into evidence.

The Judge then advised Rob that he could proceed with his cross-examination.

As Fly began his questioning, Thornton became more and more defensive and contemptuous. The witness' report stated that there was no reason to discount the value of the Mitchell land because of the nuclear testing, so Rob questioned him extensively on that point.

At one point the witness said, "I read the ridiculous report that Shea Claremore prepared for the taxpayer, claiming a huge discount in the Mitchell land value because of the nuclear testing. So I checked land records and found many sales of land within a five mile radius of the test site that were sold at no discount. I found timber cut within that area sold at no discount. There is no basis for any discount."

Rob said, "Mr. Thornton, I see in your report that you have cited 31 sales of timberland that you assert are comparable to the Mitchell lands?"

Confidently and with obvious pride, the witness answered, "I sure did. My associates and I found 31 sales of timberland that we consider comparable. We made adjustments to the sales price of each of those sales and averaged the prices of the 31 sales to get our comparable price."

"Where in your report is information that this Court can use to determine what those adjustments were or how they were made?"

"Well, I didn't think it necessary to fill up my report with all that stuff."

"Then your report is incomplete and means nothing, sir," Fly responded.

"I can get all that information from my work papers. Our comparables are tracts of from about 160 to 200,000 acres, so we adjusted their sale prices for location, size, and so forth."

Rob asked, "Do you have those work papers with you? Are they here, so that you can show them to the Court?"

"Well, no, I don't have them here with me, but they are in my office."

"Mr. Thornton, are you familiar with IRS Revenue Procedure 79-24?" Rob asked.

"No."

Somewhat sarcastically, Rob said, "That is interesting. Rev. Proc. 79-24 is the final word of the IRS as to the method of making appraisals for tax purposes." Fly handed the witness a copy of the Rev. Proc., asked him to turn to page 16 and read paragraph 4.02.

"An appraiser should use two or three sales that are the most reliable and comparable to the subject property," the witness read.

Rob said, "Hmm, two or three that are most suited to be comparable to the situation—not 31 different properties that may or may not be relevant and truly comparable?"

"We wanted to be thorough."

Pausing a few moments for effect, Rob continued his attack. He asked, "Did you go and inspect each of the 31 properties you consider comparable to the Mitchell lands, or did you send one of your associates?"

"No, I did not inspect all of those properties. You know, we divided them up. We saw some of them in person, though. I don't think that Claremore looked at every comparable sale either."

"How many of the comparable properties did you personally inspect, sir?"

"Well, any of them in the area that we could look at, we went to look at. Some of the larger sales we were familiar with by our involvement in the timber industry over the years. A lot of this data was accumulated over years of working in the timber business. We have a lot of years' experience, the same as Ms. Claremore."

Rob asked Thornton to explain how, in his report, he adjusted his comparable sales back to the Mitchell lands. The witness directed Rob's attention to a page in the report that showed the sale price of each comparable, a second column that said the amount of the adjustment, and a third column that showed the adjusted sale price.

"Where does that amount under the adjustment column come from?" Rob asked.

"Where it was appropriate, we adjusted for location, size, and so forth. That figure in that column is the total of all adjustments for each comparable."

"Let's look at your sale number four." The witness turned to the details of that sale in his report. "Tell me, Mr. Thornton, what kind of road access does that property have, how does its topography and the improvements on that land compare to the Mitchell land?"

"Uh, without my notes, I can't tell you any more than is written in my report."

"So, are you saying that you cannot tell us how you got to that total adjustment amount for each of the properties?"

"Well, I could go back to my notes and tell you."

"Yes, Mr. Thornton, go ahead. The Court and the honorable Judge will wait for you. And while you are back in your office getting all the pertinent information your report should haveclearly shown in detail from the beginning, why don't you pick up some coffee for us all on the way back?"

"Objection! Badgering the witness!"

"Sustained."

Fly said, "There should be no need to go to your work papers, should there, Mr. Thornton?"

"Well, I guess I should have included that information. I just didn't want the report to be so long and tedious that you couldn't get to the relevant facts."

Rob then laboriously reviewed each of the 31 sales Thornton had used as comparables, asking many questions about each. With each question, the witness' answers became more vague and evasive. As Rob's questions became more pointed and specific, the witness answered either that he did not know the answer, or that one of his associates would know the answer to that question. The witness' feeling of competition with Shea Claremore was very apparent. For whatever reason, he did not miss an opportunity to criticize Claremore's report.

When he had completed his interrogation, Rob advised the Judge that he had no more questions of the witness, turned to the counsel table and confidently sat down.

Judge Lansdorf asked government counsel if they desired to question Mr. Thornton on re-direct. Westover answered that he did.

Being led by Bob Westover, the witness related how he learned that the nuclear tests had been conducted on the Mitchell land, pointing out that none of the Mitchell family had mentioned it, nor had any of their representatives. Thornton had discovered it while exploring the timber on the land. He and his associates cruised the entire property, putting in some 150 miles of cruise lines.

"We found stumps of timber cut in recent months, indicating clearly that the Mitchells were still cutting and selling timber, and thus, the nuclear testing had not affected the sale of timber on the Mitchell land. That was justification enough to ignore any potential discount in value because of the testing."

The questioning continued with Westover seeking testimony to try to overcome some of the witness' answers given on Rob's cross-examination. He led Thornton through a review of many of his comparables to strengthen the validity and applicability of them. Westover attempted to have the witness show that, while he was not familiar with Rev. Proc. 97-24, with the exception of the large number of comparables he used, his appraisal still met the requirements of that Procedure.

At that point, Thornton lashed out again at Shea Claremore, saying, "Claremore's report didn't use but three comparables, probably because those are all she could find. In contrast, my report shows the extensive hard work my team put into researching comparables. Her approach to valuing timberland is so outdated, it's a joke."

Chapter 64

LITTLE NIBBLES AND REASSURANCE

Emily bolted from the courtroom to the witness room. Taking Ian by the hand she urged him to come along. "Hurry!"

When he asked her why the rush, she told him, "Court's recessed for an hour's lunch, and I want every minute I can have with you in private!"

They briskly walked to the Downtown Grill. When lunch had been served, they both nibbled at their food, mostly shared smiles, caring glances, lots of conversation, and frequent touches. Ian asked, "Are there any other witnesses to testify before I am called?"

"Well, they may tie up some loose ends with the current witness, then we put Mitchell's grandson on the stand. Other than that, you're it."

Once more, with a deep sigh, he repeated his dread, "God, I just hate the thought of taking the witness stand."

"I think it will be tomorrow morning before we get to you."

"I am so nervous about what the taxpayer's attorney might ask me. Here I am, a witness for your team, Emily, testifying for the government, but I think the government is wrong. They were wrong from the start in conducting the nuclear tests in the Mitchell Salt Dome, wrong in the unconcerned attitude they took in handling the tests and the clean-up, and wrong in refusing to admit that the value of the Mitchell land should be discounted. I mean, jeez, I believe in our government and the DOE. We do some good work some of the time, but this situation is not one of those times. How can I be loyal to the Department and the government—and keep my job—and yet be truthful?"

"You can't compromise what you know is right. I know that you won't. Just tell the truth. If your testimony is hurtful to the Department in the short run, maybe the DOE can benefit from it in the future."

"I saw that CIA agent, Jack Erwin, in the hallway at the courthouse. Has he been in the courtroom during the morning session?"

"Yeah, he has been there. He's a weird guy—the way he seems to quietly, stealthily appear and disappear," she said.

Ian replied, "For sure—he is strange indeed. The depth of his involvement in the testing, and now in this trial, is impossible to understand. But it freaks me out. Like I need anything else to worry about when I take the stand. Ugh."

After lunch they walked back to the courthouse, found a bench on the lawn, and sat.

They were quiet for a few moments, when Emily said, "When you left and I closed the door to my room last night, my heart was beating so hard! I thought of you all night. How did you sleep?"

Ian said, "I found it hard to sleep, sizzling with your touch, your kisses. Then the strangest thing happened."

"Oh? What?"

"When I was in bed, trying to go to sleep, I had a weird experience—good, but odd. Maybe I was already asleep—I can't be sure. Maybe I was dreaming."

"What?"

"I heard this soft voice. Or it was more like I *felt* the voice."

"Ah, hearing voices, are we? Maybe you and I shouldn't get involved after all," Emily teased him. Ian laughed. She said, "No, really, all joking aside, what happened?"

"Well, it was as if Kay was there. Like she was with me in spirit, telling me that it was all right to, uh," here, Ian hesitated and chose his words carefully, "to care for you. I could almost hear her say that I should go ahead and not hold back. It was very freeing, a great relief."

From the smile that covered Emily's face, it was obvious that was exciting news to her. A peaceful calm settled over the couple. They sat close, mostly in silence, snuggling against the cool wind, each deep within his or her thoughts, until Ian realized that it was getting close to 1:00.

Hand in hand, they walked into the courthouse.

"Ugh. Can't we just play hookie and go see a movie?" he joked.

"You'll be fine," she said. "And like I said, I don't even think we'll get to you today. But when we do, just say what you know you have to say. The Respondent's team will either recover, or we won't, but either way, you will know you did the right thing."

"Yeah, but will I still have a job when it's all over?"

"Cross that bridge when you come to it. It's going to be okay, Ian."

Pulling him into a little alcove in the hallway, perhaps where a pay phone used to be, she stole a moment for quick kiss, knowing no one else was around. As she left him, she reminded him again, "Have no concern for your testimony. If the truth is bothersome for anyone, that's not your problem." She kissed him on the cheek and was gone.

Chapter 65

CRAIG MITCHELL FOR THE RESPONDENTS

Westover spoke with clear strength, "Respondents call Mr. Craig Mitchell to the stand."

In the list of witnesses in the Trial Memo, both sides had listed Clarence Mitchell's son, Craig Mitchell, grandson of the decedent, as a possible witness. Even though he had no specific reason to call him, Sam had included him just in case something came up during the trial that made it desirable to do so. The reason Westover listed Craig was because a company owned by Craig had purchased timber and some land nearby the test site. If Sam called Craig to testify, he would be available to the government counsel on cross-examination. When Craig was not called by Sam, the government did.

Lansdorf asked the bailiff to get Craig Mitchell.

"What relation are you to the deceased, Clarence Mitchell, Sr., who signed the original contract with the AEC for Project Apex?" Westover began.

"His grandson."

"Please tell the Court about your current occupation."

"I'm president of Mitchell Timber Company, the family business. My Dad and I grow timber on the remaining family land that surrounds the 1400 acres leased to the government."

"What is Coastal Timber Company?"

Craig responded, "That is a company that I formed a few years ago. I own it 100%. The company buys and sells timber and operates a pole and piling mill."

"Does Coastal Timber Company buy timber from Mitchell Timber Company?" Westover asked.

"Yes, it buys timber from many land owners, including Mitchell Timber Company. Mitchell Timber Company is owned by several members of our family. It sells to a lot of buyers, including me."

"Has Coastal Timber bought timber from Mitchell Timber Company since the nuclear testing on it land?"

"Oh, yes, sir. Lots."

"And did you discount the price of the timber you bought, because of the nuclear testing on the land?"

"No, sir."

"So you paid full fair market value for the timber, even though you knew that it came from land under which the nuclear tests had been conducted?"

"Yes, sir."

"What did you do with the timber you bought from the family land, Mr. Mitchell?"

"We shaped and finished it, then sold it as poles."

"When you sold the poles, did you discount the price since they had come from land near the test site?"

"No, sir, but we trusted the government reports. Lots of people had suspicions, but no one really could say if the rumors that our land and timber was contaminated were true or not. So none of us in the family ever thought to consider how Project Apex may have affected the value of our land and timber products."

Ignoring this, Bob pressed forward. "Is it true, Mr. Mitchell, that you and your company, Coastal, have bought some land close to Surface Ground Zero in recent years?"

"Yes, sir. We bought three small tracts, each located within six to eight miles of the test site."

"And, did you pay a discounted price for those land purchases?"

"No, sir."

Judge Landsdorf interjected, "Did either the federal or the state governments impose any restrictions on the sale of timber from the land after the testing was completed?"

"No, sir."

Westover asked, "Isn't it totally inconsistent, Mr. Mitchell, that your family is asserting in this case that the value of your grandfather's land should be devalued because of the nuclear testing, while here you are paying full value for timber on that very property and buying land close by at full value?"

"No, sir, we didn't know any better."

"Isn't it true that, on numerous occasions, you told people that the radiation contamination scare in the vicinity was without any basis in reality?"

"Yes, I did. I made those statements. And yes, Mitchell Timber Company sold its timber at fair value, and yes, I paid fair value for the three small tracts of land I bought. But all of that is because we relied on information given to us by the government. The AEC and later, the NRC, DOE, and EPA assured us continually, even up until now, that there was no contamination problem with our land, timber, or adjoining property. We're not scientists—we're timber people. Why would we not believe them?"

Westover had tried to interrupt the witness to say, "Yes or no will do," but Craig Mitchell had pressed on. When he finished, Westover said, "Nothing further."

Claudia moved to the lectern for cross-examination and asked, "Mr. Mitchell, you testified that for many years you believed that there was no contamination on your family's land. Do you still believe that?"

"No, ma'am. I became deeply concerned when Mr. Ross and the other experts learned that the things the DOE had been telling us were untrue. There are problems out there. Townsfolk have always suspected it, and there were always rumors, but now we know the truth. And here we are learning that the indemnification provision in the lease is probably not binding on the government. I don't see how you can deny that the land value has decreased. And the poor people who live around there who are sick and dying, like my Grandpa died— the rates of cancer among our neighbors and family are…."

"Objection." Westover demanded those statements be stricken from the record.

The Judge turned to the witness and admonished him, "Mr. Mitchell, the statement you made about incidences of cancer is hearsay, and thus it is improper. You can testify to facts of your knowledge, but not hearsay."

"Yes, Your Honor."

Sam sat back in his chair. He saw the satisfied look on Bob's face.

Part Six: Maximum Payload

Chapter 66

THE LAST NIGHT

Thursday evening, Sam told the members of his team to take the witnesses and go ahead to the University Club, that he would join them shortly. They all left, and he moved over to the desk of the Court reporter. "Tell me, about how long will it take before we can expect to receive a transcript of the trial?" he asked.

She responded, "With Christmas approaching, it will take at least four weeks."

"Thanks a lot. I just need to have some idea in order to plan for writing briefs," he said. As he turned to leave, Sam realized that Bob Westover was just leaving, so they walked out of the courtroom, down the stairs, and to the street together, making small talk. Sam asked him how he was holding up.

"You're a worthy opponent, as always, Sam." Westover said the trial had been tough, but he would make it through. He asked Sam how he was.

"I will be glad for tomorrow evening to get here. I am tired of these long days and such technical testimony," Sam responded. They agreed that the lawsuit was the most unique, fascinating, and difficult that either had ever known, and that they looked forward to finishing it.

Sam stopped and turned to Westover saying, "Bob, we have known each other a long time and have always been straight up. I've got to know: with all the proof you knew we had before the trial began, why you refused to even discuss some settlement compromise? Is someone higher up giving you directions?"

Bob started to say something, but stopped, looking around. Then he said, "Because there is too much documentation showing other nearby timberland taxpayers aren't getting any breaks because of the nukes, and plenty of evidence that the land is clear of any impediment that would affect its value, Sam—simple as that." Bob seemed to have more to say, but he didn't go on.

They chatted casually a bit more, then parted. When Sam arrived at the University Club, members of his group were well into their first drink and full of conversation.

Following a second drink, the members of the group started drifting away. As was his ritual, Sam stopped by his office to look at the stack of pink telephone message slips and determined that there wasn't anything that couldn't wait. He called Barbara.

Laurins looked forward to a nice, relaxing evening with his wife. He felt confident about the next day and planned on doing nothing but enjoying his sweetheart's company that night.

On the phone, he asked, "Have you had supper yet, honey?"

"No, I haven't even had a moment to plan a thing. It's been a busy day. I've been helping Nell and Louise with some of the final preparations for the wedding. I can't believe she's getting married in a little over a week!"

"How is everything going in the wedding-planning department?" he asked.

"Oh, good. Great, really. But you know there's always a lot to do at the last minute before a wedding, and Louise and I want to help Nell make it perfect."

Since Barbara had not started supper, he suggested that he take her to Nick's.

"Oh, you know Nick's is one of my favorites, Sam. What's the occasion?" She sounded excited.

"Well, tomorrow, this trial will be done, and I have a good feeling about this last witness." Sam told her that he would be home in about 30 minutes. Before hanging up he said, "I love you. I am truly a lucky man to have such a great wife."

Chapter 67

THE OTHER LAST NIGHT

Ian and Emily left the courtroom together to walk back to the hotel, as usual. As they walked, Ian told her that since this was their last night in Shreveport together, he wanted to make it special. He wanted to take her to dinner at what was reputed to be the best restaurant in town.

She agreed, of course. "That sounds exciting. But if it's a fancy place, give me some time to get out of this stale business suit-dress and into something pretty."

He told her that he would come to her room to get her in 30 minutes.

She answered Ian's knock dressed in a tight blue sweater and matching pants that accentuated her waist, both matching her sparkling blue eyes. Earlier, her hair had been set to perfection, pulled high on her head, but now, she'd let it down, and it draped her shoulders elegantly.

Ian stood speechless as he gaped at her. Finally, almost in a whisper, he said, "My God, you are the most beautiful woman."

She pulled him into her room, hugged him tightly, and they kissed.

"We had better go before I lock the door and forget about dinner," he said.

"What's wrong with that idea?"

Taking her by the hand and leading her out of the room, he said, "We can see about that later. Right now, I want to show you off to the world as my girlfriend."

While enjoying a cocktail at the restaurant, they talked about the day.

Soon their conversation turned to what each would be doing in their work after the trial was completed. She asked if there was any chance that he might be coming to the DOE office in Washington, soon. "You could have a legitimate reason to come visit me," she said.

"I need a legitimate reason?" Ian grinned, and Emily laughed.

He told her that there was always a chance he might have to come to the office there. "But I don't know of any reason to go there any time soon—except for you. I'll keep looking for any opportunity. I may have to create a 'very important' reason."

Many times during dinner, they sat in silence, consumed with their own thoughts, even though most of those thoughts were the same, producing feelings of sadness that tonight was their last time together until…when?

Back at the hotel, Ian asked if she wanted to stop in the lounge for a nightcap, but she said, "No, I'm not sharing you with the bar crowd. I want us to be alone."

When the elevator stopped at Emily's floor, Ian told her good-night—in jest, as if he was staying on the elevator. Starting to laugh, he offered his hand for her to shake.

"Not on your life are you leaving me here," she said, taking his hand and pulling him off the elevator.

Ian laughed. "I was only teasing."

He took from Emily the key to her room, unlocked her door, stepped aside to let her enter first, then followed her in. They came together in a tight embrace, kissing slowly but passionately. As he kissed her neck and ear, she ran her fingers through his hair. His hand went to her breast, but she backed away and suggested they sit on the couch. Ian removed his coat, and she kicked off her shoes.

Emily fixed them a drink and turned on the TV for some background noise.

She looks nervous, Ian thought.

They sat almost wedged against each other as they talked on the couch. He would kiss her, then he'd back off a bit, both lost in the aura of the other. The passion intensified.

Mouths interlocked, she finally grabbed his hand and pulled it to her sweater. Ian fumbled with the low-cut cardigan's buttons, feeling the soft cashmere and her softer skin. When he could not get all of them unbuttoned, she giggled and helped him. He eased her sweater open, revealing her shapely breasts partially hiding behind a lace bra. As he started to remove her sweater, her first reaction was to resist, but slowly and tenderly, she let him continue to take it off.

"I haven't been in this position in a while," she admitted.

"Mmmm, he said between embraces…you and me both. Hope I'm not too rusty."

"We'll see," she grinned, seductively.

Yet again, his stomach did flips, and he became very aroused. Emily untied his tie, unbuttoned his shirt, and helped him take it off. He pulled off his T-shirt. Never ceasing to kiss her, Ian reached behind her and unsnapped her bra in one swift movement.

"Nah, not too rusty," he said coyly.

"I'll be the judge of that, Ian MacGregor," she played. She pulled the bra forward and let it drop to the floor.

"Oh, my God," he said, "you are beautiful," as he caressed her breasts with his hands and his kisses.

With no awareness of who initiated it, they stood. With continuous kissing, she unzipped her blue pants and let them fall to the floor. Emily unbuckled his belt, unzipped his trousers, and gave them a tug that sent them to the floor, while all along, continuing their playful, sweet words to one another. He stepped back to admire her body in nothing but her lace bikini panties.

"God. A work of art, just as I had thought it would be," he said.

"You mean you'd thought about my body?" she asked in a demure voice, putting her hands on her hips.

He grinned sheepishly and lowered his eyes.

She turned down the bed and sat at the edge. He took a drink. Then they fell into bed, holding each other very close. Even though he was so excited that he thought he would explode, Ian tried to take it slow, tenderly loving her from head to toe. She slipped her panties aside as he squirmed out of his boxer shorts. He had bought some protection at a drug store and now reached for it in the pocket of his pants on the floor.

"Presumptuous, are we?" she said, winking, though she was glad he'd been so thoughtful.

"Just in case," he'd said.

Both of them were breathing heavily, at times almost gasping for breath. All of the sexual desires that had been pent up in her for so long were awakened, and she was ecstatic. She pulled him to her, and they were one. After a few moments they fell back on the bed, both dripping in sweat. They held tightly, each conceding that it had been such a long time since either had experienced an orgasm that it did not take long.

After a while, Emily said, "Jeez, it's hot in here."

In schoolboy fashion, Ian said, "I'll turn on the air for you, if you like."

In lieu of an answer, she kissed him again.

The lovers rested in each other's arms, and shortly Ian pulled her to him again. As they kissed long and intensely, the raging fire within once again overcame them as their bodies melted one into the other. He fondled and kissed her breasts, her neck, her ears, as she explored his body and thrust herself hard against him.

Soon, he was inside her again, this time determined to prolong this moment as long as possible. In rhythm, they whispered soft, loving words to each other to say how wonderful it felt. Emily, in complete ecstasy, kept thinking each climax was better than the one before. Finally, Ian could not hold off any longer and, with a deep groan, his body became rigid, and he let go.

Both were exhausted. They lay in each other's arms again, the only sound being their deep breathing. They both dropped off to sleep.

Ian awakened. As he got up to go to the bathroom, he saw that it was after 4:00. When he returned, Emily was awake. She held her arms out to him. He got back into bed and held her tight, excited by her soft breasts against his chest.

She said, "It feels so good having your bare skin against mine."

He asked if she could read his mind. "I was thinking the same thing."

As they lay in the arms of the other, Ian whispered, "Emily, I hope this doesn't put you off, but I have fallen in love with you and cannot bear to think that tomorrow night you will be gone. The three people that I have loved the most in the world, my parents and Kay, are both gone, and I didn't realize how lonely I was until I met you. I can't face that happening again. I must be with you again very soon."

"Oh, Ian, I am so happy to hear you say that. I love you, too. I know we haven't known each other that long, but I feel the same. I feel like we are kindred souls who've known each other forever. As soon as the trial is over, and you are back at work, you have to figure out when you can get away to come to Washington. Or let's just take a weekend and meet somewhere else instead." Pausing, she added, "It takes a brave man to be the first to say 'I love you.' I admire you for that."

"I will call you every night, beginning tomorrow," he said.

"And I will think of you every day."

With a regretful look, Ian acknowledged, "It is almost 5 a.m., my dear, and some of your neighbors may be getting out soon. I don't want to be seen leaving your room at this hour."

"They've already started teasing me about all the time I've been spending with their star witness."

"Hmm. We'll see if they still think I'm the government's star witness after today."

As he dressed, they agreed they would be together during the noon break. After a long, deep kiss, he left.

Rather than take a chance on being seen in the elevator, Ian walked up the two flights of stairs to his floor and was soon in his room. His emotions were on a roller coaster.

With one thought, he was deliriously happy—that he loved Emily, and she loved him. In the next thought, he was melancholy that in a few short hours, they would be parting. What would the future hold?

I finally found someone else to share my life with, and she lives half way across the country.

With so little time left to sleep, Ian took a long shower, shaved, slowly dressed, and went downstairs to breakfast.

Part Seven: Critical Mass

Chapter 68

RESPONDENTS CALL MR. MACGREGOR

"All rise," the Clerk declared.

"Are you ready with your final witness, Mr. Westover?" Lansdorf asked as he took his seat.

"I am. Respondents call Ian MacGregor, not as an expert but as a fact witness."

The Bailiff went to the witness room and brought Ian back.

"Do you solemnly swear to tell the truth, the whole truth, and nothing but the truth?"

"I do."

Ian took the witness chair.

Westover asked Ian, "Please tell the Court your educational and employment background."

"I have undergraduate and Masters degrees from the University of Virginia and a PhD in nuclear physics from Stanford. I've been employed by the AEC since 1962, now called the Nuclear Regulatory Commission."

"Through your employment with the Atomic Energy Commission and NRC, were you involved in Project Apex?"

"Yes, sir."

"How long were you involved in that project?"

"I started with the AEC when I completed my work at Stanford and was sent to Washington. After two months' training, I was assigned to the Project, which was in the very early planning stage. When planning for the Project was completed, I was sent to Tullos to work with the company contracted to prepare the area and make further plans for the testing. That was May of 1963. My assignment was to remain at the test site until the testing was done and the clean-up completed. I left in 1972."

"Where did you go then?"

"I went to our operations office in Las Vegas, but I was back at the Mitchell test site numerous times in 1973, 1977, and again last year."

"Why did the AEC want to conduct the nuclear testing underground?"

Ian explained, "In 1962, it was obvious that the United States was going to enter into a treaty with the Soviet Union to limit nuclear testing. In August, 1963, that treaty was signed. The treaty banned testing of nuclear weapons in the atmosphere, underwater, and in outer space. The Cold War had spurred the AEC to focus a lot of attention on radiological warfare, but the test ban treaty severely limited what they could do in testing. They realized that the language of the treaty would not prevent us or the Russians from testing underground, so they became interested in determining the best way to do that without being detected so as not to alarm the Soviets or start trouble."

Ian continued, "By the time I was assigned to Project Apex, plans were being conceived to conduct testing of nuclear weapons underground. The AEC wanted to test certain weapons and at the same time, determine how clearly underground tests could be detected."

It became obvious that Bob Westover intended to prove through this witness that the AEC had prepared well for the testing and had conducted the tests and clean-up as planned. He wanted to paint the AEC as being thorough and responsible, and he would use Ian to show the Court just that.

"Mr. MacGregor, tell us, what was the purpose of the Saline Creek tests?"

"The bomb was to be exploded to test out seismographic equipment used to detect underground nuclear explosions. They wanted to see what would register and what would not."

"How was the location of the testing selected?"

"Information from the U.S. Geological survey showed it would be most desirable to do the testing in a salt dome rather than solid earth.

The theory was that explosions in the cavity of a salt dome would send off shock waves 100 times smaller than the waves emitted by solid earth, thus reducing the chance of the blast being detected. When a survey of possible salt domes was conducted, the potential areas were reduced to three or four. The Saline Creek Salt Dome was selected as the most desirable site, so long as the property owners would allow."

Westover asked, "Did the AEC make plans for and activate very elaborate systems for monitoring both the explosions and the environment after the explosions?"

"Yes, sir. Much time and effort was devoted to a plan to monitor everything during and after the explosions."

"How did they monitor the explosions?"

"Sophisticated seismographic equipment was placed in every direction from Surface Ground Zero at locations from a half mile out to 1200 miles from the center. Ships and submarines were posted in the Gulf of Mexico. Equipment to monitor water, vegetation, earth, and animals was placed all around the area, and milk from cows located as much at 20 miles away was tested. Readings from all that monitoring equipment were taken continuously for a period of two years after the final blast."

Judge Lansdorf, Sam, Emily, and everyone in the courtroom sat with rapt attention, visibly impressed with Ian's knowledge and demeanor as he answered the many questions posed by government Counsel.

Then Westover asked, "What was done with all the data collected from the monitoring process?"

"It was incorporated into various reports written by the AEC, the U.S. Public Service, the Department of the Interior, the Geological Survey, the Bureau of Mines, the Louisiana Department of Health, and some private contractor laboratories—those are just some that I can remember."

"Were there many of those reports?"

"Stacks of them."

"Did you read those reports?"

"I read the ones that were pertinent to the operations of the AEC, but not all the others."

"Mr. MacGregor, in any of those reports, did you see a disclosure of any leakage of contamination at the test site?"

"Yes, sir. After the clean-up was reported complete in 1972, contaminated liquid was found on the ground near a couple of the test wells. In another instance, contamination was found in two REECO pits. The contamination in each of those places was cleaned up promptly. All of that information is disclosed in the reports."

"So it was cleaned up quickly?" Westover said.

"Yes, sir."

Westover then turned his attention to questions regarding the clean-up process. After numerous questions about how the clean-up plan was conceived and finalized, to whom duties of clean-up were assigned, when clean-up started, and when it was completed, Westover asked, "How did it happen that problems arose twice after the contractor reported that clean-up was completed? Was there flaw in the original plan for cleaning up?"

"The problems that were discovered after the area was declared clean arose partly because the original plan did not account for all the possible methods of contaminant travel, and partly because the contractor responsible for the clean-up did not follow the requirements of the original plan. That was most unfortunate, because it became necessary to go back in to the test site several times, and there remain concerns to this day…."

A surprised Bob Westover interrupted his witness with another question, as he did not want Ian to go any deeper into this subject. He started directing Ian's attentions elsewhere.

Though Westover had effectively changed the subject and was moving on, Sam looked up at the Judge. Sam could tell that Lansdorf and the Court had all clearly just heard an employee of the AEC who was a part of the Project say that the clean-up plan was not only flawed in design, but that it had failed because the contractor did not follow the requirements of the plan.

✹

After hours of questioning, Westover paused to review his notes to be sure he had not overlooked anything. Feeling confident he had over-come the initial damage of MacGregor's unexpected testimony, Westover announced to the Judge that he was finished with the witness.

Chapter 69

SAM TAKES IAN ON CROSS

Sam thought again about the comment Ian had made and wondered if it was possible that Ian had opposed the tests and their potential hazards to people who lived in the area. *Boy, wouldn't that be a lark— this case would be sewn up fast if Ian turned out to…well, highly unlikely.* Sam had run through every possible scenario of questioning Ian several times over the past few days. He, Rob, and Claudia had discussed it again during a break Friday, too.

"Since I don't know what the witness will say, I must be very cautious not to ask questions that might result in harmful testimony," was Sam's position.

Rob was excited, though. "Sam, did you hear what MacGregor said about the contractor not doing his job and the clean-up plans not being 100%? That MacGregor guy is on our side, I tell you. I can sense it. He's just waiting for the right questions."

"Rob's right, Sam," Claudia said.

"Slow down. I hear what you're saying, both of you, and I'm with you. I do have a good feeling about MacGregor. But the thing is, we have made a good record up to this point, so for our client's sake, I cannot take too many risks with this last witness. We shouldn't be asking too many questions we don't already know the answer to—for the sake of Mr. Mitchell." Sam felt lucky, too, but he also felt he needed to model what an older, wiser attorney should do in his client's best interests.

As Court was called back, the Judge reminded Ian that he was still under oath, and said, "Mr. Laurins, you may cross-examine the witness."

With legal pad in hand, Sam stepped to the lectern, smiled at the witness, and cautiously began his questioning. "Good morning, Mr. MacGregor. In your testimony, you told the Court a lot about how Project Apex was conceived and operated. Hoping that it will not be repetitive, I want to ask you some more about that. Who made decisions pertaining to planning and carrying out the operations of Project Apex?"

Ian responded, "The Project Group was made up of nine people, each of the operating sections of the AEC was represented, and there were three engineers, of which I was Chief Engineer. Mr. Kyle DeLoach was the Project Manager over all of us. The Group was responsible for planning and later overseeing the operations of the project. Generally, we made decisions together. The AEC always had final decision authority, of course."

"You told us the theory that an explosion in an underground salt dome would emit sound waves perhaps 100 times less than an explosion in solid earth, and that was the reason for the decision to test in a salt dome. Please tell us a little more about how the Mitchell land was selected as the site."

"As I said, the U.S. Geological Survey did a lot of research prior to these tests. After consulting with the Bureau of Mines, they determined that there were only a few salt domes in the country that would be suitable. On further consideration, one was eliminated because of problems with access. From the remaining three, their strong urging was that the Mitchell Dome was the most favorable. The Project Group spent two or three weeks studying the feasibility of the proposed site on the Mitchell land. Their decision was that the Mitchell Salt Dome would be the site of the nuclear tests, if the Mitchell family would agree."

Sam had the witness explain the role that each member of the Project Apex Team played in the development of the plan for testing. Feeling his way along, Sam asked, "What input did each member of the team have in decisions made?"

"Most decisions were made by consensus, but if necessary, a vote was taken."

When he said that, Sam felt strongly that he should pierce further. Sensing that the risk in probing was minimal, and even though he didn't know the answer, he asked the witness, "Were the members of the team unanimous in their decision to recommend proceeding with Project Apex at the Mitchell Salt Dome?"

Ian paused for what seemed like a long time, looking around in the courtroom.

With great hope, Sam remained silent. *What or who is he looking for out there?*

Ian looked at Westover and the others sitting behind the government counsel table. He saw Erwin near the back of the room, daring him to make even the smallest error.

As seconds strung out, feeling the pause grow longer and longer, Sam started to sense that he might have stumbled onto something special. He repeated the question. "Mr. MacGregor, was that decision unanimous?"

Quietly, Ian answered, "No."

The Judge instructed the witness to speak up so that his answer could be recorded.

"No," he said into the microphone.

Now Sam knew he was on to something. "How many members of the team opposed the plan?"

"One."

Sam's pulse quickened. "Who was it that opposed the plan?"

Another pause.

Again, Sam saw Ian looking around, as if the proper answer would magically appear on the wall behind him.

Finally, after what seemed a very long time, the witness dropped his eyes down like he was going to inspect his shoes. Then Ian answered, "Me."

The courtroom, already on edge by now, fell silent.

Sam shot a glance over to Claudia, Rob, and Florence, all smiling, eyes dancing with anticipation, practically gleeful. Hoping to cover up his own excitement, Sam gently asked, "Why did you oppose the plan, Mr. MacGregor?"

Clearly searching for some way to mitigate the damage done, Bob said, "I object to this testimony. It has no bearing on the issue before this Court."

"Overruled. You may answer the question, Mr. MacGregor."

Having avoided looking at her up until now, Ian knew he needed strength from Emily. Seeking reassurance to tell the truth, he caught her eye, trying to read her thoughts. She had told him to tell the truth even though it could be harmful to the government's case. Her smiling eyes and oh-so-subtle nod gave him the approval he sought.

"I had devoted a lot of time to studying the geology at the proposed site—things like the size of the salt dome, the location of the aquifers, the close proximity of the dome to the town (only six and a half miles away), etc. I kept coming to the conclusion that there was a good likelihood the wall of the dome would rupture, and the salt might melt. If that happened, it could result in an invasion of the water table by nuclear residue. The natural flow of the region's aquifers is southeast, so if any of the residue invaded the aquifers, it would flow toward the community of Tullos. It was my concern that such a possible result would be extremely hazardous to the people in the area."

"Did you share your research and conclusions with the team?"

"Yes, sir. Every time we met, I implored the team members to insist on another site, one less likely to cause harm to unsuspecting residents. But I could not convince them. I will say that Kyle DeLoach, our boss, listened to my objections and thoroughly reviewed all of my research. He tried. In fact, he even took my research to the higher-ups. Soon after that, Mr. DeLoach told me that the CIA was really putting pressure on the President, and the President himself had to insist that the project move forward. He …."

"Objection! Your Honor, this is hearsay and should not be permitted." Westover was clearly trying to contain his concern at the extent this testimony from his own witness was now damaging his case.

"Sustained."

As he told his story, Ian became more comfortable and self-assured.

It was obvious to Ian from the looks on the faces of Westover and others around government table, except for Emily, that they were more than merely uncomfortable with his testimony. He knew he'd be in big trouble. If looks could kill, Ian was a dead man—the anger in Jack Erwin's eyes matched the snarl on his face. But Emily's eyes and her faint smile discreetly reassured him.

Sam asked the witness how long he had lived in the Winnfield area.

"February, 1963, until February, 1975, though in later years, I was not there full-time."

"Over ten years—then you must be very familiar with the test site and the entire Tullos area?" Sam asked.

"Yes, sir, very. I know the people who live in that area. In fact, I married a local woman in 1967. She lived with her parents on their 40-acre farm west of Tullos, near Saline Creek."

"Is she still in the area?" Sam asked.

"No, sir. My wife died from cancer in 1974."

"Are her parents living?"

"No, sir. Her mother died from heart failure, and her father died of cancer." Ian paused for a few moments, as though he had completed his answer, but added, "I tried to persuade her and her family to move from the area, because I was afraid that they might be exposed to nuclear...."

"Objection." Westover roared. "This testimony had no bearing on this case whatsoever."

"Overruled."

Ian continued, "I was afraid they'd get contaminated through the water. The source of their drinking water was their well, and that was true of everyone in the rural areas outside the community. After the nuclear testing, they all believed that their water was contaminated."

Sam asked, "If they believed their water was contaminated, why didn't your in-laws and other neighbors move from the area?"

"I object, Your Honor. Not only is this hearsay, it is not even germane to the issue." Westover asserted, totally frustrated.

"Overruled." The Judge seemed totally enrapt with what Ian was saying.

Sam repeated, "Why didn't they move?"

"All the people in the area are people of modest means, sir. About all that any of them have in this world is their homes, and they could not sell them—no one would buy their property because the nuclear tests were publicized in the papers. In order to buy homes and farms somewhere else, they would have to have had the money from the sale of the Tullos properties. The other issue was, well, this was their home-place. Too many generations and too many memories were here. They could not just walk away from it. They were trapped. Many of those people contracted cancer. Lots of them died from it. People became so sick after the nuclear tests."

Westover was getting hoarse, shouting, "Objection."

"What is your objection, Mr. Westover?" Judge Lansdorf asked.

"Mr. MacGregor is not a medical specialist here to testify about cancer. Not only that, but this whole testimony is all hearsay, Your Honor. He is testifying to something that he doesn't know as a fact. There is no proof of any of that in the record, and the witness has not offered any proof."

Turning to Sam, the Judge said, "Mr. Laurins?"

"Your Honor, this testimony is not hearsay. The witness lived there. He said that many people in the area have cancer presently or have died of cancer, and he knows because they were his friends, relatives, and neighbors."

"How do you know that information, Mr. MacGregor?" the Judge asked.

"The people who live in the Tullos area are a close-knit group. They were friends of my in-laws, friends of my wife, friends of mine. I know them well. I know many of those who have suffered from cancer, and I know too many who have died from cancer."

"Well, I am not sure what, if any, significance this will have on my decision, but I will let it in," Judge Lansdorf said. The objection is overruled, you may proceed."

Sam asked Ian, "When was your wife's cancer discovered?"

"October, 1972," adding almost inaudibly, "She was finally going to move away, but she stayed in town because her parents got sick."

"Mr. MacGregor, I believe you testified earlier that you were at the test site during much of the decommissioning process?" Sam asked.

"That is correct."

"What were your duties during the decommissioning process?"

"I was supervisor for the AEC and Chief Liaison to the company the AEC contracted to handle the clean-up."

Still not quite sure where this line of questions was taking him, but exceptionally pleased with all the results so far, Sam asked, "I believe you have testified that there was a written plan setting forth the requirements for the clean-up?"

As he answered, "Yes," Ian thought, *I know what's coming, and I would rather not go there.*

"You testified that the contractor failed to follow the requirements of the plan completely, correct?"

Pausing and again looking at Emily, Ian answered, "Yes."

Sam's adrenaline was flowing. He felt he was about to reveal the truth that had been covered up for all those many years. Westover had moved to the edge of his chair and looked like someone about to get punched in the nose. The faces of the other government people behind Westover were also frozen as though ready to get hit by a bad storm. Jack Erwin, obviously infuriated, was almost out of his seat.

All this did not elude Sam. *Deer in the headlights*, he thought. *What have I got here?*

"How did the contractor fail to follow the plan?" Sam asked.

"First, let me back up a little. In my opinion, the plan was based on certain assumptions that I believe were false; therefore, it was flawed from the beginning. Anyone could have guessed that the dome and other sub-structures would very likely crack with the blast's impact, creating way too many fissures and pathways for radioactive waste to travel—again, all entirely too close to the water supply for my comfort level. So one big problem with the decontamination plan was simply that there were too many possible paths the waste could flow for us to be able to competently conceive of ever cleaning it all up. Once that first blast had been let loose, I suspected a fair bit of waste would simply spiral out of control to places unknown and unpredicted by us."

"Objection, Your Honor. This witness is now testifying as an expert, and he has not been pre-qualified as such," Westover shouted.

"I don't see this question calling for an expert opinion, Mr. Westover. I am going to let it go farther to test it," the Judge responded.

Ian went on, "The planned disposal of large amounts of radioactive contamination into the cavity of the salt dome was based on the assumption that the cavity was still intact and structurally sound. Without close examination inside the cavity after the tests, it could not possibly be known whether the cavity was intact, not to mention that the dome had some existing natural fractures before we ever blasted."

"Furthermore, it was also irrationally assumed that the Tullos-Urania Oil Field pumped brine into the aquifer under high pressure, and that once the contamination was pumped into the aquifer, the liquid waste would flow in a direction 180 degrees away from gravity's pull and the direction of the natural flow. I disagreed with both of those assumptions, and I told them so."

"What response did you get from your efforts?"

"The contractor relied on an AEC report that the oil field's injections were under pressure and that this pressure would somehow turn the waste water around to flow away from the population. I told them of two reports I had seen that refuted this, saying Tullos-Urania Oil Field didn't use high pressure at all, but the contractor would not reconsider. No one would listen."

"Thank you for that background information. Now, even if the clean-up plan was flawed, did the contractor properly complete the clean-up as the plan required?"

"No," Ian said, emboldened, now telling his story without hesitation.

Doing his best to restrain his excitement, but also knowing he was on a roll, Laurins said, "Tell the Court about that, please."

"The plans called for the contractor to sample and analyze the soil, water, vegetation, and animal life on and surrounding the 1400 leased acres. While they did some sampling, I do not think they did enough. At no time did I see indications that the contractor tested for any radionuclides except one: tritium. I urged that they test extensively for alpha and beta emitters, but because someone in the operations office of the AEC agreed with the contractor that their testing was adequate, it simply was not done."

"The contractor was required to excavate all contaminated soil, haul it away to an approved storage site, and replace it with good soil. Some small amount of the contaminated soil was properly hauled away, but when they encountered very wet soil where the groundwater was contaminated and had become a muddy slush, it became difficult to haul it off, and someone in the AEC operations office permitted the contractor to bury most of that soil on site, against regulations."

Continuing, Ian said, "They were required to pump all contaminated water and other fluids into the salt dome cavity. The plan called for all holes drilled into the cavity to be plugged and sealed with cement. They did seal them, but they did a sloppy job, and it was obvious to me that some of the concrete materials and labor was inferior. Not only that, but concrete just isn't enough to stop radiation, especially after the later blasts disturbed the original concrete. It should have been re-sealed after each blast, at the very least—and done with the highest quality materials possible."

"Finally, the contractor was to transport all remaining materials, equipment, debris, and other solids to the AEC storage facility in Nevada. This was not done completely, either. While I did not see them bury anything myself, I later saw barrels of some unidentified liquid that had been buried on site. Over a period of years, the soil eroded away, leaving the barrels exposed."

Sam asked, "Have all of the solid materials been shipped to Nevada now?"

"I don't think so. Here we are almost 20 years later, and I believe there is still stuff out there that the contractor buried rather than ship away to a proper containment facility."

Again, Westover was standing. With a tone of defeat in his voice, he said, "Your Honor, I object to all of this testimony. We have introduced into evidence a mountain of formal reports from the AEC, the DOE, the National Health Service, and other agencies, stating their findings, and none of them suggest conclusions such as this witness has testified. I move that his testimony be stricken from the record."

Lansdorf patiently said, "Mr. Westover, let me remind you that this is *your* witness. On cross examination, Counsel for the Petitioner may ask him almost anything, just like you were permitted to do when cross-examining Mr. Laurins' witnesses. It is my job to weigh the testimony of this and other witnesses against other evidence introduced at this trial, which I will do faithfully and objectively. Your objection is overruled. Please continue, Counsel."

"If you were the liaison with the contractor, Mr. MacGregor, couldn't you force the contractor to address your concerns and comply with the terms of the clean-up plan?" Sam asked.

"No, sir. Only my superiors in the Commission had that authority. I reported frequently my observations of the contractor's failures, but nothing was ever done. It was as if whoever was calling the shots thought, 'The tests are complete—now let's get the heck out of here as fast as we can.'"

Pausing for effect, Sam reviewed his notes as if he'd planned the witness' testimony to come out just as it had. Then he asked, "One last question, Mr. MacGregor. In your opinion does the test site and other land around it still suffer from nuclear contamination, even now?"

"I feel certain that it does."

The courtroom was silent.

No one moved, as if each person was in a trance. Looking straight ahead, Ian sat quiet and still. Erwin's face was beet red, and his eyebrows and mouth pinched into a tight scowl. Westover, Pensa, and the government staff sitting behind their table were obviously in a state of shock, except for Emily.

Emily had not known exactly what Ian was going to say, but she knew it wouldn't be good for Bob Westover. So as not to appear disloyal, she restricted her pride at Ian's courage. But in her eyes, she said, *Ian, I am proud of you. I love you.*

Fly, Claudia Stone, Florence, and Clarence Mitchell all registered looks of pleasant surprise from smiling faces, as though they had just unwrapped a birthday present. The twinkle in Sam's eyes, together with his smile, conveyed feelings of relief and accomplishment.

After what seemed like an eternity, Sam broke the stillness by announcing, quietly for effect, that he had no further questions of the witness.

Chapter 70

ESCAPING THE AFTERMATH

Laurins led his co-counsel and all of his associates out of the courtroom. As they gathered in the hallway, there were outbursts of elation from the Petitioner's team.

All of the government team, except for Emily and Erwin, quickly gathered around Westover and began whispering wildly. Meanwhile, Emily was at the door, motioning to Ian to come outside. Erwin stood facing Ian in the center of the aisle, never taking his eyes off of him. Ian could almost feel the heat from Erwin's glare.

Ian managed to walk across the front of the courtroom and slip down the other aisle to avoid Erwin. He and Emily met in the hall, quickly walking down the flight of stairs to the ground floor and out of the courthouse. Once outside, they slowed their pace. They were afraid to hold hands with all these colleagues around, but they managed to touch lightly, standing close as they caught a taxi around the corner.

Emily had said quickly, "Listen, everyone's going to The Sandwich Shop. Let's get a cab and head away from downtown a bit."

A few minutes later, Ian led her to a booth in an out-of-the-way diner.

"Well?" he asked.

"Well, what?"

"Well, what'd you think? I told you I was worried. Now you see why."

"Ian, you did the right thing. That's all I can say. But what about you—after dreading it for two weeks, how did it feel up there on the witness stand finally?"

Ian said, "I was very uncomfortable."

Expressing surprise, Emily responded, "That's hard to believe. You seemed completely at ease, very composed, and totally forthright with your answers. Of all the witnesses I have seen the past two weeks, you appeared to be one of the most comfortable."

"I guess my outward appearance belies what is going on inside me. I will be so happy to get it all behind me. Boy, I didn't think Erwin was going to let me leave the courtroom alive. I made some enemies today—that's for sure."

"If it angered some folks for you to tell the truth—and it did—well, that's their problem. I mean, I know I'm on the government team, but having heard all the testimony and read all this evidence, especially what you had to say today, Ian, I think the last thing the government deserves is extra tax money from that poor family, what with all they have done to the Mitchells and that town."

"Somehow I don't think Jack Erwin will think I'm blameless. I tell you, this is the kind of thing people suddenly disappear over. I mean, we're talking about the CIA. I'm telling you, I'm worried."

"Now, don't go getting all conspiracy-theorist on me. It's just a tax law case. They're not going to hunt you down over that."

"Oh, really? Wasn't it tax evasion that they finally got that old mobster on—Capone, right? Tax law is important business! It's a lot of money we're talking about. Besides, I still have all afternoon to go. They may hang me yet."

She laughed. "Let's change the subject. I mean, after all, is that all you have to say to me after last night?" Emily winked at him.

Ian grinned. He now realized this was, after all, their first moments together since their unforgettable time in each other's arms last night. His tenseness softened. Making sure that no one from the trial was around, he kissed her as he stood. "I have more to say—and do—on that subject than our short lunch break will allow, my dear. Now, what do you want to eat? I'll go place our order."

He placed their orders at the window and returned to her. Sitting close, they kissed lightly, gazed lovingly into each others eyes, and moved even closer until their legs rested against each other, sharing the same side of the booth.

"After last night, I have been forever marked by you, Emily. I have fallen hard for you."

Snuggling close, she responded, "I have to say, I'd almost given up hope that I would ever again love and be loved, but now I know that God has blessed me another time by bringing us together." Then, with a sly grin, she said in his ear, "I figured I'd forgotten how to make love."

"Well, you sure helped me re-learn! It was wonderful," Ian whispered.

"A couple of sandwiches for the lovebirds?" the waitress said.

She left, and Emily giggled, "Is it that obvious?"

After a while, she said, "I was proud of you this morning, Ian. You told the truth. That's what you swore to do."

"I guess I stirred up a hornet's nest with my testimony. I am surprised that CIA guy, Erwin, didn't have a heart attack. He was so purple in the face, I thought he was about to explode. If his looks had been daggers, I'd be lunch meat. I cannot understand how he could hate the Soviet Union so much and carry that intense vindictiveness for so long that he still, even after all that's happened, does not see how wrong they were with Project Apex. I really do think he and others like him just pressed ahead with Project Apex because they couldn't see the forest for the trees."

"May be."

"Hey, would you still want to date me if I'm poor? You know, I may not have a job after today," he said.

"Oh, hush—of course," she said.

Lingering as long as they could, they threw their paper plates into the garbage bin. Ian pulled her close, kissed her, and told her that he couldn't wait to be with her again, alone, when all this was behind them.

Then they headed back to the courthouse.

Emily said, "This may have to be goodbye for now. I don't know if I'll have a chance to see you when we're done today. I'll be leaving the courthouse at 4 o'clock to get my luggage at the hotel and get to the airport to catch my 6 o'clock flight. I expect to be in my apartment in Washington about 11:00. I hope my phone will be ringing shortly thereafter."

"Well, kiss me good and hard now, then, just in case. And yes, I'll call. At 11:01 p.m."

After one more embrace, standing hidden around the side of a building, he suggested they not walk across the courthouse lawn together. He sent her ahead.

Ian watched her walk away.

That is the last time I am going to let you walk away from me, Emily Carter.

Chapter 71

WESTOVER REDIRECTS

"All rise," the Clerk exclaimed.

Judge Lansdorf asked, "Mr. MacGregor, being reminded that you are still under oath, please take your seat. Mr. Westover, do you have any further questions of this witness on redirect?"

With less than great enthusiasm, Westover replied that he did. Walking to the lectern with yellow pad in hand, Bob Westover began a lengthy series of questions.

Trying to make Ian appear like the lone nut for such outrageous testimony, he had Ian acknowledge again in several ways that he was the only one of the nine-person team who had opposed testing in the Mitchell Dome.

"And you were the only one to continue having ongoing concerns with the Project?"

Ian replied, "Yes, I guess I was."

"Mr. MacGregor, you said that you were worried that the wall of the salt dome might rupture and melt, making it possible for contamination to seep into the water supply. Didn't the Project Apex Team possess detailed studies from the Geological Survey and the Bureau of Mines determining that this would not happen?"

"Yes, sir, but…."

"Yes or no, Mr. MacGregor. And, again, you were the only one, looking at the same information as the other eight people, who had any concern after reading these numerous reports?"

"Yes, sir."

'So, are you just smarter than the others—or perhaps, not as smart—or what?"

"Objection," Sam said.

"Sustained."

Westover continued, "So then, you merely think that the other eight people on the team were wrong in their conclusions, some of whom are sitting in this courtroom today?"

"No, I am not saying that. And as I mentioned before, Kyle DeLoach shared some of my concerns after reviewing my findings. And he believed me enough to raise those issues with people higher up the ladder. But in the end, I just think most everyone was more ready to accept what they thought appeared to be logical conclusions of what would happen upon detonation. I saw other possible outcomes that some of them weren't willing to see. And unfortunately, I turned out to be right—I wish that I hadn't been."

Westover questioned Ian extensively about how the clean-up plan was conceived, who worked on it, who approved it, and so on, trying to show how much time and thought had gone into the planning. "Would you have accepted the majority point of view on the team as long as the assumptions on which the plan was based were accurate?"

Ian tried to think of a way out of that question, but he knew Westover had him. He admitted, "I guess so."

Emphasizing his point, Westover clarified, "So you don't think there was anything wrong with the plan if the assumptions on which it was based were accurate?"

Choosing his words carefully, Ian said, "No, there wouldn't have been anything wrong."

"You testified that, in your opinion, the contractor did not properly carry out the requirements of the clean-up plan. Since you have now testified that there wasn't a flaw in the plan…"

Ian tried to jump in to clarify and change the emphasis of that statement, but Bob wouldn't let him.

"…And you've said that the plan was clearly written, and you and others from the AEC were there to observe everything, how could it be that the contractor didn't complete the clean-up operation as directed, with such good oversight from you? Who failed: the contractor or you?"

"Mr. Westover, I and others from the AEC couldn't be present every minute of the clean-up process. There was no way we could see everything that was done or left undone. In addition, as I said this morning, there were several major incidences when I found the contractor was not complying with the requirements of the plan, but I was told by our operations office to forget about it, let it go. I could not control everything."

Ineffectively concealing his disappointment in that response, Westover now knew he would have to hit below the belt. "Mr. MacGregor, you told this Court about your wife and father-in-law, who died of cancer. It is obvious that those deaths have been very painful to you, and of course, they would be. Your resentment toward Project Apex as a possible cause of those deaths comes through clearly. Isn't it quite possible that the resentment you feel has clouded your memory of some facts, clouded your judgment, and is reflected in your testimony?"

Before Bob could get the words out of his mouth, Sam was on his feet objecting to the question forcefully. However, Ian's passionate answer broke through the din of all three men's voices, "That is not what's happening here. I have told nothing but the truth."

"Objection overruled. The witness must answer the question," Lansdorf ruled.

"I realize it might seem like I have some deep-seated hostility toward the project, but I tell you, I would be answering the same way regardless of whether or not Kay—my wife—and her family had lived. Every household in town was affected by what we did, and those people were my friends. I lived beside them. Not to mention that I have an ethical obligation as a professional to report that I had serious concerns from the very beginning—long before I'd even met my wife! Project Apex was flawed in its very conception. No, sir, my personal losses are not clouding my judgment," Ian finished adamantly.

Ian had responded so dramatically that Westover could tell everyone in the room empathized with the witness. Bob ended up wishing this had not gotten into the record—he was sorry the Judge had let MacGregor continue. Westover resumed his questioning nonetheless.

Try as he might, even though he made a diligent effort, Bob was unable to recover from the hurtful testimony Ian had given on cross-examination. Finally, he announced that he had no further questions.

"Mr. Laurins, do you have any further questions of this witness?"

Feeling quite confident, but desiring to put one final nail in the government's coffin, Sam answered, "Yes, Your Honor, I have one."

"Mr. MacGregor, having been a part of this Project Apex from start to finish, what do you think caused the project to go wrong?"

After a few moments hesitation, Ian answered, "The government was being pulled in every direction by all these Cold War forces we now know amounted to nothing in the course of history. The U.S. thought we had to test those bombs in underground salt domes because the Soviets were surely testing bombs in their own underground salt domes. It was the same old 'my gun is bigger than your gun' game. And all of it was circumventing what was supposed to be a Nuclear Test Ban Treaty. What purpose did any of these tests serve, in the end? We destroyed the environment, made people so sick, and for what? I think our government had a blindly-driven mission to conduct these tests, seized on a place to do it too hastily, and were so determined, they ignored the warning signs I saw. Without regard to the safety of their own citizens, they pressed onward."

"Thank you, sir," said Sam as he closed his notebook and walked to his chair.

The Judge looked questioningly at Bob Westover, who shook his head no.

Westover merely stated, "Respondent rests its case."

Judge Lansdorf said, "Thank you, Mr. MacGregor. You may step down."

Part Eight: Shockwave

Chapter 72

CLOSING & CHAMBERS

Judge Lansdorf said, "All right, folks. This case stands submitted. Counsel, let's talk about filing briefs. I want to use seriatim briefs unless the parties seriously object: an opening brief by Petitioner, a responsive brief by the government, and a reply to the Respondent's brief by the Petitioner. Any objections to that, Counsel?"

"No, Your Honor."

"No, sir."

"How much time does Petitioner want to file?"

Sam responded, "A lot."

"Well, the record is quite voluminous. How much time is a lot?"

"120 days?"

"Very well. Mr. Clerk, what will that date be?"

The Clerk advised, "That would be April 12, 1985, Your Honor."

The Judge asked Westover how long he would need for his responsive brief. Westover said that he wanted 90 days. The Judge agreed and the Clerk advised that date would be July 20.

Sam was asked how much time he would need to file his reply to the government's brief. When he asked for 60 days, the Clerk said September 9.

"All right, then. This concludes the Court's special trial session in Shreveport, Louisiana. For the record, the Court would like to take this opportunity to tell Counsel for both sides that I believe you have done an excellent job with a very difficult case—not to mention the most unusual case any of us has ever seen in the Tax Court. I thought both sides were well represented. The parties were prepared and effectively presented their positions, and I appreciate that professionalism from all of you. This Court stands adjourned."

✳

Stepping from his bench, Judge Lansdorf requested Counsel for both sides to meet in his chambers. As they entered the Judge's chambers, he motioned for them to sit. "Ladies and gentlemen, as I said on the record, you did a wonderful job in trying this case. It is the most interesting case I've ever heard. I want to share my thoughts about it for whatever benefit it might be to you."

"If I were to render an opinion today, I would rule that the 1400 acres leased to the government are probably contaminated by nuclear waste, and that some portion of the land surrounding the 1400 acres is likely contaminated, too. My feeling now is that the value of the 1400 acres is zero. I am not now prepared to render an opinion as the value of the remaining 18,600 acres. I will do that after you have filed your briefs, and I consider all the facts."

Laurins struggled to hold back the grin that he felt coming, but Westover looked like a man who had just been kicked in the stomach.

The Judge continued, "We have set the dates for filing of briefs. If the parties can talk further and reach a settlement before then, I will enter my decision based on the agreed settlement. But if you want to file the briefs, I will render my decision after reviewing the briefs and the entire record. Do you have any questions?"

Both Laurins and Westover responded, "No, sir."

"Very well, then. You are dismissed, and thank you again for your excellent work."

✳

Outside chambers, the Respondent's attorneys sulked out of the courtroom while Sam's team remained behind, congratulating each other. Bob and Sam exchanged glances as Bob left, and Bob just shrugged his shoulders, looking defeated, as he saw Sam's team patting one another on the back.

Clarence Mitchell, Jr. was elated, and everyone was expressing relief that this was finally finished. Amidst all the hand-shaking and high-fiving, Clarence said, "Sam, if he'd beat that cancer and lived to see this day, my Dad would be so happy. I thank you—my whole family thanks you."

"Well, it's not over til the fat lady sings, now, folks," Sam reminded them.

"Ah, we've got 'em, Sam, and you know it!" Rob said.

Chapter 73

A DIFFERENT KIND OF CELEBRATION

Ian immediately left the courtroom once excused by the Judge. On the one hand, he felt as if he had been beaten with a stick, completely exhausted, longing to sit in a quiet place; on the other hand, he was wishing he could see Emily before her plane left. But first of all, he wanted to get out of that courthouse.

He walked briskly, remembering that Emily planned to leave the hotel at about 4:00. Looking at his watch, he saw that it was almost that time. If he ran, maybe he'd catch her before she left for the airport. He ran, dashing into the lobby of their hotel and to the front desk. As he gasped for air, he asked if Emily Carter had checked out.

The clerk said, "She drove away in a taxi less than five minutes ago."

Crestfallen, Ian went to his room. He didn't turn on any lights or the television but sank into the easy chair. As he stared into space, in his mind, he reviewed the key questions and his answers while on the stand. *I know the government people did not want me to say all that I did, but I did not shade the truth. It needed to be said.*

The longer he sat, the more he relaxed. When he was finishing going through the day's events in his mind, he got up. Finally, he felt normal again. Darkness had fallen outside, and he realized that he was here alone with no lights, getting hungry. He thought how much he would enjoy a cocktail—or two—but he would not go near the hotel lounge, expecting Van Skiver and DeLoach to be there, maybe even Erwin. *That's all I need.* Next week would be soon enough to have to face them.

Ian turned on the lights and the TV. The evening news was coming on. It soon became obvious that the news program had nothing exciting to report, so he got up, took off his tie and put on a sweater over his shirt. *That drink sounds good. Maybe if I go out the parking garage exit and walk to a restaurant a few blocks away, I'll avoid seeing anyone who wouldn't be happy with me right now.* He got his coat, turned off the TV and lights, and left.

The bar was crowded with happy hour patrons, mostly young people who worked in the office buildings close by. The noise, laughter, and loud conversation evidenced the fact that they were enjoying themselves. He soon had the scotch and soda that he had been anticipating. Several of the young couples at the bar were hugging, touching affectionately, and exchanging an occasional kiss. Ian felt envious, but he thought how happy he was to have a woman in his life now. *And I will be talking to her tonight, as soon as she gets home.*

Slowly, the bar crowd started clearing out, most of the noise leaving with them. Ian asked the waitress for a table in the restaurant. *Might as well kill time and fill this growling belly since she's not home yet.*

When he had finished dinner, it was 7:30. *Three and a half hours to wait until Emily gets home.* Ian walked another block to a movie theatre. It didn't matter to him what was showing.

Arriving back at his hotel room, he checked his watch. Only 10:15. He picked up a magazine to read, but it was difficult for him to concentrate—so many thoughts of the trial, Emily, the future of his job, Emily.

At ten minutes to eleven, he could wait no longer, just in case she arrived early. He dialed her number. It rang several times. Finally Emily's voice on the answering machine announced that she would return the call as soon as possible.

Ian left the message, "I love you, and I will call you back in a few minutes. I hope your flight was good. It is lonesome here without you."

Forcing himself to wait until 11:05, Ian dialed her number again, hoping she would be there to answer this time. After the third ring, just as he was anticipating hearing the answering machine again, Emily answered, breathless from rushing in the door.

"What perfect timing—I have just walked in my door," she said.

"You will hear the message I left on your machine a little earlier. I had waited as long as I could stand, so I called a little early."

They talked a good while. Emily said that when she left the courtroom to go to the hotel and check out, he was still testifying. "How did the day end?"

Ian told her about the last part of his testimony and how he had left the courtroom as soon as the Judge dismissed him. He said how rung-out he felt, and how he'd dashed to the hotel, hoping to see her before she left, and how he'd cleverly avoided seeing the Nuclear Regulatory Commission people.

"You poor baby," she said. "I wish I could be there with you, to hold you tight."

"I wish I could take you out to celebrate this whole thing being over, but I guess hearing your sweet voice over the distance is celebration enough."

The next hour seemed to simply fly by. It was like talking with someone you've known forever. They hadn't skipped a beat, though they were now miles and miles apart.

As they were finishing their conversation, Ian told her he would check out of the hotel the next morning to move back to his apartment in Winnfield. "Now, you have that address and telephone number there, right?"

"Yep."

"I guess I will find out Monday if I still have a job with the Commission."

Then, exchanging their pledges of love for the other, they said goodbye.

"For now," she added.

Chapter 74

DOWN THE AISLE

On Monday, Barbara flew to Atlanta, where she and Louise busied themselves completing the final details with Nell and Lyn. Sam arrived Wednesday after finishing his big trial the Friday prior. The siblings all got in Wednesday, too.

Sam and the others soon learned that it was best they stay out of the way unless—and until—called upon to do something. Around the dinner table one night when the wedding planner was giving directions, Sam joked, "Hey, I learned a long time ago that at weddings, men should do what they're told."

Someone called out, "What about after the wedding?"

Nell quelled that discussion with a playful retort, "We'll just have to see about that!"

On several occasions prior to the wedding, Sam saw Nell carefully observing Barbara, Louise, and him, as they laughed, talked, and joked together. *Please, God, let her see how far her mother and I have come in forgiving and reconciling. I hope she can see we are all family now.*

The night before the wedding, just before they left for the rehearsal, Sam said very somberly to Barbara, "I guess I am not going to have the pleasure of giving my daughter away. She has said nothing to me about it, and someone said she heard Louise's brother will do it."

Barbara stopped what she was doing, went to Sam and held him in her arms. "I am so sorry, darling. I don't know what Nell is thinking, and I can't fathom why she hasn't let go of the ill will she feels toward you. There is no doubt in my mind that she loves you, despite all this, deep down. Some day she will show you. I had prayed that it would happen before now."

Gathered at the church, the wedding party was instructed by the church's consultant as to the etiquette and order of the ceremony. The consultant then led the groomsmen through the process of escorting the grandmother and mothers of the bride and groom to their seats, expressing some surprise when Nell told her that both Louise and Barbara would be escorted and seated together. Sam was told to follow Barbara and sit next to her.

When the groomsmen and bridesmaids practiced walking in and finding their places, the bridal march started playing, and the maid of honor came down the aisle, playing the bride's role with Nell's uncle as an escort. Sam was devastated.

Once the wedding consultant was satisfied that everyone knew what he or she was to do, she dismissed them for the evening.

On the way to the rehearsal dinner, Sam was quiet. Barbara consoled him best she could and asked him to make every effort to be pleasant. At dinner, he was pleasant enough, and though he probably visited the bar a little too often, it didn't show. Sam, Barbara, and Louise spent all the time they could visiting with Nell, Lyn, and his parents. Through his pain, Sam was glad to feel at least a touch of warmth from Nell, though she said little to him.

✳

When the rehearsal was over, back at the hotel, some of the children came by their Dad's room, ostensibly to say goodnight, but actually to console their Dad in his hurt. Earlier, they'd all tried to act like nothing was wrong, but they all knew Sam was brooding behind the scenes. After visiting a while, they all hugged and said goodnight.

Sam and Barbara undressed and got into their night clothes. They talked for a while about the day and how excited they were about the wedding, though Sam was still sulking and forlorn.

Just as they turned off the lights, they heard a knock at the door.

Assuming that one of the children had come back for something left behind, Sam got out of bed and went to the door. To his surprise, Nell and Lyn were standing there.

"Can we come in?"

"Of course," he replied. "Come over and sit down."

Nell sat on the couch next to Sam, took his hand, and looking him straight in the eyes, said, "Dad, I have come to ask you to forgive me for my coldness and all the hurt I have put you through. I have been totally unreasonable and self-centered, holding grudges that should have been given up a long time ago. I love you—I never stopped loving you, Dad. I was just very angry and immature and wanted to punish you because we could not live together as a family. I am so sorry."

Sam's spirit soared. His hopes and dreams had come true. *Thank you, God.* He took Nell in his arms and hugged her tightly. "Sweetheart, I can't thank you enough for this moment. I love you so much and have missed being close to you. I want to make sure you know I have apologized to your mother, as she has done with me. The past is the past. I just want to be part of your life."

They hugged and talked some more through tears.

Then Lyn spoke up, "Sir, there's one more thing."

"Sure—and you don't have to call me 'Sir' anymore. We're family now!"

Lyn looked at Nell, who said, "Yes, there is one more thing, isn't there?" She paused. "Dad, I can't walk down the aisle with Uncle Mark tomorrow. I can't do that with anyone but you. Will you please give me away?"

Sam couldn't help it. He broke down hard, crying. "Well, you bet! I did not know how I was going to get through your wedding without walking you down the aisle and giving your hand to Lyn! There is nothing in this world that I would rather do. Thank you, Lord, for answering my prayers, for bringing my child back to me."

Barbara was crying, too. The four of them laughed, hugged, cried, and talked for a good while, until, seeing the time, Barbara said, "It is getting very late, sweetheart, and tomorrow is your big day, hopefully one the happiest days of your life, so you had better get to bed. We all need our beauty sleep tonight."

They all agreed. With one more hug, Nell and Lyn left. When the door was closed, Sam grabbed Barbara off her chair and danced her around the room as he giggled with glee.

✳

The next morning, as he met Nell inside the bridal room at the church, Sam was speechless. As he stood there staring at her, she was the most beautiful bride he had ever seen, and he said so to Barbara.

"What about me?"

"Well, I…you were gorgeous, honey, you know that, but…," he started to recover from the social fumble he knew he'd just made, but Barbara grinned and interrupted.

"I'm just kidding, silly. Don't take me so seriously, dear. I know what you meant. Our children are always special." She kissed him.

He watched as Nell's attendants busied themselves with last minute touch-ups of hair and makeup, straightening her long, flowing dress. They were soon directed to the rear of the church to prepare for their entrance. Sam took his daughter's hands into his, and looking into her eyes, with tears running down his cheeks, said, "My dear girl, you are so beautiful, and I am so happy for you. My heart had an empty corner for years because I have not been able to share your life. Regardless of the many ways I fell short as your father, and the ways I know I've been a disappointment to you, I always loved you as deeply as I knew how. I tried, honey, I just didn't know how to be any better back then. Even though my past may not evidence it, I will always be here for you, and I want to be as big a part of your life as you will let me."

With a tear in her eye, but a smile on her face, Nell squeezed her father's hands and whispered, "Thanks. I love you, Dad." Then she said, "Now stop it before I start crying again and mess up my mascara." She smiled so big Sam's heart nearly burst.

Sam wanted to dance and shout, but it was time to walk his daughter to the alter where she would begin a new life with Lyn. He was so excited, his knees were shaking, but Sam's smile covered his entire face.

Chapter 75

A PHONE CALL

About three weeks after the wedding, Sam was back home and working in the office when he received a call from Bob Westover. After passing pleasantries, Bob said, "Sam, I am real busy with a very heavy caseload, and I've been thinking about how much time I would have to spend writing the briefs for the Mitchell case. I want to ask if you would be interested in talking about settling it."

Sam responded, "Of course, Bob. I am always open to talk, and you know I have an obligation to my client to consider any offer. But I'll tell you, unless you have had a huge change of heart since our previous talk, you might be wasting your time."

"No, we're serious. Things are a little different now. I think you realize that. I just need to get this behind me. Let me put my pencil to it, and I'll get back to you with something definite in the next few days."

"That will be fine, Bob. Just give me a call."

Chapter 76

NEXT TIME I SEE YOU

Emily was awakened by the telephone at 8:00 a.m. She picked up the receiver and heard the sweet voice of Ian, saying, "Happy Birthday, darling. I know that it's early, but I could not wait to talk to you."

"I was sleeping later this morning than usual, but you can wake me any time you want—and any way you want," she added in a groggy, seductive morning voice. "The roses you sent were delivered last night. They're gorgeous. Thank you so much."

"Good. I'm glad the flowers turned out pretty. I just wish I was there to see them—and you. How are you?" he asked.

"Except for missing you, I am fine. It is a beautiful day here. There is still snow on the ground, and it is cold, but there's a wonderful bright sun," Emily said. "I am so glad the weather is nice because winter can be depressing to me. Does it affect you that way?"

Ian said, "I feel the same way and have since I was a child. What are you going to do today?"

"I'm going to church this morning, then my friend, Hallie, and I are going to have lunch and go to a movie," she answered. "What about you, what are going to do?"

"There's a special musical service at church, then a group of friends from church are going to a restaurant here in town to have dinner together. I will probably go to a movie later, too, or maybe watch the ballgame—something to pass the time. I'm enjoying seeing all the old friends Kay and I had when we lived here. There's something healing about it. But I miss you terribly."

Emily said, "I miss you, too. When can I see you?"

"I am coming to Washington Tuesday after next. My boss—you know Kyle—has called all of us involved in Project Apex to meet to review what has happened. By the way, I did not get fired! The whole group is going to discuss what is happening at the Mitchell salt dome and what to do about it. So I will get to Washington Tuesday night and will be there until Sunday. Any chance we can get together—you know, if you can squeeze in some time for me?"

"Hurray," she excitedly shouted. "Ha! *Can* we get together? Only every minute you are not in meetings. You will stay here with me. I am so happy. Only ten days from now—I can hardly wait."

"I can hardly wait to hold you in my arms. I miss you and love you," he said.

"Once you're here, we can figure out a way for us to see each other more often, long term, right?" she ventured.

"Nah, I was thinking of breaking up after this one trip."

"Ian!"

"Oh, Emily, you know where my heart lies. I want to be with you as long as you'll let me."

The lovers talked a while longer, until she had to go get ready for church. Eventually, they hung up the phone, both excited that in just ten days, they would be together again.

I have a feeling I'll be with her for a very, very long time indeed, Ian thought as he put the phone back in the cradle.

Chapter 77

CONCESSION

Three days after their last phone call, Westover called Sam again and outlined the terms he proposed to settle the case.

Sam noted those terms carefully, and with no emotion in his voice, read them back to Westover. "I'll study the proposed settlement, Bob, and talk to my client. Can I give you a call back in a few days?"

"Yeah, sure, Sam."

Immediately, he could see that, taking into account the refund of Louisiana taxes that would result from the proposal, Bob's offer was a very attractive one. Sam made some detailed calculations, which revealed that in addition to eliminating the supposed tax deficiency, Bob's proposal would result in a refund to the client totaling about $3 million, including interest. So he called Clarence Mitchell to tell him that Westover had made an offer that appeared worth his attention.

Sam told Clarence, "I want to show the terms of the offer to your accountant and ask him to double check the effect of the offer to verify my own calculations."

"Yes, do that right away," Clarence agreed.

Sam did. The following Monday, Clarence came to Sam's office. Sam explained in detail the terms of the offer and the amount of the tax refund the estate would receive if they accepted. He said the family accountant had verified his own calculations.

"I feel these figures are reliable."

Clarence was bowled over, just as Sam had been. Clarence asked, "What is your opinion of the best result you think we might get if we did not accept this offer and let the Judge decide?"

"Of course, I have no way to know what the Judge might decide, but there is a logical way he could conclude that you are owed a refund of $5 million to $6 million, including interest. That would be the maximum. But, of course, he could arrive at something a lot less."

"What do you recommend, Sam?"

"I am torn. This is the only case of this kind that will ever be reported on the record, and especially because of the government's negligent handling of the whole testing program, and their complete disregard for the safety of innocent people, I very much want to have the trial record published, which can only happen if we leave the decision to the Judge. Trouble is, I cannot guarantee your family a better result than the proposed settlement, and in the end, it's about doing what is right for my client. So I guess I'd have to recommend that you accept the proposal."

"Ah, I hadn't considered that." Clarence paused. "On the one hand, I want to let the world know what happened out there. Part of me really wants to have the Judge decide the case so that the record would be published for all to see." Here, Clarence stopped again, clearly thinking everything through. "But I guess I need to do what is best for the Mitchell family first and foremost. Tell him that we will accept his proposed settlement."

"I will try to squeeze a little more out of him, but if I can't, I will accept the offer."

"Thanks, Sam. I knew you could do it."

Sam wondered why the government decided to be so generous to the Mitchells. Later, he tried to ask Bob, but he never got a satisfactory explanation. In his heart, Sam was convinced the reason was that this way, settling out of Court, the trial record would never be made public—the American people would never know what really happened.

✳

The next day, Sam called Westover. "Bob, I have talked to my client about your settlement proposal, and while we think it is pretty good, I think it is still a bit short. From what Judge Lansdorf told us of his opinion, he already said he will determine that the 1400 acres are worth nothing. I believe I can show him in my briefs that the surrounding land, maybe as much as 5000 acres, should also be valued at next to nothing. If he accepts that suggestion, his decision would result in a refund of more than $5 million. That is more than you are offering."

Westover interrupted, "Sam, let me stop you. My authority is to make the offer I have proposed. I cannot concede one penny more. So, can you accept the offer, or should we have the Judge decide? My hands are tied."

Sam paused a few moments, letting Bob squirm just a little, then said, "Okay, Bob, we will accept. Prepare the decision document and send it to me to review."

"Glad to hear it, Sam."

"By the way, Bob, tell me, I need to know: did you know what the government was hiding behind all of those inaccurate reports—did you know they were lying?"

"I don't know what you are talking about, Sam."

"I mean, did you know the truth, the things Ross and MacGregor and the others revealed, or were you in the dark? What I really want to know is—were you being directed by somebody higher up to keep things concealed?"

Westover just said, "Sorry, old buddy. I've got to go. I'll get the documents out to you in a week or so. See you."

Sam could still hear Bob on the other end.

"Hey, Sam…" Westover began, then stopped. Sam could hear Westover's contemplation in the static on the line.

"Yes?"

"Sam," began Westover again, "why don't I meet you in person to pick up the documents—say over a drink at Tommy Rupps' Bar, downtown? They have specials on Tuesday nights. I hear the house favorite is the Atomic Blast."

Sam almost laughed. "Tuesday night it is, Bob."

"It's a date," said Westover and hung up.

Chapter 78

FULFILLED

It was 6 o'clock when Sam called Barbara. He asked what the plans were for dinner.

"The kids all have something going on, so it's just you and me. Why? What's up?"

"Because you and I are going to celebrate. Can we eat at home? I would rather be there and have a nice meal with you in private."

"Sure we can eat here. What are we celebrating?"

"I am leaving here in 30 minutes to come home. I will tell you when I get there."

As he arrived home, Barbara met Sam at the door with a big hug and kiss, filled with expectancy.

"Tell me what we are celebrating! I have spent the last hour trying to imagine."

"Let's get a drink and get comfortable first," Sam said, popping the cork of the champagne he'd brought home.

"Champagne—wow, this is a special night!" Barbara exclaimed.

Settling down on the couch together, champagne glasses in hand, Sam started, "I want to tell you about this big case I've been so preoccupied with lately—Project Apex."

"Okay…," Barbara said, curious.

"When Clarence Mitchell came to me two years ago to represent his father's estate and contest the IRS, it was a routine dispute over the value of the Mitchell land. The situation was that when the estate filed its tax return, they paid a lot of tax, but the IRS came back asserting that the land should be valued much higher, saying the Mitchells owed more. The government was looking for some $7 million more in taxes than what the Mitchells had paid. That is what we were fighting over."

"All right. Sounds like what you do every day, Sam. What's so special?"

"Just wait. We engaged some competent expert witnesses to help prove our case, and we thought we were ready for trial. Then, one day about a month before the trial was to start, one of our experts casually mentioned to me 'the test site.' When I asked him what he meant, he was surprised I didn't know. He told me the government had conducted tests of nuclear bombs under the Mitchell property in a salt dome."

"What? You've got to be kidding me!"

"I know—I have never been so shocked. When I found out that it was true, we got a continuance and went back to the drawing boards to determine how that testing on the land would affect its value. We located some new experts, a lot of experts, who we felt could prove to the Judge that the land should be devalued because the nuclear testing created a stigma. Our experts did that and more. They convinced the Judge that there is a probability that some part of the land is contaminated with nuclear waste. Anyway, to make a long story short too late, we won. Today we agreed to settle the case. Rather than the Mitchells having to pay the IRS even more, the government attorney agreed to pay my client a big refund."

"Oh, honey, that's wonderful news. What an interesting case!"

"It really has been interesting. There were a lot of mysterious things going on, too."

"Like what?

"Well, for starters, there were all these government people present for the trial. What I'd call high-up-mucky-mucks from the IRS and CIA and more. Then another curious thing: the IRS lawyer, a guy I have known a long time, someone who is pretty reasonable, refused to even talk about reducing the land values or the taxes owed—not until the very end, when the government's own witness basically testified material that helped us win the case for the Mitchells. Even after the IRS lawyer had information from our expert's reports, he would not listen to my proposals to compromise the tax deficiency they were proposing. They fought us through the entire trial, refusing to relent. When the trial was completed, the Judge told us lawyers on both sides that he was convinced that some of the land was contaminated. Then three weeks later, the IRS lawyer called me and proposed a settlement—I think so the government could avoid having the case go public like it would when the Judge's decision was published. Because the case was so fascinating, and there will never be another like it, I wanted to have the Court enter its decision, so that the decision would be preserved for posterity and public record, and Mr. Mitchell did, too. But, they offered us a settlement that we could not refuse. Anyway, here I am going on and on. I am just thankful to have had this unique experience and to have recovered a large refund for my client. That is the reason for our celebrating."

"That is just amazing, Sam. I'm so proud of you."

"Well, I just wanted you to know about what's been consuming me these last few weeks. I know I've worked a lot of long hours again lately, and I didn't want you thinking I was backsliding into my old workaholic ways."

"No, I knew something different was going on. I could tell it was something unique driving you, a situation you were clearly passionate about. You still felt connected to me in spirit."

"Thanks. Oh, one other thing. I just want to tell you how good it is to be able to come home to my beautiful wife and share things about my day. You have been good to me through thick and thin, and I'm grateful." He gave Barbara a long kiss with the kind of zeal they'd had when they first met.

She said, smiling, "Goodness. What's got into you?"

"Just happy and really content with life, that's all."

"Glad to see it. Give me another one of those." And she kissed him again. "Well, then, a toast—to a job well done and to justice!"

"To justice!" Sam said, taking a drink. "Hey, while we're celebrating, here's a toast to Nell and her wedding going off so successfully."

"And to the restoration of your relationship with her. That couldn't have made me happier to see, Sam. I'm really glad for you. Hey, did I tell you she called? They're back from their honeymoon. She said it was wonderful."

"Oh, good! I'm glad they had a nice time and are home safe again."

Settling in, fully relaxed with his arm around his wife, Sam said, "I tell you what, Nell finally coming around filled a deep void in my heart. I have a good job, a nice house, good friends, but if I had to choose, I would gladly give up all the other good things for my daughter's love. "

They snuggled on the sofa and talked all evening—about the law suit, Nell, and life in general. Later that night, looking at Barbara, Sam said, "I am a man blessed by God—I have a wonderful loving wife, great children, a law practice that is fulfilling and enjoyable—I can't think of anything I don't have in my life." He stood and took Barbara by the hand.

"Where are we going?"

"To bed, my love. I have some more celebrating to do."

✻

THE END

✻

ABOUT THE AUTHOR

Lauch Magruder enjoyed the practice of law for 40 years. Feeling the pull of the mountains, he retired from his practice and moved to North Carolina with his wife, Jane.